Maliha Anderson

BOOKS 1-3

By

Steve Turnbull

To my family (you know who you are).

TABLE OF CONTENTS

MURDER OUT OF THE BLUE

BOOK 1

CHAPTER 1

Maliha Anderson glanced down at her watch. Temperance and Lochana were late. RMS *Macedonia* was scheduled to launch at three o'clock local time, just half an hour away, and the great Peninsular & Oriental Steam Navigation Company were strict about their schedules. She looked out at the sun-bleached streets of Khartoum, almost devoid of life in the heat of the day. Flat roofs lay all of a height except for the domes and minarets of the mosques. To the west, the sun's light shimmered on the rippling surface of the White Nile.

She leaned forward against the polished wooden rail that curved around the stern viewing lounge of B Deck. A Deck above—for the truly wealthy—had a similar lounge but fewer and larger berths. Those in the cheaper second and third class berths below had no lounge at all; only the Promenade and Observation decks were available to them, with no privacy to speak of.

All together they were 300 souls packed into a steel and glass container thundering through the sky at 100 miles per hour and an altitude of 3000 feet, courtesy of the Faraday device and the steam-driven rotors on the ends of the six stubby wings.

The purser had given them a tour after the vessel had lifted from London three days ago. The *Macedonia* was the latest passenger vessel of the P&O line, flaunted in its newspaper advertisements as a marvel of the skies: a floating Sky Liner with its rotors to take it vertically into the clouds, then swivel to drive the vessel across the firmament. It was, they said, a miracle of engineering.

Maliha sighed. Always they were "miracles of engineering". Then she smiled. This truly was a miracle of engineering, and it did indeed please her. She ran her fingers along the painted iron underside of the rail, feeling the bumps of the letters that spelt out the name of the Belfast shipbuilders: Harland and Wolfe.

Movement outside caught her eye.

The two lost sheep emerged in sudden colour against the washed-out shades of ochre. They hurried arm in arm towards the ramp. The Welsh copper heiress Temperance Williams, intense with the certainty of a *zenana* missionary, was travelling to India to save the souls of the Hindu womenfolk. And beside her was Lochana Modi, of Indian birth and nurse to General Makepeace-Flynn. It seemed Temperance had decided to begin her missionary work with Lochana.

They were unaccompanied again. It had been the same in Constantinople. Temperance was a very modern young woman and did not consider a male escort to be required under any circumstance. And it seemed the general did not mind his nurse going ashore with her; certainly he felt no compunction in co-opting Maliha to push his wheelchair, despite her injury, when Lochana was unavailable. He seemed to think that because she was young, just 19, he could ignore her need for a walking stick when in port.

"The wanderers have returned, eh?"

Maliha did not turn to look at the general, who rolled into place beside her, propelled by a steward. He pulled on the cigar clenched in his clawlike fingers and blew a cloud of white smoke at the glass. He ordered the steward to fetch him a whiskey, and the man slid away like a ghost. Maliha leaned forward to watch as the women approached the ship.

The two figures outside reached the shadow of the liner. One of the ship's officers appeared from the belly of the vessel and strode down the ramp. He offered his arm to Miss Williams. She ignored him and marched into the ship without even a sideways glance.

"Certainly has her own mind, that filly," the general said. Maliha did not need to see the grin on his face to know it was there. "Needs taking in hand. Touch of the crop, eh?"

"Excuse me, General." Maliha took up her walking stick from where it leant against the ironwork. Before he had the opportunity to say something even less decent, or call her back, she turned away and limped briskly towards her cabin.

She slipped between the red leather wingback chairs that would not have looked out of place in a gentlemen's club; they were so tall one could disappear into them. She strode past the bar on the port side and, beyond that, the small but eclectic library. Not that there was a great deal of time to read on this trip, as she was only travelling as far as Ceylon. They would arrive in a couple of days, but those heading on to Australia had another week to occupy themselves, plenty of time to become bored with deck quoits.

But, she admitted to herself as she stepped into the stairwell that climbed up to the Observation deck, she had yet to grow tired of the ship launching itself into the blue. It was not as elegant as a seagull catching the uprising winds against a cliff and hovering in space, but it was a "miracle of engineering". And, once they were in flight, the strain on her leg was so reduced she could forego her stick completely. As there was no one nearby, she allowed herself a smile.

ii

The ship's warning klaxon sounded with two long bursts, indicating the Faraday device would be engaged in just two minutes. Maliha was one of very few people on the Promenade deck; others were scattered along both the port and starboard sides, peering through the gleaming glass that protected them from the outside air. Most passengers disliked the transition to light-weight when the device was activated; they would be in their bunks, in their beds, or at least in chairs. Maliha enjoyed the tranquillity and the unspoken camaraderie among those souls who braved the event.

She took her place leaning against the rail that separated her from the wide expanse of glass and steel stretching overhead and fully enclosing the open decks. The earlier emptiness of Khartoum had been replaced with crowds, five or six deep, around the perimeter of the air-dock. In their bright clothing they were like a multi-coloured ribbon.

Beneath her, visible through the glass, distributed along the ship's hull, were the three port-side wings: each one perhaps half the width of the ship again. At the end of each wing, enclosed in sheaths of beaten steel, were the massive steam-turbines that drove the rotors. For landing and take-off the turbines were turned to the vertical position with the rotors parallel to the ground.

The klaxon sounded a single long blast: one minute to go. The ship shook as steam tore through the pipes and into the turbines. The rotors resisted for a moment, then reluctantly began to rotate. At first she could follow the individual movements of the blades, but they accelerated quickly and were soon nothing but a semi-transparent blur glittering in the sunlight.

The klaxon gave three short blasts. There was a count of ten, and the Faraday device was engaged. The sensation was like being at the top of a swing, about to descend. It was like falling without movement. It was not uncommon for people to feel sick at least initially, but Maliha revelled in it; it felt like freedom. She had experienced a less powerful form of the effect in the school and at a fair. However it had been only three days before, travelling in the atmospheric train from Bournemouth to London, that she had felt it at full. Now she was an old hand.

Further along the deck, near the enclosed Ladies' Reading Room, a young lad—perhaps only 10 years old—leapt into the air and touched the ceiling of the Observation deck. His father, his clothing marking him as third class, caught him as he descended with the lightness of a bird.

The rotation of the propellers increased. The ferocious down-gusting wind from them whipped up clouds of dust and sand, but the glass dome that enclosed the whole of the upper decks protected them; while, outside, Khartoum became nothing but a phantom beyond the ship's own private sandstorm.

The ship listed to port slightly, and she felt herself pushed against the rail. This was it. Somewhere adjustments were made; valves opened or closed by tiny amounts to adjust the ship's attitude, and the deck straightened once more. The rotor noise increased again. She knew they were airborne now, but the wind-driven sand filled the air around the ship.

Then they rose above it. Khartoum lay below with its streets laid out in the form of the Union Jack—the legacy of Lord Kitchener. The Blue and White Nile rivers reflected the intense sunlight. The clouds of sand drifted along the streets but settled out quickly. The ribbon of people had become a ribbon of upturned faces. She resisted the urge to wave back to the children that ran back and forth below them, though in her heart she was as excited as they.

The klaxon sounded once more to indicate a successful launch, followed by the ship's steam siren that blasted their farewell to Africa. The ground below twisted as the ship changed its heading towards the east and slightly south to cross to the Red Sea, where it would turn south to follow the coast.

The central rotors swivelled a few degrees towards the horizontal, giving them forward propulsion and Khartoum slid away beneath them. Maliha lifted her walking stick, held it at its centre as she took bold steps, towards the bow and the Ladies' Reading Room. As she passed the enthusiastically bouncing boy, he paused and stared. Maliha heard the *sotto voce* words of a child that has not learned to whisper. "That lady's been out in the sun too long."

"Quiet."

"But why…"

She slipped into the reading room, which was mercifully empty. Most of the ladies would be suffering the vapours after the trauma of launch. This final refuge was near the prow of the ship, just behind the superstructure occupied solely by the captain and his senior crew.

Although it was called a reading room, reading was perhaps the least indulged-in exercise. When it was occupied, the most common activity was gossip, not that she was invited to take part—not that it would have been an undertaking she would have enjoyed. Being the subject of such malice quickly disabuses one of its merits.

"Excuse me, miss?"

Maliha jumped. There was a maid holding cutlery and a cleaning cloth.

"Yes?"

"This area is for first-class passengers."

No escape. If only her skin tone had taken after her father's more than her mother's.

"I certainly hope so. Now, if you will go about your own business, I will go about mine."

The girl's face reddened, though whether from embarrassment or anger Maliha could not tell. She turned away and strode to the windows nearer the bow. It did not really matter anyway. In two days they'd be in Ceylon, and another couple of days after that she would be back home. No more "respectable" women judging her by the colour of her skin.

The ship had reached its cruising altitude. The propellers were fully rotated to the horizontal and the ship threw itself through the clear blue sky. The sun hung almost directly above and ahead of them while, in the distance, mountains peeked above the horizon.

The afternoon passed quietly. By three o'clock, the reading room boasted some twenty occupants, from ladies as young as

Maliha with their chaperones to women of a certain age and beyond. Maliha felt uncomfortable; there were too many pairs of eyes glancing in her direction.

Maliha took one last look at the African landscape gliding away beneath them to the thrumming of the six powerful turbines. The temperature inside the ship had dropped as the air they now breathed was vented from the outside and driven through by the pressure of their movement.

Light as a feather she managed a gentle bound across the room, successfully negotiating maiden aunts and highly strung debutantes. She smiled to herself as she took hold of the door handle, then composed her features to perfect neutrality as she opened it and stepped through onto a deck thronging with passengers from all classes.

She walked the length of the Promenade deck, skirting the central games area. High above, the triple domes of glass and riveted steel allowed the sun to pour through. A few hardy souls played quoits in the blazing light, but nothing more energetic. Through the glass ceiling, she could see the starboard funnel, near the stern, churning out smoke from the furnaces. The speed of their progress ripped it into a horizontal trail.

iii

Maliha reached B Deck through the port-side stern stairwell. She considered returning to the lounge as there was a good chance it would be empty at this time of day, or at least there would be a chair in which she could hide. She turned towards the stern but had gone only a few paces, long bouncing ones though they were, when she grabbed the brass rail to bring herself to a halt.

The afternoon sun and the porcelain sky were so bright that everything inside the lounge was nothing but shadow. Dark against the blinding backdrop was the wheelchair-bound figure of the general, facing the slim silhouette of his nurse. As Maliha watched, he gestured violently at her, his hand outstretched and open upwards. Lochana turned towards the window and took a step away.

The roared words of the general—"Don't you turn your back on me!"—penetrated the thrumming of the rotors. The rest of his words were lost. Lochana turned back and took his hand, clasping it in both of hers. Maliha could almost imagine the touch as if it were some performance of Shakespeare, as if they were star-crossed lovers.

The outrageous ill-manners of her eavesdropping struck her. She turned on her heel, embarrassed by her own behaviour and the scene she had witnessed. In an instant she resolved to return to her cabin; the real world was too full of emotion, too full of care to be easily borne. She tore herself away from the thing she should not have witnessed.

"Miss Anderson?" The sharp nasal tones of Mrs Barbara Makepeace-Flynn—a woman of few words and considerably less empathy—sliced the air. Maliha almost stumbled over her own feet as the woman emerged from the passageway that led to her cabin.

The general and his wife occupied separate cabins a short distance down the passage from Maliha's room. The nurse's cabin was next to the general's, with an adjoining door. It was an arrangement that now took on an entirely different meaning in Maliha's thoughts. The unbidden images that surfaced in her mind would have made a paler woman visibly flush.

Not quite understanding her own motivations, Maliha took a few more steps before turning to speak to Mrs Makepeace-Flynn, arranging herself so the woman would have her back to the lounge, her husband, and his nurse.

"Can I help you, Mrs Makepeace-Flynn?"

"You will accompany me to afternoon tea."

A lady did not eat in public without company. Maliha was in no doubt that if it had been Temperance Williams who had crossed Mrs Makepeace-Flynn's path, she would have been a more acceptable choice. Miss Williams was a far better option, with her Britishness unmistakably marked by her pale skin. As that wise child had commented, the best that could be said of Maliha was that she had been out in the sun too long: an offense almost as bad as having an Indian mother. The fact that her Brahmin mother was a member of the Indian aristocracy meant nothing to the pure-blood British.

"You are too kind."

The woman harrumphed as if she were well aware of just how demeaning it would be for her. But Maliha was not paying attention. The lovers had moved further towards the wide expanse of glass at the rear of the vessel and out of sight behind a pillar, with the general wheeling himself easily in the reduced gravity. But it was not they who caught her eye now, but the Indian-born steward who leaned out from behind the bar and stared unashamedly at the general and his nurse.

Another harrumph interrupted her and was also noticed by the steward who disappeared back into the bar. Maliha turned to see Mrs Makepeace-Flynn paused and waiting. Maliha fell into step half a pace behind the general's wife who did not deign to continue their conversation. Maliha knew she was a convenient sop to convention and nothing more.

iv

Maliha made her excuses to Mrs Makepeace-Flynn as soon as it was decent to do so: after two cups of tea and a delicious macaroon. She headed back to her cabin, calculating the hours to Ceylon in her head. It did not require any amount of cleverness to see why the general might prefer a younger woman to his wife. But that said, if one were

- 17 -

treated so abominably by one's husband, how could one not become bitter? The Bard had it right about tangled webs woven by deceit. One could only hope the outcome would not resemble that of the Bard's most famous tragedy.

Maliha unlocked and entered her cabin. While not one of the best first-class accommodations, it was far from unpleasant: a comfortable lounge area with a sofa, armchairs, and a coffee table; a writing desk; a small bookshelf; a double bed behind a screen; large windows that could be opened in a pinch; and a separate room for one's toilet. A palace, compared to the dormitories of the boarding school.

She smiled as she placed her walking stick by the door. How pleasant it would have been if her roommates had succeeded in their plans to have her removed to a room of her own. She arranged her skirts and sat lightly in an armchair, the large rectangular window giving her a clear view of the blue sky and brown earth of the Sudan. The prejudice of the other girls blinded them to the irony of their plan. The teachers, however, were not easily swayed, and unfortunately the plan had not succeeded.

Still, best not to dwell on such things. Absently she rubbed her thigh through the layers of her dress. The ridges of the scar pressed into her skin though she could not feel them with her fingers. No, it is best not to dwell on the evil that could inhabit the minds of immature girls.

A good Buddhist did not concern herself with material things, at least so her studies had suggested. Nor did a good daughter of the Empire dwell on misfortune. Perhaps she should just remain in her room for the rest of the journey. She opened her copy of *Romeo and Juliet*, slipped the bookmark to one side, and continued to read from where she had left off.

There came an abrupt rap on the door, interrupting Romeo's vengeance on Tybalt. Was it possible the universe connived against her? With a sigh, she lifted her feet from the comfort of the footstool and headed for the door. She glanced at herself in the usefully placed mirror by the door—her hair needed some attention, but she would do.

"Who is it?"

"Temperance," said the light, Welsh-accented voice.

Maliha fixed on a smile and pulled open the door to the pretty and slightly flushed face of Temperance Williams. She inhaled deeply on the ivory cigarette holder between her lips and removed it, holding it delicately in the fingers of her right hand. There was an awkward pause as if Temperance were waiting for something. She breathed out smoke.

"Do you want to come in?"

"No, no, *cariad*, I won't disturb you more than I must."

There followed another awkward silence; Temperance took another lungful of smoke and glanced up the companionway to where one of the maids had appeared around the corner, wiping handrails. Temperance looked down at the book still clasped in Maliha's hand.

"Do you have one of those Shakespeare plays I could borrow?"

Maliha suppressed her surprise. "Of course, any one in particular?"

Temperance glanced again at the maid. "Oh, I'm not so bothered. I just fancied something to read until dinner. Just like you. Thought I'd sit in the lounge. Something light?"

"*Twelfth Night*, perhaps?"

"Just the thing."

Maliha stepped away, feeling awkward leaving her visitor at the door. It took only a moment to find the volume. Temperance waited and watched. She reached out her hand as Maliha returned.

"A couple of hours of Shakespeare, what could be better?" With that, she turned away and bounced lightly past the maid and into the port-side companionway.

Maliha closed her door with a click, looking at the Do Not Disturb sign that hung on the inside handle wondering if she dared hang it outside the room in the middle of the day. "Indeed, a few quiet hours with Shakespeare. What could be better?"

CHAPTER 2

i

Maliha had no one to help her change for dinner. Most of the first-class passengers came with at least one personal servant, if not an entire retinue. But she was not alone in doing without; even the general's wife had no one. Irascible she might be, but she was self-sufficient. Or perhaps they simply could not afford it. They would rather travel first class without staff than second class. And the vessel did provide personnel on request. That, however, was a facility Maliha did not feel comfortable with. The school required them to look after themselves (although obviously the other girls had helped one another). This was no hardship.

She stared into the mirror one more time and adjusted her hair. She wondered whom she was trying to impress. Certainly no one on board this ship. But was it wrong to have pride in one's appearance? At what point did making oneself look pleasing turn into hubris? But was life itself not a form of art? Should one not deport oneself as pleasingly as possible?

She had been born into a family of two religions, Hindu and Scottish Presbyterianism, and she had spent the last years being forced to behave like a good Anglican. She found the teachings of the Buddha to be more to her taste.

She cut herself short by pulling open the door. She closed and locked it behind her, slipping the key into her reticule. It was twenty minutes before seven, enough time to order a drink in the lounge as the other passengers would do. She would have avoided it, but it was important to conform, at least for now.

As she approached the junction between her side passage and the port-side companionway, she found her way barred by the steward she had noted earlier displaying the unexpected curiosity regarding the general's private conversation. He moved to block her way, forcing her to arrest her motion by gripping the rail, but her momentum carried them inappropriately close. So close she could smell his breath. His wrinkled uniform seemed a size too large for him.

"*Sahiba?*" His voice was pitched high, and his eyes flicked nervously from somewhere near her feet to her face.

He did not seem menacing, and Maliha suppressed her fears. The idea that anyone would attempt something unpleasant in such an open place was not sensible. Still, she stepped back until a more suitable gap opened between them.

"What do you want?"

He put his hand in his pocket, pulled out a folded envelope, and thrust it at her.

"For Lochan."

"Lochana Modi?"

The steward hesitated then nodded. "*Ji haan.*" He spoke in Hindi.

With an effort (it had been a good many years), Maliha made her best effort to reply in kind, though her native tongue was Tamil. "Give it to her yourself."

Unfortunately that was the exact moment Mrs Makepeace-Flynn chose to float past. The older woman stared at the two of them—an eyebrow raised in admonishment—before her momentum carried her out of sight towards the lounge. Maliha was grateful the general's wife seemed unable to grasp the simple science behind movement in reduced gravity. She turned her attention back to the steward.

"I cannot," she said.

But he pushed the letter into her hand, and she clutched it reflexively as it slipped when he released it. He spun around and headed away from the lounge. He was clearly experienced at movement under the Faraday effect.

Maliha spread the envelope out in her hands. The name "Lochan Modi" was written in careful English in the centre. She turned it over and examined the back: it was one of the older sort of mass-produced envelopes where the sticking was left to the purchaser. That was another deprivation living in India would impose, unless she chose to spend a great deal of money on the imported pre-gummed envelopes. In this case, the sender had chosen to seal the envelope with a large splash of common wax.

She wondered whether it came from the steward or someone else. If it was the steward, why had he not attempted to deliver it in the previous few days? The answer was clear enough even as the question presented itself. She did not recall having seen him before; therefore, he had come aboard at Khartoum. His confidence on the vessel, however, indicated he was a genuine employee of the P&O line.

She examined the envelope again. The handwriting was quite precise, but the pen must be old since the letters were uneven and scratchy. Most likely written by one of the street-corner scribes she had seen in Pondicherry when visiting with her mother.

ii

"Seen my nurse? Blasted chit's disappeared off somewhere."

The general hove into view, wheeling himself. This was no great exertion with the ship in flight, although he still seemed to expect someone to do it for him if such were available. Maliha pushed the letter into her reticule, and when she looked up the practiced smile was once more on her face.

"I'm sorry, General, I have not seen her. I've been in my room since tea."

"Be a dear and shove me up to the lounge, would you? We'll see if she's there. Couldn't dress myself for dinner, had to get one of the ship's boys to give me a hand."

"Of course, General."

She got behind him and propelled him effortlessly to the lounge.

The buzz of polite conversation grew as they approached, small knots of people discussing everything and nothing. She scanned the room for the group to which they belonged. She spotted Mrs Makepeace-Flynn talking to the Spencers, Valerie and Maxwell. They were newlyweds moving out to the Fortress in Ceylon. He was an engineer engaged by one of the many companies that had sprung up around the British void-port, for the construction work of the Queen Victoria station hanging thousands of miles above Ceylon on the very edge of the void itself.

As they passed the bar Maliha glanced across to see if the steward was there. He wasn't.

"It's really terribly exciting." Maxwell Spencer's voice was the kind that penetrated background noise like an angry wasp or, in his case, a happy wasp. Maliha couldn't decide whether the perpetual bonhomie of the Spencers was genuine. "They keep the station with its Faraday device continually activated, and it stays up there at about seven thousand miles. We'll be able to see it on clear nights, I'm sure."

Maliha let the wheelchair roll to a gentle halt beside the small group.

"That seems an awfully long way," said the general's wife. She did not acknowledge her husband's arrival.

"About the same distance from London to Bombay, in fact."

"So it would take five days to get up there? That would be wearisome, without even a change of scenery or stopovers."

"Oh, not at all."

Maxwell Spencer was warming to his subject and given half a chance would talk all evening. Maliha had experienced the same effect when she had been cornered by Valerie and made the mistake of mentioning she had never read an Indian romance by Bithia Mary Croker. She had come away reeling from the onslaught of plot details and character names.

"You see, this top-of-the-range Sky Liner—the pride of the P&O fleet—has a maximum speed of a mere one hundred miles per hour. But a vessel built to travel the void, even one that only travels between the ground and the station, can achieve speeds of *five hundred miles per hour* or even more: Less than a day is required to reach the station."

"And you will be going up?" asked Mrs Makepeace-Flynn innocently. There was no doubt she already knew the answer and sought only to pierce his good humour.

There was a distinct lag in Maxwell's enthusiasm. "Not personally, no."

The general chose that moment to cut in. "Evening, Barbara. Max. Seen Lochana by any chance?"

If Mrs Makepeace-Flynn's tone with Maxwell Spencer had been subtly cutting, her response to her husband was undisguised malice.

"I have not. Perhaps she fell overboard."

Valerie Spencer chose that moment to turn away and take a long sip from her glass. Her husband, on the other hand, completely failed to recognise the menace.

"Oh, nobody can actually fall overboard, can they? I mean, the upper decks are fully enclosed and do not open."

"Who's fallen overboard?" Temperance arrived from deeper within the lounge, a freshly lit cigarette burning in the holder dangling from her left hand; she wore a very modern dress with a distinctly French look about it and no corset. Mrs Makepeace-Flynn's face reddened with the effrontery of such a provocative garment, and even Valerie looked shocked. The general seemed unmoved.

"Seen my nurse, Miss Williams?"

Temperance looked down at the general as if he had just crawled out of a sewer. Then her face relaxed, she placed the tip of her cigarette holder delicately between her lips and drew a leisurely breath.

"She came through the lounge earlier, said she was feeling a little under the weather. She said she might take a turn about the Promenade deck."

"Oh dear, she's not well?" Valerie chimed in. "Perhaps someone should check on her." And her eyes flew to Maliha. "Don't you think so, Miss Anderson?"

Maliha smiled. One thing one could be sure of with Valerie Spencer; she would never use Maliha's first name. "I'm sure I wouldn't know, Valerie; besides, who would push the general?"

"Quite right," said the general. On cue, the dinner gong sounded, and like Pavlovian dogs the ensemble drifted towards the companionway. "If you wouldn't mind, Maliha."

iii

The dining salon's round tables had been transformed. Where they had held the simple adornments for tea earlier in the afternoon, they now carried a ravishing selection of china and cutlery. There were huge flower arrangements that towered, thin and spindly, up to the ceiling with a minimum of support. Elegant glassware—made especially for the vessel—with images from Greek mythology engraved into each piece, artistry of the finest quality, finished off the place settings in fine style. Rows of Greco-Roman columns supported the ceiling and the walls were decorated with Greek frescoes. During the day, the pictures were covered up using curtains, to give the room a cosier aspect.

Being forward of the main cabin areas, the port side of the room was lined with windows that looked out on the darkening sky and the Red Sea; they were now travelling south-east along the African coast. When they reached Abyssinia they would turn north-east, following the Gulf of Aden and thence to the Indian Ocean and Bombay.

Stewards moved swiftly but without haste, seating travellers in the oak chairs and providing drinks as needed. Maliha wheeled the general into position as one of the stewards removed a heavy chair from the table; then she took her place between him and Maxwell Spencer.

Each person at the table positioned themselves in their usual configuration. There was a vacant seat on the other side of the general that would have been occupied by Lochana, and beyond that Mrs Makepeace-Flynn. Beside her on the other side was William Crier—a banker or an accountant, Maliha wasn't sure which. He disconcerted her in that he did not express the natural prejudice of his peers, and always took time to be interested in his companions— an interest that seemed quite genuine.

The general's wife had taken to him, and apparently he never tired of listening to her complaints. Continuing clockwise around the table, there was Temperance who was another confusing character: she was passionate in her faith but fond of Parisian fashion. She had been very friendly towards Maliha on the first day but turned cold quite quickly. After that, she had turned her attentions to Lochana.

Then came Valerie Spencer and finally Maxwell. It was easy to prod Maxwell into talking for a long time before he wound down, and to Maliha, at least, his talk of machines and engineering was not uninteresting, even if he did have a habit of repeating himself. As a result, the evening meals were not as arduous as they might have been. If Maxwell dried up or conversed with his wife, the general was another easy target for a pretence of conversation.

Apparently Mr Crier had commented about war wounds and set off the general.

"Not been bound to this damn chair for very long at all. Last saw action in the Transvaal, putting down that damn farmers' revolt back in '02."

Temperance's head jerked up. "But surely, General, it was their land."

"Nonsense. We took it fair and square back in the 80s; they only existed at all on our sufferance. We let them stay and farm, provided protection from the natives, and then they had the audacity to object."

Temperance looked down at her plate. "You just don't see it, do you? You started with the Welsh, then the Scots, then anywhere else in the world that isn't significant enough to give you pause. A nation of bullies." Her accent became more pronounced with every word.

"Oh look, the first course!" broke in Valerie, as waiters flooded from the door at the end of the salon. "I wonder what it is."

"Fish," said Mr Crier.

Maliha breathed a quiet sigh of relief and turned her attention towards the food.

iv

The general's nurse failed to put in an appearance during dinner and, as a consequence, Maliha was co-opted for more wheelchair management. They returned to the lounge for bridge. The tradition of the men drinking and smoking without the ladies was dispensed with on-board and, as the evening drew on, it was natural to either retire or return to the lounge. The Spencers had chosen to retire, claiming the shortened days of the vessel for their excuse.

Maliha found herself the general's partner against Temperance and Mrs Makepeace-Flynn. The other tables were occupied with games of whist and backgammon. The electric lights burned through the pall of smoke that rose from the combined combustion of a hundred cigars, pipes, and cigarettes. The steady hum of conversation filled the ears along with the occasional bark of laughter or raised voice.

Meanwhile, through the wide expanse of glass in the stern, the twin trails of smoke were lit by a brilliant moon that reflected off the Red Sea, with the dark masses of Africa to the left and Araby to the right.

It was all so civilised. So British.

Both Mrs Makepeace-Flynn and Temperance were matched in their aggressive bidding and more often than not, one or the other was dummy, forcing Maliha to remain at the table. The general was more measured, though it might have been the brandy slowing him down. Maliha bid predictably; she had learned years ago it did not pay to stand out. At around 10 p.m. they were on the last hand of a rubber, and she was dummy.

She grabbed at the opportunity and excused herself for the night. A turn around the deck to clear her head of the smoke and noise seemed wise, and she quickly mounted the stairs. She kept on past the Promenade deck up to the Observation deck. As she had expected, there were many passengers of a similar mind, but the subdued lighting protected her from their stares.

She looked over the inner balcony down onto the Promenade deck. Some young fellows were playing football, with their jackets for goalposts. It was a foolish idea in reduced gravity, but their good-humoured laughter at their own antics, bouncing high into the air and doing somersaults and making the ball fly to prodigious heights and distances, made her smile—although she judged them a little worse for drink.

Moving to the outer hull, she gazed into the dark. The moon's light sparkled on both the rotors and the sea. Here and there, along the coastline, the light of fires: perhaps tribes of African nomads, or villages of sunbaked mud buildings.

v

"A penny for your thoughts, Miss Anderson?"

"Mr Crier." He had appeared beside her, quiet as a mouse. He held a glass of wine in one hand and a glass of water in the other. To her, he proffered the water.

"I know you don't drink alcohol."

"Thank you." As she took a sip, ice clinked across the surface, and the ripples sloshed in the slow way they did under reduced gravity. He turned away from her and stared out across the dark landscape, and up at the moon.

"Like a jewel hung in ghastly night, makes black night beauteous and her old face new." He said. Maliha took another hurried sip and wondered if she should leave; that was a rather racy sonnet of the Bard's. "Oh, I do apologise, Miss Anderson, I really was talking about the moon. Perhaps you would prefer me to withdraw?"

"No. It is fine, really."

He took a deep breath and sipped his wine. "It seems a shame we should have to travel without being able to breathe the fresh air, don't you think?"

"You could travel by boat."

"I think that might be pleasant, but everyone is such a hurry nowadays, and all the quality liners are in the sky. To travel by boat would mean a great reduction in luxury."

"I do not think you would be forced to scrub the decks."

He laughed. "No, perhaps not. But one does enjoy the trappings of first class. And the company can be most pleasing."

"Sometimes, it can."

"Perhaps if we were on a coastal scow you would not be forced to replace a missing nurse and not even get paid for the duty."

The term *duty* conjured other images in Maliha's mind to those intended. "I don't mind."

He turned to face her. She felt uncomfortable beneath his gaze. "Perhaps you should."

"It is not my nature, Mr Crier." She hid behind another sip, and the cold water slid across her tongue. "It is not done." The words were placatory, but her tone was strained.

"There," he said. "I believe you are a suffragist."

"You may believe what you wish," she said. "Thank you for the water. I believe I shall retire now."

As she walked away in long, careful strides, she felt as if his eyes burned into her back. She cursed herself for reacting to him. Clearly he was playing some game: he had sought her out, as evidenced by the glass of water; deliberately engaged her in conversation; and then goaded her into reaction. It was all very inappropriate.

vi

Lochana Modi opened her eyes. Her head throbbed in a way that made even looking painful. The cabin she was in was almost complete shadow, just a hint of moonlight. She attempted to rise and instantly clutched at her lower ribs as an agonising stabbing pain ripped through her, she slumped back breathing heavily with a gurgling catch in her throat.

Her bodice was sodden, and her fingers wet with whatever the thick gooey liquid was. She stretched out her arm and stared at the dripping dark that covered the palm of her hand. Then she knew; tears filled her eyes.

It was so unfair. All she ever offered anyone was love.

Cold seeped through her, eating at her. Already her feet were like ice.

"No." She had meant the word to scare away Death as it came for her. But though the sound came from her mouth she barely heard it above the wheezing. Whimpering with the pain she took hold of the sofa's arm and levered herself to her feet. She staggered for a moment as she found her balance. Her head swam. Her training told her that she had lost a lot of blood.

She had seen men die. She did not want to die. If only she could get help.

She took an uncertain step towards the door.

CHAPTER 3

i

It was morning. The sun poured through the windows of the dining salon. Maliha sat alone at breakfast at a small table near the inner wall. The tables near the windows were filled with other passengers. The Spencers had nabbed their own while Mr Crier was eating with some people she recognised but had never spoken with. The general and his wife were at another. Maliha frowned; this was the first morning Lochana had not been in attendance. Perhaps she really was ill, as Temperance had suggested.

There was no one else in first class who would consider checking on her, and it would be inappropriate to approach the general and ask him, especially with what she had observed and Mrs Makepeace-Flynn's undisguised animosity. No, that was not a discussion to engage in. It would be best if she simply visited Lochana's cabin.

She took a final sip of coffee; it was a vice, but one could not be completely pure in the real world. Besides, the scent of fresh ground coffee was a form of beauty and there was no point grinding coffee only for the smell.

Leaving the table she headed out through the double doors into the main companionway. It took only a few minutes to traverse the distance to the cabins. She composed herself and knocked lightly. She waited a few moments, then knocked a little harder.

She waited again, a feeling of concern rising within her. She knocked firmly and more times than would be considered proper. A response was not forthcoming. She tried the door handle, but it was locked. She turned from the door, intending to find a steward and alert them to the situation, when something else caught her attention.

The sound of the engines and their vibrations had changed.

Maliha ran to the window. The ship was not due to touch down until they reached Bombay in the late evening, around eleven o'clock. The blueness of the Gulf of Aden stretched out to the horizon with not even an island in sight. But the central rotor was moving to the vertical position. She pressed her face to the glass, peering forward and then to the stern. The other rotors were also turning.

It was impossible to see what was happening from here.

She headed back to the main companionway. She had expected to see hordes of people flooding from the salon and rushing up on deck. But the companionway was nearly empty from end to end, a couple of stewards moving in the lounge to the stern and another she didn't recognise moving towards the salon.

She took the stairs to the Observation deck. She thought she could perceive the difference in the way the ship vibrated as the rotors would be fully vertical now. The ship would be drifting forward with its thousands of tons of momentum. The captain had not issued orders for reverse thrust, which would have been very noticeable, so she could only assume the change had nothing to do with anything down on the surface. It had to do with the Sky Liner itself.

She burst from the door out onto the deck; the sun beat down through the dome from the front, but Maliha's attention was immediately grabbed by the passengers spread out along the outer rail, peering down. She moved towards them. They were most closely pressed together near the stern where the windows came to an end. She could only join the group next to the nearest person standing in line with the central rotor.

Being careful not to touch the man, she stretched out across the rail and attempted to make out what they were looking at.

Unfortunately, the man was quite large, and he, too, was stretching to see around the crowd to his left.

Maliha sighed quietly. This was not the first time she'd had this sort of problem though, on previous occasions, those blocking her had been doing it deliberately. At least it wasn't malicious this time. There was nothing for it but to step up onto the railing. There was no danger to life, as the wall of glass and steel prevented anyone from falling overboard; the only risk was to her pride, and she had little enough of that. And not one iota to lose to the other passengers.

She lifted her skirt and placed her boot on the lowest metal rail, then hauled herself up with a slight twinge from her injured thigh, but that passed quickly. She sat on the rail and leaned out, pressing her outstretched hand against the cold glass for support. She looked down.

The most immediate impression she got was that there was now nothing between her and a three thousand foot drop to the sea below. Then her attention was taken by events in the side of the vessel. A hatch had been opened in the hull above the rear wing, below the level of the rotor.

A platform had been run out, and three sailors stood half in and half out, holding a rope as another crew member climbed down rungs set into the hull. At intervals, he ran his rope through attachments mounted parallel to the rungs: a wise precaution, as the down-draught from the rotor whipped his hair and clothes like a gale. She noted he had a second, much thinner, rope being paid out as he descended. A second man with a stout rope about his waist exited the hatch and followed the first down.

The rear rotor itself was running perfectly smoothly as far as she could tell, and he did not appear to have any tools; she wondered what he could be doing. It was then she saw it, flapping and fluttering under the rotor's gusting power, a collection of rags caught on the rear wing. Then she let out a gasp as she saw a hand moving, and the randomness of the air flows lifted the rags to reveal a slim body before hiding it again in the next moment.

Maliha stared in morbid fascination as the crewman reached the curved surface of the wing and stood under the battering force of the rotor. He attached the rope to another hook embedded into the metal, then took measured steps across to where the tangled clothing continued to flap about. Kneeling beside the body, he took a few moments to examine it, and then pulled on the second rope.

A stretcher was passed out from the hatch just as the second crewman made it to the wing; he reached the body and helped the first crewman guide the stretcher as it was buffeted back and forth in the wind. Once on the surface of the wing they lashed it down and proceeded to disentangle the body from where it was caught. They transferred it to the stretcher and strapped the arms, body and legs.

At their signal the rope attached to the stretcher tightened, and it rose from the wing. Holding their end of the rope tight, they managed to get the stretcher up to the hatch without bumping it against the hull too many times. The stretcher was brought inboard. But in those last moments, Maliha had seen everything she needed to see. It was Lochana Modi. Dead.

ii

Maliha stepped down awkwardly from the rail, surprised to see the much bigger crowd that now surrounded her. A man directly in front of her pushed into the space she had vacated by the rail. He didn't even look at her. But with the recovery of the body, the crowd along the rail broke apart. Only those wanting to watch to the bitter end continued to hang over the edge.

The low buzz of conversation grew steadily as those who had not been able to see were told the events by those who had. Maliha pushed through the crowd as carefully as she could. She needed to get to the purser, the only member of the senior crew that a passenger could easily contact.

Under ordinary circumstances, she would have avoided the crowded stairs that led from the Observation deck down to the Promenade, but this was no time to worry about such things. She pushed her way through the crowd and joined the queue of passengers heading down. There was barely a glance in her direction.

A jumble of thoughts pressed in on her. How had Lochana's body come to be outside the hull? If she hadn't become caught on the wing, she would simply have disappeared without a trace into the sea. Temperance had seen her in the lounge sometime between six and seven, so she had been alive then. But seemingly no one had seen her afterwards. Could she have fallen from the Promenade deck? That seemed impossible; there were no opening windows on either of the open public decks.

Maliha crossed the Promenade deck heading forward to where the purser's office was accessible from the passenger deck and the ship's superstructure.

The cabin windows had catches which were soldered to prevent tampering. They could be opened but with difficulty. Lochana's cabin was inboard and had no windows, but she did have access to the general's cabin, so if she had been able to open the window there she could have fallen that way. But would she have taken her own life?

Maliha pushed open the door into the purser's outer office. A large oak desk acted as a barrier across the cabin. A crewman of Indian origin and unhappy demeanour stood at a filing cabinet replacing a folder. He looked round as she entered.

"I must speak to the purser immediately."

The man smiled. "I am afraid he is unavailable at present, Miss Anderson."

Maliha was impressed, though she could appreciate the benefits of knowing all of the ship's first-class passengers by sight. They could be very difficult. "I expect he is dealing with the body you found on the wing."

"A most unfortunate affair."

"Yes, of course, but I know who she is."

He became serious. "You know?"

"It's General Makepeace-Flynn's nurse, Lochana Modi."

He picked up the phone on the desk, consulted a chart of dialling codes next to the phone, and dialled a four digit number.

"It is the assistant purser here … Yes … Is the purser available? … Yes, quite important … Yes, sir. I have one of the passengers here. She says she knows who the body is … Lochana Modi, General Makepeace-Flynn's nurse … Miss Maliha Anderson … yes, sir. Very good."

He slowly placed the phone back in its cradle.

"Would you mind waiting?" He indicated a row of hard-backed wooden chairs upholstered in green leather. Maliha took a seat. She felt the vibrations in the ship changing again and surmised they were underway once more. She glanced at the two clocks on the wall. One showed the time in London while the other was local time. They were now three hours ahead. She adjusted her watch; they had already gained an hour on Constantinople and Khartoum.

iii

The ship's doctor, in leather apron and with his shirt sleeves rolled up, examined the body of the woman. The examination room was crowded with the captain, purser, and master-at-arms, as well as the doctor's assistant and the ratings who had brought the body on board.

The death would not look good on his record, thought the captain. Fifteen years as the master of passenger vessels, ten years in the Royal Navy before that, and never anything like this.

The doctor cut away the tattered remains of the outer clothing, enough to examine the body. The skin was covered in pink splotches with a network of scrapes and abrasions across the entire surface.

The purser excused himself.

"All this damage is post-mortem," the doctor said to the unasked question. "Rigor mortis is setting in now."

The MAA looked interested. "So she was killed this morning?"

"Can't say, there's no rigor at low temperatures; she could have been out there all night."

"So when?"

"Hypostasis—the blotches—suggests all night, but there's no distinct pooling; she was moving around the whole time by the looks of it." He looked up at the captain. "It's a miracle we found her at all. If she hadn't got caught, she'd have been gone and you'd just have had a missing person."

"Can't say that would have been worse," said the captain. "Any idea how she died?"

The doctor smiled. "That's the easy bit. Here." He pointed to a spot just below the ribs on the left of the body where an inch-long ragged hole broke the skin. With a gloved finger he prodded and looked inside with a small electric torch. "The blade was probably about six to eight inches long, quite thick too. Whoever did it certainly made an effort to cause damage; made a right mess of the liver. She would have taken a while to die though. Very painful."

"Are you saying she was murdered?"

"Unless she accidentally fell on the blade, then wriggled about a lot before getting off and throwing herself out of the window. No? It was murder."

The captain sighed and turned to the master-at-arms while the doctor attacked the remainder of the clothes. "All right, you'd better start an investigation."

"This is a little outside my experience, sir."

"None of us is going to come out of this looking good, Chief. If we can sort it out before we hit Bombay—"

"Oh, dear God." The doctor's voice was a complete change from his previous blasé attitude. The others stared at him. "Lochana Modi was not a woman."

The MAA spluttered. "Are you sure?"

"It is a fairly fundamental factor in medical training but if you doubt me feel free to take a look at him yourself. I'm sure you're familiar with the basics."

iv

The cabin door was pushed open by a large man with a ruddy complexion and a handlebar moustache. Along with his height and girth it gave him a commanding aspect, and he knew it. Maliha did not know who he was beyond the fact he wore a uniform and was not the purser. She resolved not to be intimidated as he came to a shuddering halt before the desk. The assistant purser glanced purposefully in her direction. He turned and loomed over her.

"Miss Anderson." He thrust out his hand. She was uncertain whether he intended to shake, or pull her from her seat. She stood and placed her hand in his. It disappeared, but his skin was soft and he did no more than squeeze gently. "Please come into the office."

The assistant already had the door open and, having seated Maliha opposite the officer's chair, closed it gently after them.

"I am the master-at-arms, Charles Grey. You may refer to me as Mr Grey. I am dealing with the current situation." He stared at Maliha for a moment, as if seeing her for the first time. It was a look she had seen many times before. It came with the cognisance that the person in front of them was not as white as the viewer had previously thought. "Would you like some tea?"

"No, thank you," she said. "Perhaps we should get to the point?"

He nodded and looked down at the desk. He scanned it and, failing to find what he was looking for, opened a drawer from which he extracted a number of sheets of paper with rows and lined columns. Something for accounts, she thought. He took a pen from the rack and wrote her name at the top, the date and the two times which he took from his two wristwatches.

"I am investigating the death of a passenger."

"Yes."

"I understand you have some relevant information?"

"Did they not tell you?"

"I would rather hear it first-hand."

"All right. The woman you recovered from outside, it's Lochana Modi. She came aboard with the general. She's his nurse."

"Is she?"

Maliha frowned. "Yes, of course."

The MAA stared down at his piece of paper. "And you know this because?"

"Because I have spoken to her. I have played cards with her. I have seen her with the general."

"No doubt. But how do you know the body was"—he hesitated for a moment—"her?"

"I was watching from the Observation deck. She was wearing the same clothes as yesterday. And I saw her face, although it was a fair way away."

"The clothes were badly torn. The face was … damaged."

"Yes, but I had seen her in the afternoon, I was in the stern lounge when she came back on board with Temperance Williams. She was wearing the same clothes." Which was odd, now she came to think of it; why had Lochana not changed after the heat of Khartoum?

"You saw her?"

"I was in the lounge watching for them because it was getting late. I did not know if they had adjusted their watches. The general was there too." Maliha grasped what was behind his words. "She was murdered."

The MAA's head jerked up. "No one said anything about murder."

"And you're thinking I might have done it," she said. "What possible reason could I have?"

"The number of possible suspects is very limited, Miss Anderson."

"About five hundred, I would have thought."

"Not everyone would have a motive, Miss Anderson. I'm sure we can limit it to those who have had regular contact with the victim."

"And I have a motive, do I?"

"You admit yourself you spend a great deal of time with the general. Perhaps you would like to take the place of"—again the curious hesitation—"Miss Modi."

Something exploded inside Maliha. It was not the master-at-arms himself. It was not the fact that he considered her a suspect. It was all the times in her life that the finger had been pointed in her direction because she was different.

"Have you the slightest idea who my parents are? Do you even care?" Maliha found herself on her feet, shouting at the seated man. "I do not require a job. And if I did, I believe I could do somewhat better than a position tending the general and putting up with the constant sniping from his jealous wife. If you want someone to suspect, perhaps you should look a little closer to their home."

Her hands were shaking. She could feel tears in her eyes as the anger overcame her, anger from so many years of lies and hatred. She turned on her heel, pulled the door open, and stormed through;

finding herself floating a little too high and long, she struck the wall opposite. Inside she screamed. She could not even manage an elegant exit.

When she finally managed to get out onto the deck, the tears were flowing down her cheeks. People were looking at her. She turned away and faced the glass wall, looking out across the sea though she could barely make out where sea ended and sky began through the tears. She clicked open her reticule and rummaged for a kerchief.

Something white appeared in front of her.

"Here, *cariad.*" The soft tone of Temperance Williams penetrated her suppressed anger. She took the kerchief, dabbed at her cheeks, and sniffed.

"Sorry." She offered the damp cloth back to Temperance.

"Keep it." Maliha felt a hand grip her elbow, turning and pushing her towards the stern. "Let's go somewhere more private."

v

Temperance Williams' cabin was of a similar layout and decoration to Maliha's, but was one of the cheaper inboard ones. It lacked a rug, had fewer cushions, and less china adorned the walls. An elegant Turkish cloth had been thrown over the sofa where Maliha sat, a cloth which she recognised as an item Temperance had bought in Constantinople.

Daylight spilled into the room through a small lace-covered window opening onto the companionway, which in turn had windows at its end. The room was lit by electric lights situated around the walls. Temperance had ordered some tea and served it when the maid had left.

"Now," said Temperance. "What has happened?"

Maliha stared down into her tea. "Lochana is dead. Murdered."

"I don't understand."

"The fuss this morning, when the ship stopped they were recovering her body."

"Recovering her body? From where?"

"Outside, on one of the wings."

Temperance sipped her tea thoughtfully. "Why were you crying, *cariad?*"

"I was being interviewed by the master-at-arms. He said I was a suspect."

Maliha was shocked from her introspection by the sudden barking laugh from Temperance. "How utterly ridiculous. Anyone who knew you would know you are far too decent a human being to do such a thing."

"That's very kind, Temperance. However I'm sure anyone is capable of any act given the right motivation or the right set of circumstances." Unconsciously she rubbed the ridged scar on her thigh. "One does not always consider the consequences when one is in the grip of emotion."

They went quiet and drank their tea.

At length Temperance placed her cup down with a solid clink into its saucer. "So, Miss Anderson," she said. "What do you intend to do about it?"

"I don't know what you mean."

"You have been falsely accused."

"I'm only a suspect," she said. "Using their criteria, you would also be one."

"What about Valerie, Max, and that Mr Crier? Oh, and the delightful Mrs Makepeace-Flynn."

"Yes, of course, perhaps some of the crew as well."

"So who is it?"

"I couldn't say." Maliha wished Temperance would drop the subject but she refused to let go.

"Let's just review what we know, shall we? Why don't you tell me what you said to the master-at-arms?"

"I said I didn't know a great deal. I saw you come back from Khartoum with her. That you mentioned you'd seen her between six and seven, I suppose the times would really be six and quarter of seven because that's when we turned up."

"I think it was shortly after six."

"Yes, and she told you she wasn't coming to dinner."

"And that's it?"

"That's all, I said."

Temperance looked at her watch. "We have a couple of hours until lunch. What say we have a snoop around and see what we can find?"

CHAPTER 4

i

Maliha trailed Temperance as she strode down the main companionway. People stood around in small groups speaking quietly with worried voices. The news of the death was now common knowledge and even the word murder was uttered. Maliha considered how impossible it was to keep a secret like this. They turned into the passage that led past Maliha's cabin to Lochana's and the general's.

A crewman stood outside Lochana's door. He had a gun holstered at his side. Maliha hesitated, but Temperance did not even pause. She approached the sailor, and Maliha could not fail to notice the way he took in Temperance's slim modern form.

"Can I help, miss?" he said.

"Oh dear," said Temperance in such a soft voice that Maliha studied her face carefully to make sure she was not unwell. The woman that stood so tall and proud at all times was transformed into some meek child. She clasped her hands demurely at waist height and did not make eye contact. Clearly Temperance had missed her calling on the stage. "I'm really sorry…"

"What's the problem, miss?"

Temperance hesitated. "This is all so awkward and so sad. I really hope you can help."

"Whatever I can do, miss."

"It's so terrible, Miss Modi…" Temperance pulled out a kerchief and dabbed at her eyes. "But, oh, this is too awful."

"Should I fetch someone?" This time he addressed his comments to Maliha, having noticed her for the first time. He looked back at Temperance.

"No, I need to fetch my Bible."

"Your Bible?"

"I feel so foolish. I lent my very own family Bible to Miss Modi. You see, I am taking up a position as a missionary to the Hindu ladies of India. I was instructing Miss Modi on the wonder of God's grace. I lent her my very own family Bible. And now this…"

"Shall I fetch it out for you?"

Temperance laid her hand gently on his arm and looked up into his eyes. "Oh no, I could not ask you to leave your post. We can find it as quick as may be." She smiled at him.

ii

The door closed behind them, and Maliha switched on the electric light. Temperance regained her usual poise. "Men are pathetic."

The room was another inboard cabin without windows. In this case, it was specifically intended as servants' quarters and had a connecting door to a large cabin on the outside. The wooden floor had a rug in front of the sofa, and the armchair while off to the side was the writing desk near the connecting door to the master cabin.

Something nagged at Maliha. She stared around the room again frowning.

"Problem?" asked Temperance. As she spoke, raised male voices filtered through to them. The door slammed open, and the master-at-arms stormed in.

Temperance shrank back to become the mouse version of herself. But the MAA's attention and anger was not directed at her. His ire was reserved solely and entirely for Maliha.

"What's the meaning of this? Tampering with evidence, Miss Anderson?"

Maliha stood her ground, but her thoughts were not coherent. She knew she should be paying attention to the master-at-arms, but there was something in the room that was just not right. Temperance came to her aid.

"Oh no, sir. It is my fault."

His eyes did not leave Maliha. "And you are?"

"Temperance Williams. Missionary."

"Really."

Maliha frowned again and turned away from the master-at-arms. She studied the sofa and, with a feeling of relief, saw the thing that troubled her.

"That end cushion is upside-down, Mr Grey," she said and pointed at the left-hand end. The sofa was of the three-seat variety, with individual cushions for each position. The cushions were shaped so that each end one was an L-shaped piece that fitted around the front of the armrest. Each was patterned and when observed more closely it was clear the pattern of the left-hand cushion did not match.

The master-at-arms made a harrumphing sound. "What's that got to do with anything?"

Maliha, feeling more confident, turned back and met his gaze. "What reason might you have for turning a cushion over in a murdered woman's room?"

The man was not a fool. Two strides took him to the erroneous cushion, and he flipped it over. A mottled brown stain covered most of the surface.

"So this is where she was murdered," said Temperance.

He looked at her. "Of course not."

It was the turn of Temperance to look confused. "Why not?"

"Look around, Miss Williams."

Temperance did not look, but her eyes narrowed, and she opened her mouth for a sharp retort. Maliha interrupted before she could say anything. "There are no other bloodstains and besides, how did she get outside?" She said the words but her mind was already racing ahead because there was still something wrong with the sofa, and now she knew what it was. "Anyhow, that cushion doesn't belong in here."

The MAA looked down at the cushion in his hands and back at her. "How could you possibly know that? We use the same design throughout this deck."

Maliha knew that thoughts of her guilt were running through his mind again. It was very tiresome. "I did not kill her."

"That remains to be seen. How can you possibly suggest this cushion does not belong in this room?"

"Try putting it back the right way up." Maliha said dismissively. She turned away from him and went to the connecting door to the general's room. She turned the handle and pulled, but the door did not move.

The MAA swore in a most indelicate way. "It's a right-hand end cushion."

Temperance laughed. "There you are. Mr Grey, is it? No woman would make such a mistake."

Maliha took a piece of paper from the writing desk and slid it into the top of the gap between the door and the frame. She carefully slid it down until it reached the handle level where it met an obstruction. "It's bolted on that side. I wonder why?" She turned to where both of them were staring at her.

"Why shouldn't it be bolted?" asked Temperance.

Maliha hesitated. The secret moment between the general and Lochana that she had observed was almost a precious trust. But if it helped to find Lochana's murderer it would be best to reveal all the truth. But what of any embarrassment to the general's wife? No,

Maliha was sure Mrs Makepeace-Flynn already knew. It was the only thing that explained her attitude.

"Because I believe the general and Lochana were"—she paused and gathered her courage—"intimate."

Despite everything, she was not prepared for the surprise that took hold of Mr Grey's face, which rapidly degenerated into utter disgust. Temperance had only a look of the latter.

"That is a very serious accusation, young lady." The words seem to have been torn from the MAA's gut. Maliha felt a twinge of anger that he should be disgusted at a liaison between an Englishman and Indian woman. After all, that described her parents precisely.

"There you are," said Temperance. "Must have been the general."

iii

The captain's day cabin was equipped with various tables, chairs and desks; there was a wide sofa along one wall over which hung photographs of various ships of the Royal Navy. There were no windows. Captain Jones stood at ease behind his desk as the steward pushed open the door from the companionway with his elbow and then backed in, pulling the general in his wheelchair. As the door swung back, the steward turned the general round and pushed him into position opposite the captain.

The captain moved round the desk and shook the general's hand. The man looked grey and feeble, as if all the blood had been drained from him. His hand was cold, and it was like clasping a withered leaf. The old soldier put no effort into the formality. Captain Jones nodded at the steward and the man left.

It was a very awkward situation, thought the captain as he took his seat opposite the man. It was hard to think that this was the same irritating gentleman that had come aboard four days earlier.

"Would you like a drink, General?" The general shook his head, staring at the desk in front of him, but the captain was certain the man saw only his inner thoughts. "A cigar?"

"Say what you must say."

The question on the captain's mind was not one he could say outright. It was the kind of question that must be approached sideways. There were easier questions.

"I must, of course, ask about the death of your nurse."

The general did not respond.

"When did you see Lochana Modi last?"

The general took a deep breath. "It was in the afternoon between three and four o'clock." He finally looked up and met the captain's eye. "I did not kill Lochana, Captain."

"The ship's doctor says she died in the evening, most likely, but he was unable to specify the time with any degree of precision."

"The last time we spoke was in the afternoon."

"Can you tell me the nature of the discussion you had?"

"I do not recall," he said. "Do you have a nip of whiskey?"

The captain took a few moments to pour a drink from his private stock. It was a decent single malt. General Makepeace-Flynn took the glass and cradled it for a few moments before taking a sip. The captain resumed his seat and leaned forward across the desk.

"There is a steward who was on duty at that time who will swear that you spoke with raised voices."

"Yes, all right. I was angry with the amount of time Lochana was spending in the company of Miss Williams."

"Miss Williams?"

"Some Welsh missionary travelling first class, if you please. Full of zeal which she decided to expend on my nurse."

The emotion he expected from the man was creeping back.

"So if you did not kill your nurse, General, who did?"

"I don't know! And let me tell you that if I did then I would be doing your job for you and that person would pay!"

"She's just a nurse, General. Just a native."

"You, sir, are a fool!" The general looked very much as if he wanted to pull himself from the chair and wrap his fingers around the captain's neck.

"But Lochana Modi was not a woman at all, was she? He was a man."

The general slumped back into his wheelchair and looked, for all the world, as if he were going to cry. The captain hoped he would not.

iv

Maliha and Temperance waited outside the general's cabin. Mr Grey had not allowed them to enter though he left the door open, perhaps hoping for some insight from Maliha. The view it afforded them was better than nothing. It was quickly confirmed the right-hand cushion of the general's sofa was also the wrong one and presumably the one swapped. But as the MAA continued his search, Maliha became disinterested. He was looking in all the wrong places.

Without a word she turned away, went to the nearest window, and looked out. It confirmed what she already thought; all the cabins on this companionway were forward of the rear wing.

She judged that anything thrown from her own window would be eaten by the rotor as her cabin was slightly forward of it, but the general's cabin was further towards the stern and thus behind the rotor. From his windows, an object would be caught in the air stream, blown backwards, and probably lost forever. Unless, by some happenstance, it was a heavy object that managed to fall onto the wing and get caught on some protuberance before being thrown into oblivion.

"What are you doing?" said Temperance from the door.

"Just thinking."

"I am told gentlemen are not attracted to women who think."

Maliha looked at Temperance in her Parisian dress. "It's not something that concerns me."

The lunch gong sounded, echoing down the passageways.

"Oh good, all this sleuthing has made me quite ravenous," said Temperance. "Shall we?" She put her arm out for Maliha to slip hers through and smiled. Dutifully Maliha did so while hiding her reluctance and allowed herself to be led through the ship to the dining salon.

Friendship was a concept she understood in principle, but since leaving India and all her real friends at age eleven, it was not something she had experienced. She had soon learned that any friendship offered at the school was always a mask for betrayal. She found it hard to imagine that Temperance's offer of camaraderie was honest, though she had no sensible reason to doubt it.

There were fewer people in the salon than usual. Those who knew they were not the perpetrator considered themselves potential victims. Rationality did not come into it.

The table was set with melon. Maliha sat in her usual seat. The place to her left where the general would normally have sat contained a chair and an untouched place setting, likewise the next seat which would have been Lochana's. Mrs Makepeace-Flynn sat in her place with Temperance beside her. Maliha was somewhat surprised, since that would normally have been where Mr Crier sat; he was one place further along. Max and Valerie were not in their places. Maliha was on her own.

Mr Crier stood up. "Miss Anderson, would you consider it inappropriate for me to sit next to you; otherwise there will be no one for you to talk to."

Maliha did consider it inappropriate and had a great deal to think about, but those were not words she could say. "You are very thoughtful, Mr Crier."

Which is how she found herself having luncheon with a man. He dug his spoon into the melon. Waiters drifted in and removed the food from the other settings.

"A most unpleasant business," he said.

"Yes."

"Do you have an opinion on it?"

"I see no value in having an opinion, Mr Crier. This is not art, it is murder." She punctuated her comment by cutting into the melon with her spoon and taking a mouthful. A dribble of juice escaped her lips and she hurriedly dabbed it with her napkin. One benefit of reduced gravity was that dribbles travelled at a very unhurried pace, which meant it was easy to catch them before they became too obvious.

"I understand you are travelling home."

"That is correct."

"Do you disembark this evening?"

"No, at the Fortress in Ceylon. Then I take a flier to Pondicherry and a carriage home." She concentrated on the melon, but the outer skin was soon stripped clean. The plates were cleared without a fuss and replaced with plates of various sandwiches, cheeses, and light biscuits.

"You attended Roedean I believe, Miss Anderson."

The sandwich she was lifting to her mouth came to an abrupt stop. He knew. This was really too much. Was there nowhere she could go to escape the notoriety? She felt the scar on her leg begin to itch. She frowned in annoyance.

She set down her sandwich and looked across at Temperance who had her lips very close to Mrs Makepeace-Flynn's ear and was whispering something with a look of self-righteous pride on her face.

On hearing the words, the general's wife's face distorted into a mask of complex emotions that were hard to fathom. But there was pain and anger in there, perhaps hatred and loathing too.

There was a commotion at the main entrance to the salon. Maliha was forced to turn in her chair to see. The general had been pushed through the doors by a steward, who had managed to make a meal of it, scraping the wheel against the wood of the door. Maliha noted the shell of a military uniform that encased the pale, wasted figure the general had become. She barely noticed Mrs Makepeace-Flynn getting up from her chair.

Maliha watched long enough to see the general's wife approach her husband, raise her arm, and slap him with all her strength—an act to which he did not react. She then strode from the room, head high. Maliha turned back in her chair and saw the faces of all the diners watching the event. Including Temperance, her lips pressed into a thin, humourless smile.

v

The general dismissed the steward and locked himself in. He glanced at the connecting door to Lochana's room. He rolled himself to the drinks cabinet and poured a large whiskey. He held the glass between his knees and pushed himself over to the writing desk.

He took a sheet of paper and the steel-nibbed pen his wife had given him for his fiftieth birthday, the finest pen produced from the Birmingham factories. He unscrewed the ink pot and charged the reservoir. Now his secret was known to so many, the ignominy would be too difficult for his wife to endure. And the law would not be far behind.

It did not take long to write what he needed to say. He pressed the upturned sheet into the blotting paper. He considered addressing it to an individual but concluded it would be futile. It had his signature at the bottom, and that was all that was required.

Retrieving his pistol from the case he had placed under the bed required more effort, but the reduced gravity of the ship eased the task. He unlocked the door, then took the gun and his whiskey to the armchair and pulled himself across into its welcoming cushions. He checked the pistol carefully to ensure everything was in good working order, and loaded a single bullet. It wouldn't do to have a misfire, nor to have someone else accidentally fire it when they found him.

He took a long comforting mouthful of the whiskey and placed it on the side table. Raised the gun and placed it at his temple. And pulled the trigger.

CHAPTER 5

Travelling so fast through the sky from west to east had a curious effect on time. The seconds, minutes, and hours became compressed. It felt like mid-afternoon as they cruised across the Indian Ocean, and yet the sun already dipped towards the horizon.

Their table for the evening meal was barely half full as Maliha took her usual seat. She was not hungry since, in reality, lunch had not been very long ago. And it had been a very unpleasant lunch. Temperance was the only one who seemed in good humour as she helped herself to the food.

"So, the general did it," said Temperance. "Good riddance to the sodomite."

There was a sharp intake of breath from Valerie. Maliha was stunned by the remark. What was this? A factor in the murder of which she was not aware. Was the general a sodomite? With whom? Oh.

"Please, Miss Williams!" asked Max. "There is a lady present."

"I think you'll find," said Mr Crier, "there are three ladies present."

"I do not require you to defend me, Mr Crier," said Temperance. She pointed her knife at the Spencers. "You are the worst type of snob. You're worse even than Mrs la-di-da Makepeace-Flynn. It's taken generations of breeding to make her into the cow she is today. You two have only your own bourgeois aspirations to blame."

Max stood up, grabbed his wife's hand, and pulled her to her feet. "If you were a man, Miss Williams, I would demand satisfaction."

"If you were a man, Mr Spencer, I would oblige."

Max looked as though he might strain something looking for a suitable retort. He failed. "Come, Valerie" was all he could manage. He turned on his heel and stalked off with Valerie fluttering beside him.

"Thank the Lord," said Temperance, and returned to her meal.

"You are a curious missionary, Miss Williams," said Mr Crier. Her only response was to glance up at him, her eyes devoid of discernible emotion. He turned his attention to Maliha.

"So, Miss Anderson, what do you make of it all?"

"I do not believe I have anything to add, as I said at lunch." She attempted to make her statement as final as possible, but he seemed immune. She needed to think about this new idea, Lochana was a man?

"A queer business though. The general is having an affair with his nurse. That much is understandable given the disagreeable nature of his wife. But in a most sordid turn, it seems his nurse was a man in disguise."

"It wasn't a disguise," Maliha said absently as memories surfaced of her old life at home: all the different people who visited and consulted her mother.

"I beg your pardon?"

"I was just saying it wasn't a disguise, Mr Crier." Maliha felt awkward as she had made herself the centre of attention; even Temperance was listening. "Sometimes, an Indian might feel they are in a body of the wrong sex. I believe they are called *Hijra*."

"Ridiculous," said Temperance. "Primitive. Now you see why I am a missionary to these people, Mr Crier."

Mr Crier smiled and nodded in her direction. "Then something happens between them and he kills her."

"Yes, of course," said Maliha. "Except..." She trailed off, as thoughts played hide and seek in her mind. Silence hung about the table while, around them, the chink of crockery and scrapes of cutlery on porcelain went on.

"Except what?" demanded Temperance.

"I wonder what time she died?" Maliha said. "You saw her at six and no one saw her again. So the general probably didn't do it."

"That's what he wrote," said Mr Crier.

Maliha's eyes narrowed. "You've seen his suicide note?"

Maliha could almost read the excuses that ran through his mind as he thought of them and rejected them again. "I haven't seen it. I was told what it said."

She nodded. "I imagine he also said he had returned to his room after bridge and found her dead in his room. Realising the scandal that would ensue if he were to report it, he got the window open in his cabin and pushed the body of his lover out, expecting it to be gone forever."

"How did you know?"

"It only takes a logical mind, Mr Crier."

"I knew it was you," he said, and Maliha's excitement drained away. "You were the one involved in the Taliesin Affair. They said it was a schoolgirl but never said who."

"I was not *involved*."

"You?" Temperance could not have been more incredulous. The revelation also caused her to frown, and she seemed to be contemplating something.

"If you'll excuse me," said Maliha, "I think I will retire." She rubbed her fingers absently on the napkin and dropped it beside her plate. She found Mr Crier ready to remove the chair from under her as she stood. There was nothing she could do to stop him, so she allowed it.

She did not look back as she headed for the salon door.

ii

Maliha pressed her back against her cabin door in a futile attempt to keep the world at bay. Would this nightmare trip never end? Now they knew she was the "schoolgirl investigator". She hated the journalists but for once her Anglo-Indian heritage had helped: they had not used her picture or her name.

But still. The general had stated he did not kill Lochana. It made sense because the timings were wrong; there was no motive and—she realised she had no idea how Lochana had been killed. Had she been shot with the general's gun? Or stabbed? Or even poisoned? Probably not poison, murder would be hard to prove. And a gunshot would doubtless have been heard unless it were done in the engine room; it was a sound that would reverberate and carry in the metal of the ship—just as it had with the general's suicide. Would a gunshot wound bleed more than a stabbing? Probably it would; if it were going to kill at all it would do a great deal of damage.

Most likely stabbed, then. Sufficiently badly to be fatal, but not enough to kill her immediately, as she still had the strength to go from where she had been attacked to the general's cabin. It couldn't be too far, or she would have been seen.

Maliha cried out and kicked the door with her heel. Not having full access to the facts that were clearly known to others was a significant disadvantage. She stopped at the thought. Turned and faced the mirror.

"What am I doing?" she asked her reflection, but her simulacrum looked as confused as she felt. "The general will be blamed for the murder, and they will wrap it up with a nice red bow.

His wife will have to live with the social ignominy of being married to a murderer, a suicide, and a sodomite. And the real murderer will go free."

She nodded at herself. It would be unfair if the general were to be found guilty of both crimes, though what befell Mrs Makepeace-Flynn was neither here nor there. But that the true murderer should go free? That could not be borne.

She would need to act quickly because as soon as the vessel was in radio range of Bombay they would report the murder, and police would come aboard as soon as they landed. If her previous experience was anything to go by they would settle for what was convenient and any further investigation would be stifled. Only a few hours remained.

With new purpose coursing through her, she equipped herself with a light jacket and a hat, pinning it firmly in place. She hefted her walking stick; she might not need it for walking, but it always lent her positive strength when dealing with others. Thus armoured, she stepped through her cabin door and locked it.

iii

It was Mr Crier's custom to take a turn around the Observation deck after meals. It took him a moment to recognise the lady striding purposefully in his direction swinging her cane. He almost started when he realised it was Miss Anderson. It looked like her, yet her demeanour was that of a different woman to the one he knew.

He touched his cap as she approached. "Good evening, Miss Anderson."

"Mr Crier. Please walk with me."

She walked past him without slowing. He had to overcome his momentum and almost run to catch her up.

"How can I assist you?"

"You must tell me everything you know about the death of Lochana Modi and General Makepeace-Flynn." He was quite taken aback at her demanding tone.

"Shall we have a drink?"

She stopped abruptly by ramming her cane into a ridge between the planks of the deck. Once more he was forced to dance to her tune as he sailed further along the deck and had to turn back. "This is not a social matter, Mr Crier. All I require is your information."

"Naturally I was not suggesting anything of that nature. I thought you might prefer somewhere a little more private."

Miss Anderson looked about at the scattered groups of individuals, families, and couples promenading. "This is quite private enough," she paused, considering. "Perhaps if you were to offer me your arm we might continue. If you do not feel it would reflect badly upon you."

Mr Crier extended his arm and felt the lightest of touches as her thin fingers brushed his arm. She did not come in close, but that was to be expected. She was most certainly a strange woman.

"Where would you like me to start?"

"Do you know when Lochana is believed to have died?"

"I understand the best estimate is early evening but that the nature of her death makes it hard to judge accurately."

"And can I ask how you know this?"

"The doctor is an old school chum," he said. "May I ask why you want to know? This will not help the general now, or his wife. It can only cause more upset."

"The apprehension of the real murderer is paramount, wouldn't you say?"

He sighed. "What else do you want to know?"

"How was she killed? Was she stabbed? With what? And how many times?"

She sounded almost ghoulish in her demand for detail. "Yes, she was stabbed. It was something with a very thick blade and quite long."

"How many blows were delivered?"

"Only one, I believe."

She fell silent. He stopped and turned towards her pensive face. "I do apologise, are you feeling well?"

She returned from wherever she had been. "What? Unwell? No, of course not. The facts must be evaluated one against the other."

"It does not disgust you?"

"Of course, I am disgusted. Can you imagine the mind of someone who could commit such a crime?" She did not pause for an answer. "It is just a matter of considering the motive, means, and opportunity. If they cannot be divined we only lack sufficient information."

She gestured to him to continue walking.

"Your involvement in the Taliesin Affair has given you a taste for mystery then?"

"I was not *involved*, Mr Crier. There was a great deal at stake and I was the only one to see it."

They had come around to the forward part of the deck and crossed in front of the Ladies' Reading Room.

"Perhaps you would like to watch the sports?" he asked and paused for a reply that did not come.

Thin clouds hid the stars, and all that could be seen of the moon was a whitish glow, but the electric lights kept the dark at bay across the deck. There were shouts and cheers from the game players. He walked on and she followed along with him.

Miss Anderson remained quiet, wrapped in a cocoon of thought. He had never before associated with a woman with such a power of concentration. It was almost unnerving. They approached the starboard stairwell. She finally spoke, but "Ah" was all she said.

Back in her room Maliha retrieved her reticule from where it lay in the dressing area. She poured a glass of water and switched on all the lights. With the glass beside her, she sat in the armchair with her reticule open in her lap. She pulled out the letter. The name on the outside, Lochan Modi, now made sense.

She broke the seal and withdrew a single sheet of folded paper. She examined the interior of the envelope briefly, then discarded it. With delicate fingers she opened the letter and stared at the strange characters for a few moments, then dropped it with a sigh. There were so many languages in India and as many different scripts to go with them. If she had been educated there, she might have known this form of writing.

It was critical she speak with the steward who knew Lochana.

For the first time in the journey, she eyed the push button on the wall near the bed that would summon a member of the staff to her room, but there was no guarantee he would be the one to respond.

She stuffed the letter back into her reticule and headed towards the stern lounge.

Beside the bar, she paused and looked out across the empty room. All was quiet—far quieter than would be expected at this time of night. The deaths and the imminent arrival at Bombay had cleared the decks. Except for one chair, facing the huge windows, from which a thin line of cigarette smoke rose. On the small table next to it was a small glass of something green, a liqueur no doubt. The chair's occupant, however, was hidden by its high back.

"Can I help you?" The steward behind the bar was not the one she needed. He was English and sported the thin moustache favoured by the lower middle classes.

She turned to face him. "Yes. I need to speak to one particular steward. Indian by birth, I believe he came aboard at Khartoum, and his uniform is too large for him. Do you know him?"

The man's look was difficult to decipher but after a short pause he turned and went through a door into the back. Moments later he returned, followed by a nervous-looking man, the very steward she required. Maliha glanced at the library door. The lamps inside were still lit.

"Come with me." She opened the door and entered. "Don't shut the door."

"Can I help, *Sahiba*?" He was sweating.

"What's your name?"

"Pravangkar Modi, *Sahiba*."

"You are family to Lochana?"

"Lochan was my brother, *Sahiba*."

Maliha removed the letter from her reticule and offered it. "Here."

He took it. "It is open."

"What does it say?"

"It tells that our father is dead. Lochan should help the family. He should send money."

"Nothing else?"

He shook his head. "Will you tell the captain about me, *Sahiba*?"

"Were you on duty here yesterday evening?"

He nodded. "I deliver orders to rooms."

"Did you see anything?"

He shook his head and looked towards the door. "Why do you ask me these questions, *Sahiba*? Only bad things can happen."

"Do you want the murderer to go unpunished?"

He frowned. "The general?"

"Nonsense. Whatever you may think of his nature, or the nature of your brother, I saw them together. They loved each other. Besides, the times are all wrong. So what did you see?"

He did not answer.

"If you do not tell me, then I will tell the captain of your connection to Lochana. What will they think then?"

Maliha was not proud of the shiver of terror that shook him as the thought sank in. After all, how much more convenient for the police to have an Indian as the murderer?

"Please do not, *Sahiba*. I beg you." He dropped his head and pressed his palms together fingers pointing towards her.

"Then tell me what you saw."

"I saw nothing of value, *Sahiba*. The engineer and his wife returning to their cabin."

"You mean the Spencers?"

He nodded.

"That is not unusual; they did not come to the lounge that evening. They said they were retiring." He shuffled his feet.

"What else?"

"Please, *Sahiba*…"

"Very well," she said, and took a step towards the door, he instantly looked relieved. "I will go straight to the captain."

The relief turned to terror. "They went to their cabin!"

"But?"

"They went to another place first."

"Where?"

"I do not know—"

"Oh, for heaven's sake," she took another step towards the door. His arm snaked out, his hand gripping her forearm.

"They came from the passageway with your cabin, with the general's cabin, with Lochan's cabin. They were not coming from the salon."

She stopped, and his fingers fell from her arm. "What time was this?"

"Between nine and ten o'clock."

"How many minutes after nine?"

He thought for a moment. "Perhaps thirty or forty."

"Very good."

CHAPTER 6

i

Maliha hesitated at the door to Mrs Makepeace-Flynn's cabin. She was a formidable and unpleasant woman at the best of times, and this was not the best of times. However there was no alternative; the ship was only an hour from Bombay. She knocked firmly then took a step back.

A few moments later the door was opened by a maid. Maliha recognised her as one of the ship's crew. She was not Indian. "Can I help, Miss?" She spoke with an over-emphasised "h" as if being particularly careful not to drop it.

"Miss Anderson to see Mrs Makepeace-Flynn." She spoke loudly enough that the general's wife would be able to hear her.

"Let her in," said the harsh voice from within. "And leave us. Come back in the morning to pack." The maid stepped aside to allow Maliha in, and then left, shutting the door firmly.

The cabin barely differed from the others: same furnishings, same rug, and no windows as this was an interior room similar to the one Temperance had. Barbara Makepeace-Flynn rose to her feet from the armchair.

"What do you want?" she said. "Have you come to gloat?"

"It must be difficult."

"What?"

"Can I offer my sincere condolences, Mrs Makepeace-Flynn?"

She seemed taken aback, as if the fire in her had been extinguished. She sat down.

Maliha noticed that tea had been brought but not served. She splashed a small amount of milk from the delicate jug, poured the tea, and passed it to the older woman, who took it almost without noticing. Maliha did not pour any for herself but perched on the edge of the sofa.

"It's a terrible thing to happen."

The general's widow ran her finger delicately around the rim of the teacup. Maliha could see her hand shaking.

"Forty-three years we were married," she said, almost talking to herself. "In all that time he never even held my hand. The last time he touched me was at the wedding ceremony when he put this ring on my finger." She held out her left hand and looked at it as if it did not belong to her. "Do you understand what I am saying?" She jerked her head up at Maliha who met her eye but only trusted herself enough to give a slight nod.

"I had no idea what he was really like. I was naive. We travelled so much: the soldier's life, y'know. I did what any good wife would do. I kept his house, and I waited for him."

She brushed her fingers against her cheek leaving a trail of dampness. "Then came the stories. You think I am harsh and cold, Miss Anderson, do you not? Don't deny it. That may be so, but among officers' wives there is seldom great friendship. We do not remain in one place more than a year, and always there is the competition and the cutting tongue. So I came to hear the stories about my husband and his … preferences. And they laughed behind their false sympathy.

"But then, finally, after all those years of torture he succumbed to the wheelchair. Judge me how you may, Miss Anderson, but I was glad when he was shot because he would be mine at last." She went silent and took a sip from her cup.

Maliha wanted the whole story. "But that was not to be—"

"No! That was not to be, as you say." Her voice was acidic with anger and pain. "No, because he brought that woman … that nurse. Lochana Modi. And it was she that tended him. She who spent her hours looking after him. She who was with him day and night."

She looked up into Maliha's eyes again. "I hated her."

"But your husband loved her."

"Yes!" she hissed. "That much was obvious. I tried to console myself at first with the thought that, after all the stories and innuendo, at least he now loved someone of our sex." She gave a humourless laugh. "But that was false. She was a man after all. I did not kill that pervert, Miss Anderson, but I assure you I would have happily wrung her neck."

"I can't imagine how you felt."

"No. I doubt you can," she said. "When I was informed of her true nature, I felt as if I would break. And to have my husband enter at that very moment. To make a public scene."

"I am truly sorry."

The general's wife looked her in the eye. "I believe you are." She gave another half laugh, as lacking in humour as the other. "You are a surprising young woman, Miss Anderson. Most extraordinary." She paused to drain the teacup in an undignified way, then quickly dug out a kerchief to dab her eyes.

Maliha smiled gently. "Would you like more tea?"

ii

Through the port-side panorama of the Observation deck, Maliha watched the lights of Bombay glittering through the rain and the dark. It wasn't monsoon yet; if it had been she probably wouldn't have been able to see a thing.

Laid out before them was the rectangular landing dock, lit with the dazzling brilliance of dozens of electric lamps. Landing at night, and in the rain, would be nearly impossible without the lights. The rotors along the side of the ship had pivoted into their upright hover position; the ship drifted into place through its momentum and the guidance of smaller rotors located strategically around the ship's hull.

As they moved over the landing field, she had to lean farther out to see below. The ship continued to descend. Whenever it drifted off station the sure hand of the captain easily brought it back into position.

Below them, she knew that hatches were being opened, and sure enough the ground crew ran out through the torrent of rain and under the ship. She contemplated for a moment what would happen to a man if he were crushed by 35,000 tons of Sky Liner, but then they reappeared, running back from the ship holding the hawsers that had been thrown from the open hatches. These were rapidly attached to winches firmly anchored to the dock. The winches turned under steam power, gathering up the slack in the lines.

Now began a battle the vessel did not intend to win. While the rotors were kept up to speed, the winches pulled the ship down towards the dock. The brilliant lights gleamed off the wings, turbine housings, and rotors. Finally, when the Observation deck was no higher than the surrounding buildings, the power to the rotors was finally reduced, and the ship settled the final few yards to the ground with barely a bump.

The ship's klaxon sounded three times in quick succession. Maliha grasped her walking stick firmly by its end and braced herself against it. On the bridge, the captain gave the order and the Faraday device was deactivated. Maliha felt her full weight return; the pressure on her leg made it ache. The iron and steel of the ship groaned in sympathy as its weight settled.

Bombay. The seven islands of the archipelago had been subject to extensive land reclamation through the last two hundred years and were now almost all connected by broad land bridges. The port where the ship now rested, to the north-east of the city, had been swamp a few years before, and sea only a little before that.

She looked out into the city streets, lines of darkness delineated by dim gaslights. While in the distance, the frontages of the larger buildings were illuminated by electric lights. At first glance one might believe it was London or any other city in Britain with the grand Victorian buildings rising above the streets lined with lower three and four story structures. The railway station, not far away, was a slab of gothic architecture dwarfing the buildings around it.

But then you looked closer and saw the pillars and towers of the Jain temples that would never be seen in England, and the curiously garbed people passing occasionally under the street lights.

Under normal circumstances, those disembarking would leave the ship almost immediately, but not this time. Once the vessel was secured, perhaps twenty Indian police officers emerged from a building marked Immigration. They deployed at a fast trot around the ship facing inward, clearly to prevent anyone attempting to leave without permission.

After them came another group of men: one in the uniform of the P&O line, another in a brown suit, and the remaining six being uniformed police. They crossed the distance to the ship and disappeared beneath it. Little doubt this was the inspector and his men.

"An unpleasant night, Miss Anderson."

She turned. "Just a night like any other, Mr Crier."

He leaned on the rail and looked down at the loose circle of policemen, already dripping wet in the rain. "I fear those who are planning to leave are in for a long night, unless they managed to get to the front of the queue."

"Interviewing them is a waste of time and energy," she said following his gaze.

"Because you know who the murderer is?"

"Because they don't."

It was six o'clock in the morning, Bombay time, when the *Macedonia* once more took to the air. Maliha remained asleep. She had not watched the slow trickle of passengers leaving the ship as each was interviewed briefly and allowed off. She was not aware of the fraying tempers and stern words.

An hour later she woke, dressed, breakfasted in the near-empty salon and—grateful for the reduced gravity once more—emerged for a short constitutional around the deck. She took her walking stick with her, even though she did not need it.

The view from the Promenade deck revealed the Indian Ocean to the starboard dotted with fishing vessels and the occasional sea-bound steamer. To port and ahead, the ragged strip of the wide Indian coastal landscape was crisscrossed by rivers that mixed and separated in a great confusion while punctuated by villages and towns. Further inland was the mountain range that paralleled the coast and ran all the way to Kerala.

The Reading Room was thankfully quite deserted. She was expecting a summons from the inspector quite soon, so there would be little point getting tied up in Shakespeare just now. However, as she had hoped, there were a dozen copies of the latest edition of *The Times of India* on a table.

She took a copy to a reading desk, her back to the window but facing the door.

She glanced at the front page. There was an article about the proposed Indian Press Act to limit what stories the native newspapers would be permitted to print. She was familiar with the story and *The Times* spoke in a similar way to the newspapers back in Britain: the natives were restless and could not be trusted; cut their ability to speak to the ignorant populace, and their talk of revolution will be similarly suppressed.

She moved on. She read quickly, a talent that had earned her even more scorn at school from the teachers as well as her fellow pupils. She rapidly absorbed the local Bombay stories and those having wider importance. She reached page five and stopped.

TRAGIC ACCIDENT IN PONDICHERRY

Her mother and father's names leapt from the page as the words of the article burned into her mind. *Fire … all dead.* A cold hand reached out and clutched her heart. She could not move and stared at the words. The only image in her mind was her home with fire ripping through the wooden walls and floors.

"Miss Anderson?"

She jerked her head up. She had not noticed the three men enter. The moment of outrage at them entering the women's domain passed. This was not the *zenana* of an Indian household where a man could not enter.

"Yes." She blinked twice. She recognised the inspector from last night. There were dark circles round his eyes, he was insufficiently shaven and his cheeks seemed to droop. "Inspector." She realised the man next to him was Mr Crier, which was somewhat surprising; then again perhaps it was not, as Mr Crier was most certainly not an accountant. The man behind was one of the policemen, a sergeant by his stripes, and he looked equally tired.

She looked down at the newspaper article again, hoping vainly it had been nothing but a fancy. The words still sat on the page. She inhaled deeply, held it for a moment and breathed out.

She took hold of herself, forced herself to stand and held out her hand to shake. The action took the inspector aback, but he rallied and took hers in a loose grip. She could feel calluses on his hand; he had seen hard manual labour in his time.

"Inspector Forsyth, miss. I'd like to ask you a few questions."

His Glaswegian accent was a further shock. He sounded just like her father.

"Yes, of course."

He led the way to a group of leather settees. They arranged themselves at an appropriate distance from one another. The sergeant remained standing.

Forsyth's questions were the standard sort one came to expect from the police: times, places, what was seen, questions about relationships. Normal, of course, if one had come into contact with the police before, which she had. Then came the one she was expecting.

"Mr Crier here tells me you're the young lady behind the Jordan case."

She found herself warming to the inspector. He did not use the sensationalist title the press had attached to the event in Brighton.

"Yes."

"You're a little young, aren't you?"

"I am 19, Inspector. I did not have a particularly demanding social life at my school, as you may imagine. Thus I had much free time and I read a great deal. I believe this gave me a suitable grounding."

"And you have been investigating this case?"

No point in denying it with Mr Crier sitting there. "Yes."

"And what conclusion have you reached?"

"That General Makepeace-Flynn did not kill Lochana Modi, and if we reach the Fortress without apprehending the real murderer, they will escape scot-free."

"Can you prove he did not do it?"

"There was no motive; no sign of a murder weapon, let alone any idea what it might have been; and the opportunity aspect is uncertain."

"But you cannot prove he did not do it."

"No one can prove a negative, Inspector."

"So do you know who did it?"

"I think so. But I cannot prove that either, yet."

"So who do you think it is?"

"I'm sorry, Inspector. I can't tell you."

He frowned. "And why not, Miss Anderson?"

"You won't believe me," she replied. "However, you may find it useful to ask the Spencers what they were doing lurking around our cabins the night Lochana was killed."

"You think they did it?"

"I doubt it. But you can be sure they have something interesting to tell you."

iv

The inspector had left her and gone about his business—probably to make life difficult for the Spencers—leaving her in the Reading Room. Now she simply stood and stared out at the landscape drifting by. But she saw none of it; news of her parents' deaths had numbed her. Her fingers curled around the railing were cold.

All these months, years even, she had dreamed of going home; it was the one thing that made school tolerable, and now there was no home to return to. Her father's estate would go to someone in Glasgow who would not even want to know her. And if he had been conscientious enough to make his will, then anything left to her would be in trust for the next two years, if she ever managed to see a penny of it.

"It's an amazing land."

Maliha did not turn at Temperance's voice. All she wanted was to shut herself away, from everyone and everything but she did not have energy to move.

"Miss Anderson, you are crying."

Am I? she thought. She raised a hand to her cheek and touched the wetness. *So I am.*

"Whatever is the matter, *cariad?*"

Maliha choked as she tried to suppress a sob.

"Was it that policeman? Men have no feelings."

Maliha shook her head. "No... no, not him."

"Come on, let's get you somewhere private," said Temperance and put her arm around Maliha's shoulders. "You can't go making a spectacle of yourself. Not when you're almost home."

Her solicitations forced another bout of sobs from Maliha. Temperance turned her towards the door. The room was now quite busy and the spinsters and debutantes were looking.

"My walking stick," said Maliha pointing back towards the rail. Temperance walked back and picked it up, putting it gently into Maliha's hands before guiding her through the door, across the deck, and below to her cabin.

CHAPTER 7

Temperance unlocked the door and pushed it open. "In you go now, *cariad.*"

She studied Maliha as she stepped into the dark interior just inches from her, breathing in the soap-smell of her skin. She followed Maliha inside, switched on the light, shut the door and turned the key gently so as not to alarm her guest. The room was a mess. She had left her empty cases open on the bed ready for packing and her sewing box was still open on the desk.

They would be landing in only a few hours but there was still time.

Maliha had stopped a few paces into the room, so Temperance gently took her by the elbow and guided her to the sofa and settled her into it. She relieved her of her walking stick and placed it along the side of the sofa just out of Maliha's reach.

"Shall I send for tea?" she asked.

"Just some water, if you don't mind."

"We don't want to be disturbed, now do we?"

Temperance went to the glass-fronted drinks cabinet. She had resisted the temptation to pour every last drop of the foul liquor into the basin lest the servants think she had drunk it herself. She folded down the front, took out a lead crystal tumbler, and poured water from the jug. She hated the way it moved so sluggishly, it was so unnatural.

She looked at the reflection in the glass as she put down the jug. She saw her dress-making scissors in Maliha's hands with the blades wide apart. She seemed to be examining them. Temperance smiled, it would be amusing to catch her in the act.

"Do you sew?" she said.

Maliha shook her head and put the scissors back. Temperance sat down beside her, passed her the glass, and placed her hand on Maliha's. She had beautifully delicate fingers, but her skin was cold.

"Why don't you tell me what is wrong, *cariad?*"

Temperance saw the tears well up again. Poor thing was in such terrible need.

"Have you a kerchief?" Maliha asked sniffing indecorously.

Temperance stood up and went to the dresser; she took a handkerchief from one of the smaller drawers and switched on the bedside light. Then she went to the door and switched off the main lights. She did not mind that her cabin did not have more windows, as darkness brought her closer to God. As she turned back, she noticed Maliha staring at the small window as if she had seen something. Temperance pulled the small curtain across it.

"Here you are." She passed Maliha the kerchief and watched as she delicately wiped the tears from her cheeks. She sat down close beside her, feeling the comfort of Maliha's thigh pressing against hers. But she was not the one in need of solace. She placed her arm around Maliha's shoulders and rested the other on her leg. She knew from many years of experience that those in grief were the easiest to manipulate. Listen to their sorrows, give them succour, and they could be commanded.

In her quietest but most insistent voice she asked again. "Tell me what has happened."

Temperance allowed the silence to stretch out. Sometimes it took a while for them to gather the courage to speak.

"It was in the paper. My parents are dead. My home is burned," said Maliha. "I have no parents and no home."

Temperance almost laughed; that made it so much easier, but now was not the time for laughing. That would come later. "And no income, I'll wager."

Maliha shook her head. "I don't know what the arrangements are. It was only a newspaper."

The two of them remained silent for a time. Temperance watched her, seeing the downcast eyes, still on the verge of tears, and felt her own confidence grow. The girl had not thrown off her arm; she even seemed to be nestling deeper into the embrace. Neither had she removed the hand from her leg, the presence of which should be considered a great impertinence.

Temperance kissed Maliha's cheek. Maliha closed her eyes. Temperance's heart leapt with joy. She had not been rejected. So many times she had been, and the pain was hard to bear.

Maliha opened her eyes and turned to face her. Those eyes, still glistening with tears, looked searchingly into her own. Their lips almost touching, preparing for that first kiss.

Maliha spoke: "It must have been a terrible shock when you discovered Lochana was a man."

ii

Temperance's arm about her shoulders became rigid, and the hand on her thigh tightened. Maliha pulled away from Temperance so she could see her full face more clearly in the half light. The look of excitement had been replaced by confusion and something much harder and sharper.

"What?" Temperance's voice grated as if someone had gripped her throat.

"You killed her because you found out she was a man."

Temperance jerked away from Maliha as if she were poison. She jumped to her feet, grabbed her cigarette holder from the table, and put it in her mouth even though it contained no cigarette. In annoyance she removed it again.

"The general killed the pervert," she said. "Everyone knows that. You are weak in the head."

"No, he did not. He loved her."

"Love?" she screamed. "*Thou shalt not lie with a man as with a woman; that is an abomination.*"

"The fact remains. He cared for her. He did not kill her. He could not have. You did."

Temperance fumbled with her cigarette case, jammed a cigarette into the holder and lit it. She took in a deep breath of smoke, blew it out, and felt its energy flowing through her, calming her. She laughed and sat down facing Maliha.

"You're a very dull girl, you know? You think you're so clever with all your books. Well, if you remember I was reading your Shakespeare in the lounge all afternoon until dinner."

Temperance sat as if tied. Ankles and knees tight together, elbows pulled in.

"That was to cover the tryst you had arranged with her. Lochana was found dead in the same clothes as she'd worn into Khartoum. If she had been killed in the evening, she would have changed. No. You arranged to meet with her immediately after your excursion. The chairs in the lounge are big enough that you could leave your cigarette holder there with a drink, and anyone would think someone was sitting there."

Temperance glanced at her cigarette holder. Then back at Maliha. "Or I was sitting there reading all afternoon. And you're wrong. I saw her in the evening she said she was going for a walk."

"You made that up to confuse matters," said Maliha.

"You dare to accuse me of lying," she cried. "I do God's work."

But Maliha would not be side-tracked. "You came back to this room where she was waiting. And you ... discovered she was a man and in a rage you grabbed up the nearest thing you could and you stabbed her. You thought you'd killed her then and there, and went to cover your tracks. But when you came back she was gone."

"You can't prove any of this. You're an ignorant half-caste daughter of a demented father."

Maliha ignored the insult. It hurt to be reminded of her father but in her years at the school the girls had been far more imaginative in their attacks, and Maliha had all that time to learn to let them roll off her.

She changed tack. "Where's your rug?"

"What?" Temperance looked down at the bare deck and then at the door. "There wasn't one."

"All the cabins have rugs, Temperance," said Maliha. "You got rid of it because it was stained with Lochana's blood. The seals are broken on one of the outer windows in the companionway outside; you threw it out the same way the general disposed of her body. I noticed when the master-at-arms was examining the general's room."

Temperance sat back, her muscles loosening. She took another deep drag on the cigarette holder, held the smoke in her lungs, then blew it out smoothly. "You still have no proof, Miss Anderson."

"That's true, everything up to now is strongly indicative that you killed her but not an absolute certainty. Except you made a mistake. An independently verifiable mistake."

"I don't make mistakes," she said.

"You made a mistake with me, didn't you? You thought I would succumb to your seduction, but I have to say, you are not my type."

Temperance leapt to her feet and slapped Maliha across the face so fast, she had no time to pull back. "Not your type? You ugly little whore. I do God's work. I give God's love where it will best serve His purpose."

Maliha's cheek stung and she almost regretted the moment of facetiousness. But again, she hadn't survived school without more than her share of physical mistreatment. A slap was nothing.

"So what was my big mistake?" demanded Temperance.

iii

The pathetic little girl held her hand against her cheek. She had to die, of course: she would not accept the absolution of God's love. She could not be allowed to prevent the spreading of the Truth. Maliha was nothing but a disgusting half-breed.

Temperance took a long pull on her cigarette. It relaxed her. She saw her scarf on a hook on the far wall. Stabbing may not kill someone fast enough, but choking the living breath from her would be effective and satisfying.

She strode across the room and took the silk scarf delicately in her hands. She loved its sensuous feel.

"Well? What was my mistake?"

It was almost as if Maliha accepted her fate. She did not turn about as Temperance twisted the scarf into a tight band.

"You told Mrs Makepeace-Flynn about Lochana."

She could not have erred. "It was common knowledge."

"When you told her, no one outside of the crew knew."

"She told me herself." Yes, that was it; the pervert had revealed the truth to her.

"No, she didn't. For two reasons: In the first instance, she did not consider herself to be male; and in the second, you dislike men. If you had known, you would not have given her time of day."

No. She could not have made a mistake. The little half-breed needed to die.

In the dim light, a scarf whipped over Maliha's head and tightened about her neck. The pain shot through her along with the terrifying knowledge she could no longer breathe.

Temperance hissed in her ear. "Goody Two-Shoes. Let me help you to Hell where you'll find your dead mother and father." Maliha tried to pull the cord from her neck but it was too tight, too thin, she could not grip it. Spots danced before her eyes and there was a rushing in her ears. The muscles in her chest desperately tried to drag air into her lungs but could only spasm uselessly.

It would be so easy to just let go. Why bother fighting? What was there about her life that really mattered? Then she remembered the child jumping high to touch the ceiling. And, as the noose tightened still more, Maliha reached back with both hands and gripped Temperance's dress. She hooked her heels under the sofa and hauled as hard as she could. Temperance's grip was so tight on the scarf her feet lifted from the deck and she flipped vertically in the air over Maliha's head.

The pressure lessened on Maliha's throat and she released her grip as Temperance descended in front of her, facing away. She crashed to the floor and released her grip on the scarf. Maliha took in a grating, howling breath as Temperance tried to regain her feet. Maliha grabbed her walking stick, brought it up and then down in a sideways sweep that cracked against Temperance's temple.

The murderess collapsed to the floor. Maliha drew a second breath that rasped through her crushed windpipe. Temperance moved her arms, trying to gain purchase and climb to her feet. Maliha swiped her head with her stick again as hard as she was able. Temperance went limp. Maliha struck her one more time with immense satisfaction, though she was sure she would regret her gratuitous behaviour later.

Then the door broke open and two police constables fell into the cabin. The inspector and Mr Crier stood in the doorway, and behind them was Lochana's brother.

v

Maliha stood in the corner of her cabin watching two maids packing her things. She had not wanted any fuss, but the captain had been insistent. He assured her that both he and the P&O line would be forever in her debt. It was a kind thought, but she doubted it. The company's executives would want to forget the whole affair as quickly as possible. Still, she was not ungrateful for the help. Her neck hurt, and she wore a high-necked blouse to hide the bruising.

The only good thing to come out of this was that she could disembark well before the press got hold of the story. She was content to let the inspector take the credit. The dried blood in the hinge of the scissors had settled the matter once and for all. The last thing Maliha wanted was her name known and the connection made to the Jordan case. She would never hear the end of it.

Someone appeared at the open door, hesitated, then knocked.

"Yes, Mr Crier?"

He put his head around the door. "Good afternoon."

"Can I help you?"

"It has been suggested on more than one occasion that I am quite beyond help, Miss Anderson."

"What do you want?"

He glanced at the maids. "Shall we take a turn about the deck? For old time's sake?"

"You do not have your stick," he said as they reached the Observation deck. The sun beat down through the glass ceiling.

"I don't require it when we are underway."

"And yet you had it with you when you confronted the monster."

Maliha did not reply. She touched her fingers to her neck.

"You are an extraordinary young woman, Miss Anderson."

She felt that comment, too, was best left unremarked.

They reached the port rail and looked out. The vessel was equidistant between India behind and Ceylon ahead. Halfway to the horizon, two spits of land—one from each coast— reached out to one another but did not quite meet. But British industry was dealing with that issue: the bridge was taking shape.

"Will you be returning to Pondicherry?"

"There will be legal matters to deal with."

"Will you stay there?"

"I cannot say." There was nothing left there except memories and she carried the best of those with her.

"Do you have money?"

"I'm not sure that question is entirely appropriate, Mr Crier."

"But if you are in need...?"

She turned to face him, her face quite stern. "I am quite capable of looking after myself."

"Of that, I have no doubt."

She turned away again. "Besides, Barbara has offered me a room until such time as my future is known."

"Barbara? You mean Mrs Makepeace-Flynn?"

"The very one."

"You are indeed remarkable," he said, "to have tamed that beast. So you will be staying near the Fortress?"

"That remains to be seen," she said.

EPILOGUE

i

One disadvantage of disembarking was that you did not get to see the place from the air as the ship approached. Instead Maliha was in the depths of the ship in the wide disembarkation lounge with the other first-class passengers.

Her baggage had been collected and, together with Mrs Makepeace-Flynn—dressed in mourning, complete with veil—she had descended three flights into the main cargo area which contained, via a carpeted and enclosed companionway, the disembarkation lounge. Despite the very best efforts to make the lounge comfortable, the throbbing of the nearby engines and the heat of the furnaces could not be kept entirely at bay.

The lounge did not lack in facilities. There was the bar, leather chairs and sofas, and staff constantly checking to ensure all their needs were satisfied. But still she was reminded of her trip to Brighton one Saturday morning and how she had stumbled on the cattle market. She had seen the animals penned tight, ready for sale and slaughter. It was not their ultimate destination that concerned her; it was the conditions they had to endure to get there.

Of those people she had met during the journey, only Mrs Makepeace-Flynn remained. It had come out the Spencers had seen Lochana staggering from Temperance's cabin to the general's but they had kept quiet. What they were doing in corridors away from their own while everyone else was at dinner, she did not know, but it was apparently something the police were investigating; as a result, they were not disembarking with the rest.

Temperance was in the ship's brig, awaiting transport back to Bombay with Detective Forsyth. Now that all had been revealed she was quite unrepentant. There was little doubt she and the gallows would become intimately acquainted very soon. It was difficult to understand how a person could be so broken.

The one person unexpectedly missing was Mr Crier. She had not seen him since he had taken his leave of her this morning. She imagined he perceived their relationship as some sort of ship-board romance. She could not deny being flattered. Such a thing had never occurred to her before, but the idea was ridiculous.

ii

Her introspection was interrupted as the ship's klaxon sounded three times in quick succession, and those standing in the lounge made for their seats. A few young men remained on their feet in an attitude of bravado while children were called and grabbed. Mrs Makepeace-Flynn adjusted her posture in anticipation. Maliha ensured her walking stick was to hand.

The Faraday device was disengaged and she sank deeper into her chair. There were various exclamations from around the lounge as full weight returned. She glanced about to see one of the young men climbing to his feet, a look of chagrin on his face. More disconcerting was the groaning of the ship's structure as it settled. Here, in the depths of the vessel, the sound was quite alarming.

Those disembarking on foot formed orderly lines, but Maliha waited with Mrs Makepeace-Flynn until a steward arrived to tell them their carriage had arrived. They followed him to an area filled with horse-drawn carriages driven aboard to collect the passengers. Her earlier assessment of the state of the Makepeace-Flynn's finances was further evidenced by the old-style growler waiting for them, now loaded with their baggage. It was drawn by a pair of chestnuts.

On the far side of the area, a hearse waited to collect the general's body. It was not in funeral colours (that would come later), but the four black horses stood waiting. One of them pawed the deck in boredom.

As the carriage descended the ramp, the hot, dry air invaded the inside. The afternoon sun beat down and the temperature in the carriage became intense as they drove out across the vast commercial landing field. There were another two large passenger ships on the ground some distance away along with some smaller cargo ships of different design. They exited the field between large administrative buildings and the Fortress came into view.

iii

It was named *Sigiriya* in Sinhalese, the native tongue of Ceylon, which meant "Fortress in the Sky". It had been acquired by the Empire to become the Royal Navy's prime base because of its position roughly equidistant from Britain's main concerns (Britain, South Africa, and Australia), while mainland India provided the workforce that Ceylon itself could not. And because of its position relative to the equator, it was a similar distance to the Queen Victoria void station above.

Sigiriya was a lump of rock—it could not be described otherwise—jutting six hundred feet from the flat landscape around it. It was encased with modern buildings that towered the same distance again. Encircling it at various heights were artillery guns on platforms.

Surrounding the Fortress itself was the Compound: a roughly circular area with a diameter of over two miles. Apart from the commercial port, there was the naval shipyard; a hospital that catered for both military and civilian needs; and a segment for the British Army, containing barracks and training ground. The governor's residence had been relocated from Columbo ten years earlier and was now surrounded by a residential area for the great and good. Barbara's home was there.

The Compound was contained within a concrete wall. The whole structure was reminiscent of a medieval castle but on a colossal scale.

Outside the Compound lay all manner of shops and houses created by those who could not live in the Compound but who serviced its other needs.

A shadow passed over the carriage. She looked up. A vessel bearing the black cross of the Imperial German Sky Service blocked the sun. The Zeppelins utilised the Faraday effect but used gas for their lift and only used engines for driving and manoeuvring. It was more efficient but had its risks. It was probably heading for, or returning from, German New Guinea with a refuelling stopover at the Fortress.

Mrs Makepeace-Flynn also looked out and up. Then sat back.

"Can you see if that's the *Hansa*, my dear?"

Maliha squinted up. The gothic German lettering was difficult to make out against the bright sky.

"Yes, I think so."

"Ah, good. We shall have some company tonight. Captain Voss is a cousin."

Maliha sat back in the carriage. Barbara's kind offer of accommodation was very welcome but this place stood on the edge of a war that was certain to come. There was nowhere for her to go, but how could she remain here?

BLOOD SKY AT NIGHT

BOOK 2

PROLOGUE

The invitation to visit Guru Shahin came through the post within days of Maliha's arrival in Ceylon. It had been a little awkward explaining to her host, Barbara Makepeace-Flynn, where she was going. This was a rare instance where she felt honesty might not be the best policy. Instead she claimed she was visiting a religious site, which was not entirely untrue.

The building to which the letter guided her stood on the road to Anuradhapura, north-east from the Fortress, just beyond the city with no name. Her destination looked as if it had once been a farmhouse but most of it was collapsed, probably in an earthquake. The abandoned structure had been taken over by a *hijra* colony and makeshift constructions made the least-collapsed rooms serviceable.

A *chela* in a bright sari but with very masculine features guided her from the gate to the main building and through into a room where the guru sat in a large armchair that must have been liberated from a European home many years before. The guru herself had very dark-hued skin that was deeply creased where it wasn't drawn tight against her bones. Her hair was white, covered with a loop of her sari.

Maliha pressed her palms together slightly above her waist. "*Namaste, guru Shahin.*"

"*Namaste.*" The guru matched her palm position, indicating this was a meeting of equals.

The guru waved her arm and Maliha took the indicated seat across a low table. One of the guru's *chela* came forward carrying a glass of water balanced on her palms in the approved style. Maliha took it carefully and sipped.

"Thank you for accepting my invitation, Miss Anderson." The guru's voice was frail but carried authority. "You honour us in accepting it."

The *hijra* community did not send out invitations, which meant this could only relate to the recent murder aboard the sky-liner.

"You knew Lochana Modi?" said Maliha.

"She was one of my *chela* before she decided to pretend to be a woman."

Maliha was surrounded by men and boys, *chela*, dressed in sari. Her confusion must have been obvious.

"Miss Anderson, we are *hijra*. We have no need to pretend to be women. We do not deceive, whatever choices we make."

"Lochana did."

"She tried hard to please me when she became one of my *chela*, but she was hungry for a sustenance we could not provide." Guru Shahin sighed.

Maliha felt the need to defend Lochana. "She trained to be a nurse, she met a man to whom she could give her love and who returned it."

"A married man."

"She was happy."

"But she trailed unhappiness."

Maliha could only nod. Barbara Makepeace-Flynn was the unhappy widow.

"But you discovered her murderer."

"There will be a trial and, I have no doubt, a hanging."

The guru climbed to her feet and pressed her palms almost at neck height indicating great respect. "Maliha Anderson. Lochana was as a daughter to me, I am in your debt. If there is any way I can repay you, please ask."

Maliha stood as well and bowed her head.

CHAPTER 1

i

Mary Carnforth adjusted the blinds and peered down into the thoroughfare below. She scanned the street as best she could from the protection of the window blinds. No one loitered or stared up in her direction. Instead the early morning sun beat down on the brightly dressed traders and customers as they laughed, argued and shouted to one another.

She turned back to the dim interior of the room. Ngurah had packed their few belongings into the basket the fisherman had given them. It still smelled of the sea despite being thoroughly rinsed, but it was all they had. Mary's only set of clothes had been washed overnight and returned in good condition.

She knew the Indonesians, like Ngurah's own Balinese people, were generally trustworthy, but after their recent experiences with the Dutch it had been difficult to let go of the only connection she had with her former life. Having spent the night in the vulnerable position of having nothing to wear in the event of an emergency she felt suitably armoured in her blouse, heavy skirt and boned undergarments.

Ngurah stood up and smoothed her silk blouse. Mary was envious of the child, dirt and grime did not seem to attach to her. Ngurah reached down and pulled her *kris* from under the mattress. It was a vicious weapon with an undulating blade about fourteen inches long and intricately decorated from the hilt to the tip, but lethal nonetheless. She wrapped it in a cloth of white cotton and laid it carefully in the basket.

Mary found it strange that a fifteen year-old girl should have such a thing. But all her family did. Or had. They were dead and most by their own hand, using their own *kris*. The mere idea made Mary sick. It was so un-British, so *unnecessary*, to consider that surrender was a worse fate than death? Abominable.

It was just as well she had been escorting Ngurah on a trip to the coast when the Dutch had attacked the palace, otherwise she too would be lying among the dead. One thing Mary did understand was politics. Perhaps "understand" was going a little too far, but she had been very interested in history at school and one thing she had learned was that when one royal dynasty took over from another they would seek out and eliminate any possible competitors. And now Ngurah was the only surviving heir.

The girl finished tying up the basket. "I do not like *kris* in basket."

"You should say 'I do not like being separated from my *kris*.' "

"I do not like being s-seprated from *kris*."

"From my *kris*."

Ngurah imitated the sigh Mary gave when she was tired of correcting repeated mistakes. "Yes."

"If you wear the *kris* they will know who you are. And they will not let you carry a blade openly on the Zeppelin."

"They should know me. I am Ni Dewa Ayu Ngurah."

"Be glad they do not."

It had taken a week to sail from Bali to Makassar, the capital of Sulawesi, in the fishing boat. A terrifying journey with the three of them on the tiny vessel crossing three hundred and fifty miles of open sea. They had eaten raw fish and Mary would be happy to forget the indelicacy of the "arrangements". Since their arrival two nights ago they had been in hiding. She had persuaded the lodging-house staff to buy the tickets and it had cost Ngurah's bracelet. She had, of course, complained.

If only they could have afforded tickets back to Britain. Instead they would disembark in Ceylon where she would have to rely on Jack. That, of all the things that had happened, gave her most concern. And even when they reached Ceylon they would still need to be careful. There were plenty of Dutch in the British territories.

ii

Maliha Anderson sipped a glass of iced water on the verandah at the rear of Barbara Makepeace-Flynn's bungalow. The view was slightly inclined downhill across the well-tended lawn and its simple flowerbeds to the summer house.

The distant view looked out towards the Fortress. It was named *Sigiriya* in Sinhalese, the native tongue of Ceylon, which meant "Fortress in the Sky". It had been acquired by the Empire to become the Royal Navy's primary base. Its position placed it roughly equidistant from their main concerns across the globe: Britain, South Africa and Australia. And because of its position relative to the equator, it was a similar distance to the Queen Victoria Void Station above.

The Fortress was a lump of rock—it could not be described otherwise—that jutted six hundred feet skywards from the gently undulating landscape around it. Since time immemorial it had been used by local kings as their power base. They had cut staircases into its sides; tunnels through it; carved statues in the cliffs; and constructed great buildings on the flat summit. Now it was all but encased with modern buildings of cut-stone, steel and glass that almost hid the original foundation. Encircling it at various heights were artillery guns on platforms. At night it was a beacon of light and it never rested.

Surrounding the Fortress was a roughly circular area with a diameter of over two miles. Within that space was the commercial port, the Naval Shipyard, and a hospital that catered for both military and civilian needs. The Army had one segment containing barracks and a training ground. The Governor's residence had been relocated from the Sinhalese capital of Columbo ten years earlier and was now surrounded by the homes of the great and good. The bungalow belonging to Barbara Makepeace-Flynn was one of them.

The whole Compound was contained within a stone and concrete wall with few gates. The whole was reminiscent of a medieval castle but on a massive scale. Outside the Compound, an entire city had come into being. It provided all manner of shops, workplaces, and houses created by those who could not live in the Compound but serviced the city with no name.

Maliha's eye was drawn back to the Fortress glittering against the black sky.

"It is a mighty symbol, is it not?"

"I imagine it can be seen that way, Mr Brouwer."

She glanced sideways. It was too dark to see him clearly but the lights from the interior highlighted his large nose and extensive moustache. He held a half-full glass and smoked a cigar; the end glowed bright as he drew on it.

She turned back to the Fortress and watched a cargo vessel rising, light as a bubble, from its summit. It paused at a few hundred feet, shining in the spotlights trained on it. Smoke poured from its smoke stack and its four rotors, motionless until then, engaged, spinning up to speed. The tethers that held it in place dropped away and it accelerated smoothly upwards. Within a few moments it had vanished on its way into the void.

"I do wonder how that is achieved," said Brouwer.

Barbara Makepeace-Flynn had a wide selection of acquaintances among the residents of the Compound including the Dutch trade attaché, Wim Brouwer. He was a pleasant-enough man who did not feel the need to fill silences with his own voice. Something Maliha found admirable though rare.

From the room behind them came the sound of scraping chairs.

"Excuse me, Mr Brouwer, I believe they are sitting down for games."

Mr Brouwer turned towards the door and presented his arm. Propriety insisted she took it and allowed him to guide her in. As with all things freely given, Barbara's generosity in allowing Maliha to stay in her home had its price.

iii

Mary opened the second letter from Jack and held it up to the oil light. He had never had a very delicate hand when it came to forming words—nor in his dealings with her—yet this scrawl was the worst she had ever seen. He had insisted she meet him, not something she looked forward to, but if he gave her the money that was all that mattered. It was in a public place so she had less concern over his behaviour though the location was outside the wall.

She let her hand, holding his letter, drop to her knee. It was sweltering hot in the room that was barely more than a hovel, the floor covered with sheets of old newspapers instead of straw. It was the best they could afford. The small amount of money Jack had sent with his first letter was barely enough to keep them in board and lodging. Damn him, if only he had just sent her what she needed, instead of playing games

She sat back. The cry of the *muezzin* calling the faithful to prayer penetrated the room. She had heard it so frequently now that it was almost background noise despite being so close.

She wished they were back aboard with *Hansa*. Their two-day journey from Makassar to the Fortress had been heavenly. They had had a cabin with attached servants' quarters which meant she could have some privacy. There was clean running water and as much food as they could eat. The company had been pleasant, with bright and well-informed conversation. Apart from that one chap, some accountant or other, who had looked at her askance more than once.

Now it was all gone as if it had been nothing but a pleasant daydream. She was hungry again, and her clothes were wet with perspiration. She mopped her neck with a kerchief that could not absorb any more.

If she had married Jack Bainbridge last year none of this would have happened. She looked up at Ngurah who was holding the *kris* absently, running a cloth along the blade. But if she had married Jack, Ngurah would most likely be dead. And she herself would have been miserable. Jack would not have been a good husband no matter how much he declared his love for her.

That one evening he had been so drunk a monster had emerged and revealed to her what a terrible mistake marriage would have been. She had been forced to hide from society for a week before make-up was sufficient to hide the damage he had done to her face.

She glanced down at the newspapers. There was a photograph of a woman in mourning, her face veiled, but next to her a young woman leaning on a walking stick. There was something about the girl's face. Mary reached down and picked up the crumpled sheet. She spread it out, smoothed away the wrinkles and almost cried out with the relief of seeing a friendly face.

"Wasn't there another sheet of writing paper?"

Ngurah looked up. "Bored."

"Nonsense, only boring people get bored." Not for the first time Mary wondered when she had become her own mother, though she did not think her mother would have found herself in this pickle. She read the attached article.

It was her, Alice Anderson, though the article referred to her as Maliha. The girl had been two years below her at Roedean. The story was about the unfortunate death of the older woman's husband, General Makepeace-Flynn (a hero of the Boer War) and the General's nurse aboard the sky-liner from Britain. According to the article Maliha Anderson had helped discover a murderer.

That settled it. Although the Taliesin Affair had happened after Mary had left the school, she knew from gossip Alice Anderson had been the key to its resolution. This must be the same person. Then Mary recalled how unpleasant the other girls had been because Alice was half-caste. It was entirely possible the girl hated anything to do with the school.

But beggars could not be choosers and this was too good an opportunity to let pass. Perhaps she would not have to deal with Jack after all.

"Let's find that other sheet and the pen. I have another letter to write."

Ngurah handed her the paper and pen. "Why stay when your people close?"

"Because the Dutch are here as well. We will not be safe until we reach Britain."

"What I do in your Britain?"

"You will become the Princess your father wanted you to be."

"That is good. I ask your King give me army then *aku bakal mbales dhewe ing Landa.*" She punctuated the last word striking her fist into her palm.

"English, dear."

iv

Maliha would have preferred a game of Bridge, but Barbara never played that at home now. It brought back too many unpleasant memories. So it was whist. The advantage of Bridge was that at least some of the time one could step away from the table.

Barbara's bungalow was not one of the largest so the dining room doubled as the games room once the ladies had returned. The hot air, now stiff with cigar smoke, was kept circulating by the *punkhas* hanging from the ceiling. In the old days the rope that kept them swinging would have been pulled by a *punkhawala* in a nearby room. But now she could hear the miniature steam-engine chugging away below them. She had taken a look at the engine—much to the horror of the servants—but apart from its diminutive size there was nothing special about it.

To assist with cooling each of the wide-open windows was draped with a grass mat, these were kept wet so the evaporation of the water drew the heat from the room. Barbara could not afford a permanent *bhishtee* but hired one for her dinner parties. He walked around the verandah and soaking the mats. As a result the room was acceptably cool for the European guests.

Because of Maliha's tardy arrival the least unpleasant players were already taken and she found herself playing opposite Jack Bainbridge. His father, Cecil, was seated at a table with their hostess alongside that confounded Mr Crier. She frowned at him but he wasn't looking at her.

This was only the second time she had seen him since she had returned from Pondicherry, having had to travel into India to deal with legal matters after the death of her parents. On both occasions he had barely spoken to her beyond the expected pleasantries. Clearly he felt the acquaintance they had achieved on-board ship was not something he wished to continue. She had been rebuffed enough times in her life that this new instance was of little consequence.

She forced her attention away from Mr Crier to Cecil Bainbridge. He was a business entrepreneur of the sort that had built the British Empire. He ran a fleet of "ice buckets" as they were colloquially known—cargo vessels that fetched ice from Tibet and the Himalayas and sold it across India, Ceylon and even further afield throughout the East Indies, and even parts of Africa. For the British, Germans and Dutch, ice was as essential as coal in the tropics, not only for its luxury but for its benefits in food preservation and transportation. They could have done with some of his company's products this evening.

She was jerked from her musings into the here and now by Jack Bainbridge knocking the table as he sat down, jabbing it into her damaged thigh. She drew in a sharp breath at the pain. She looked at him, he was drunk as usual and oblivious to the consequences of his actions.

He lifted his head until he focused on her, apparently with effort, and smiled. He was undoubtedly quite handsome, but that did not compensate being his partner. Their opponents in this game were Herr Brouwer and the German Zeppelin commander, Captain Voss.

Despite the animosity between Germany and Britain, Maliha could not find it in her heart to dislike the Captain. He was always willing to discuss his vessel, the *Hansa*, which he clearly loved. He had even promised to give her a tour in the near future. Besides, he was second cousin to Barbara so any show of animosity would have been improper even if he had been as rude as Jack, which he never was.

Play passed from hand to hand, she and Jack won two while Brouwer and Voss took just one. In the pause between play Maliha took a sip of her iced water. Jack prepared to deal. He passed the second deck across to Maliha while he clumsily distributed thirteen cards to each of them. She shuffled carefully and placed the deck to her right, beside Mr Brouwer in preparation for his turn. Jack picked up the last card from his hand and turned it face up: Three of clubs. Maliha glanced at the cards in front of him and frowned. There was something odd about them.

"Clubs trumps," he said then drained his glass and waved it in the air. An Indian servant, also hired for the evening, moved quickly to his side and replaced his glass with another filled one.

She picked up her hand and sorted the cards by suit and rank.

"I have fourteen," said Voss, with a smile. Jack focused his wandering attention on the German.

"Damned if you have," he said, drawing gasps from surrounding tables.

"It can happen." Voss smiled and studied those in front of Jack. "There you are, you see, Mr Bainbridge, you have only eleven plus the trump card. Twelve."

"You accusing me of cheating?"

Maliha glanced at Barbara. Most eyes were now directed at their table and all play had stopped. Barbara laid down her cards and stood. Maliha took a firm grip on her walking stick.

Voss made another effort at placating Jack. "Mistakes happen, Mr Bainbridge. It is nothing. Please deal again."

"Didn't like the cards?" Jack climbed to his feet. He made to step around the table's corner and loom over Voss. His attempted threat came to an end as he stumbled and fell forwards. He reached out to steady himself with the table, missed and flailed as he went down. The card table was upended and cards flew as he impacted the floor. Maliha untangled her stick from Jack's legs and leaned heavily on it as she climbed to her feet.

She stepped away to the window as Cecil Bainbridge ordered servants to remove his errant son. She noted a certain stiffness in his features and a dullness in his eye. She wondered briefly about Mrs Bainbridge; it occurred to Maliha that she had never encountered the woman at any social event.

The servants hesitated since Bainbridge was not paying their wages. Barbara gave a slight nod after which they acted quickly, lifting the unconscious man and carrying him out. Cecil Bainbridge and Barbara went with them. As another servant righted the table and recovered the cards, Voss and Brouwer stepped out of the way and joined Maliha at the window.

"I have never seen him this bad," said Brouwer, shaking his head. "He never recovered from being rejected by his *bruid*."

"Bride?" said Voss. "He is married?"

"No, not yet bride."

"Fiancée?" said Maliha.

"*Ja*." Brouwer glanced across to the door. "He suffers."

"He must find another love," said Voss.

"She would have to be strong. Like you, Miss Anderson." Brouwer smiled as he said it but Maliha felt her skin crawl at the thought of being close to such an unpleasant fellow. Her feelings must have shown as Brouwer's smile disappeared. "My apologies, I did not mean to – embarrass."

There was an awkward moment.

"Perhaps the Englishwoman from Sulawesi?" said Voss. "She was robust."

Maliha wished her glass of water had not been knocked over; it would have been convenient to hide behind a sip.

"I'm sorry, gentlemen. I am quite disconcerted, if you would excuse me?"

Voss clicked his heels in salute while Brouwer gave a nod. She detached herself from them and left the room, her walking stick clicking on the wooden floor.

v

Persuading Ngurah to stay in the room had taken work. It was like trying to look after a spoilt adolescent tiger. She was still a child but with claws that could kill. It took a firm hand to keep her under control. But in this she had finally acquiesced.

Mary made her way through the tight slum streets outside the Compound. The city itself had no name and neither did the streets, if they could be called such since there was no planning. It was as if the buildings had been gathered up in the hand of some Hindu god and thrown down. Most of the structures were built from wood and rough stone while a few were of brick. They were one or two stories only, and there was no sewerage system save the streets themselves. Something really would have to be done about it.

In the eighteen months she had been in the Far East she had become used to seeing brown faces instead of white. But she was not used to being stared at, no one in the palace had done so. Here, it seemed, everyone she encountered seemed fascinated with her.

She looked down at the instructions in Jack's letter. She had found the metal and glass tube that comprised the atmospheric railway stretching from the Compound west towards Columbo. It was the only sign of the Empire in this place. The atmospheric had a decent roadway alongside it, for transporting coal to the pumping stations placed at regular intervals along its length. She followed the line back towards the Compound wall until she found the makeshift Islamic temple. A train thundered through the tube and she looked up, wishing she were inside.

Beyond the temple she saw the building Jack had described. Most of the streets were full of people yet this place was surrounded by emptiness. It did not stand out in its style of construction—it was as haphazard as any of the others—yet a pervasive aura of unpleasantness emanated from it. She approached but could not bring herself to step out into the wide alley that ran alongside it.

"How about a kiss, Mary?"

Jack stumbled out of an alley, grinning in that way she had once considered so endearing. He grabbed her by the shoulder, more to prevent himself from falling than out of any affection. He was dressed for a formal dinner but his clothes were stained and there was mud down one side of his jacket. He must have been out all night; his eyes were deeply shadowed and he needed a shave. There was a bruise on his left cheek.

She shrugged off his hand and backed away.

"Have you brought the money I need?"

"What money would that be?" His eyes slid away from her and focused somewhere beyond her right ear.

She felt herself on the brink of tears. She had broken off their engagement because of this, why must she be forced to endure it again?

"Do you have the money or don't you, Jack?"

He brought his focus back to her face. "You owe me!"

"Owe *you*?" She shook her head while tears poured down her cheeks.

"Come back to me, Mary. I promise I'll be better." His face twisted into a mask of innocence.

The fury in her boiled over. "Look at you! It's not even nine o'clock, you haven't been home, you're dirty and you're drunk. Just tell me whether you're going to give me the money."

Jack's eyes focused behind her and he frowned. He jumped forward and grabbed her wrist. She pulled back but could not break his grip. "Jack, let go!" Terror overwhelmed her. He could have killed her the last time he was like this. Was this to be the time? He dragged her towards the solitary building.

She stumbled and fell, crashing into the dry mud and filth. Her arms were grabbed and pulled behind her. She was struck violently from behind, she felt something snap, but before a cry could reach her lips, paralysing pain shot through her head. Then there were crashing lights and crushing blackness.

CHAPTER 2

"*Sahiba?*"

"What is it?" Maliha pushed herself up on her elbow. The room was dark but Sathi had left an oil lamp outside and stood silhouetted in the open doorway. There was no light through the windows. "What time is it?"

"Very late. Very early, *sahiba.*"

"What's wrong?"

"A visitor, *sahiba,*" she said. "In the kitchen."

Maliha sat up. "A visitor? Now? Who?"

"A visitor for you. She is in the kitchen."

"Tell her to come back in the morning."

"I am sorry, *sahiba.* You must come. She has a sword. My father ask you come quick."

"A sword?"

Maliha sat up on the edge of the bed, slid her feet into her slippers, pulled on the light dressing gown and took hold of her walking stick. Sathi moved out of the doorway and picked up the oil lamp.

"You have not woken Mrs Makepeace-Flynn?"

"The visitor ask for you, *sahiba.*"

"You did the right thing."

The kitchen was on the other side of the house. Maliha glanced at the long-case clock in the hall as they passed. Twenty minutes to two. The air that wafted in from outside was pleasantly cool.

There was light streaming from the kitchen. Maliha allowed Sathi to enter ahead of her. She reached the doorway and stopped. The visitor stood by the kitchen table. She was dressed in what had once been good quality silk and, though somewhat ragged, still retained its bright colours. She appeared to be of pure Asian birth but not Indian or Sinhalese.

She held a large knife to the throat of Old Vidu. Maliha looked more closely, it was not just a knife, it was a kris. That meant she was from one of the Dutch islands, Sumatra or Java perhaps. It also made her a person of importance. The girl's eyes darted here and there, to Sathi, to Maliha, to the old man.

Scared and trying not to be.

Maliha stepped into the room. Her stick prevented a proper greeting but she bowed her head. "You wished to speak with me?"

"You are just girl."

Maliha sighed, was there no escape from one sort of prejudice or another? She walked forward, stick tapping loudly on the tiled floor and took a seat at the table opposite the visitor.

"I am Maliha Anderson," she said. "And you have had a long and difficult journey."

The girl's head jerked up, and her eyes narrowed. Then she glanced down at her clothes. "Yes."

"Why don't you put down your kris and take a seat? No one here is a threat to you. You asked for me and I am here. Let's have some tea and you can tell me what you want."

Sathi took the hint, filled the kettle from a jug and placed it in the embers. She stoked the fire a little to build it up. The girl watched her, then removed the kris from the old man's neck. He did not move but fixed his eyes on Maliha. She nodded and he slid away to stand by the door to the verandah.

The girl sat down and placed the kris on the table within easy reach. Maliha decided it would be best to keep the control on her side.

"What's your name?"

"I am Ni Dewa Ayu Ngurah." She said it proudly as if it should mean something, Maliha could almost feel the anguish pass through her when she realised her name meant nothing. "I am princess in Bali."

Bali was one of the smaller islands in the chain, but still a stronghold for the Dutch, and a major producer of opium. Maliha knew the Dutch were in the process of consolidating production by taking it out of the hands of the farmers in order to reduce consumption. And that the ruling classes were not happy with the Dutch government's actions.

"And who was the British woman who brought you here in the German airship?"

This time the girl was impressed.

"My teacher. She is Mary Carnforth."

ii

Maliha's leg throbbed in sympathy as she was assailed by memories of Roedean. She remembered Mary Carnforth, just as she remembered every name and every face of every pupil and teacher in that school in detail. Her perfect memory was both a blessing and a curse. Mary had not been among those who played practical jokes; the ones who laughed or spat at her; however she was also not among those very few who had treated Maliha as a human being.

Mary Carnforth had been studious though not particularly clever, and perhaps a little unworldly. She had been ahead of Maliha in the school and left before those last two years when things had become interesting. Sometimes Maliha saw her schoolgirl-self as a different person: that person was not Maliha, she was always Anderson, or occasionally Alice. The school's purpose was to mould her into the perfect daughter of Empire yet they would never let her belong.

Sathi placed a cup of tea in front of her and the clink of the china broke the spell.

"Yes, I knew Mary," she said finally. "We were not friends, but neither were we enemies."

She took a sip from the porcelain cup. "What's happened to her?"

"She went to man who give us money to go England. She not come back. I wait long time. I wait whole day. I find you. She say you help."

"What man?"

"You help?"

Maliha looked her in the eye. She was proud, aloof, and quite desperate. Maliha looked back at her tea. Mary and the girl were on the run, most likely from the Dutch government. Mary was not thinking clearly if she thought being in Britain would keep the girl safe. And what on earth was she doing being a governess to a princess, and in Bali of all places? Maliha looked up again.

"I don't think I can help."

The girl jumped to her feet and grabbed the *kris*. There was a look on her face, something that reminded Maliha of the murderer she had confronted on the sky-liner. Terror and desperation, when the future has been ripped away and one's soul laid bare.

The one we wear when all hope is gone.

"But I will try." The girl did not put down the *kris* but the desperation left her eyes. "What help do you want?"

"Find my teacher."

Maliha nodded. "Do you have somewhere to stay?"

The girl shook her head.

"And the Dutch will be looking for you."

She nodded.

"You cannot stay in the house. And the fewer people who know about you the better. Sathi, make a bed in the summer house for our guest. And find some clothes. Something less obvious. What should we call you?"

"Ngurah."

Maliha looked her in the eye while addressing Sathi who was still fixated on the *kris* in Ngurah's hand. "Ngurah will not threaten or harm you, Sathi. She is our guest."

Maliha took up her walking stick and pushed herself to her feet.

"I am going back to bed. I hope you find the summer house comfortable enough. Tomorrow we'll see what can be done about finding Mary."

She clicked her way to the kitchen door.

"Miss," said Ngurah. Maliha turned in the doorway and looked at the girl almost her own age. "My teacher teach me I must be grateful. So I thank you." She pressed her palms together and bowed. Maliha inclined her head in return and left.

Weariness surged through her as she lowered herself into the bed, but her mind would not rest. She could not think about Ngurah and the vanishing Mary Carnforth, there was insufficient information. But unwanted images of being doused with water, and other liquids, in the freezing nights of British winters filled her.

She slept poorly.

iii

If it had been the body of a Sinhalese or Indian woman discovered floating face down in one of the ancient irrigation wells that covered this part of Ceylon there would have been little fuss. But the corpse was of western origin and had suffered a particularly unpleasant death, if the state of her features were anything to go by. The fuss was going to be significant.

Detective Constable Devilal Choudhary considered policing to be a curious profession. He had the authority to speak to any member of society and yet must undertake tasks that only the lowest caste should perform. He made notes in his pad on the state of the woman's battered body. Another ritual cleansing was in order for him once this day was over.

There was a click as the photographer took another shot on his big Kodak then gathered up the tripod for the next picture.

Remnants of the woman's soaked clothing clung to her legs and lower torso and a small scrap of blouse still encircled her upper arm. There were rope marks around her wrists, ankles and neck. The cloth was clean of blood but that was undoubtedly due to immersion in the irrigation tank. All her wounds, the cuts and tears in her skin, were equally clean.

They might never know who she was if no one came forward. Her face had been beaten severely and lacked any distinctive features.

And then there were the seven parallel cuts across her abdomen each one precisely the same length. There was no question they had been inflicted deliberately and they were marks Choudhary had seen before, though not what he would expect to find on this corpse. It was easier just to think of her as a corpse and not someone who had been breathing a few hours earlier.

"Turn her over," Choudhary told the two untouchables who had been co-opted for the task. Her back had been flayed extensively. There was no way of counting the number of strikes. The bones of her ribs and spine were exposed to the air in a number of places. The photographer took more shots while Choudhary made further notes.

Finally the photographer indicated he had finished so Choudhary instructed the men to wrap her body for delivery to the morgue. The sooner she was on ice the better. In this heat corruption set in quickly.

Inspector Forsyth arrived in a carriage as Choudhary mounted the bank surrounding the well. Forsyth was a recent addition to the Sinhalese force having transferred from Bombay. His arrest of the murderer aboard the RMS *Macedonia* had attracted a lot of attention.

"Where's the body, constable?" The Inspector's strong Scottish accent was sometimes hard to follow but he tended to use short sentences which was helpful.

"On the cart, sir." Choudhary nodded at the two-wheeled cart.

"You made notes?"

"Yes, sir, and the photographer has plenty of shots."

"Show me where she was found."

Choudhary led the way back down the slope towards the water. The irrigation well was a small lake, and though it had a gently sloping beach area the bottom dropped away a short distance out.

"They were probably trying to dispose of the body permanently, sir. If they had succeeded in weighing her down she might never have re-surfaced. Some of these wells are over a hundred feet deep."

"Any clue as to where she was thrown in?"

"The water doesn't flow in the wells, sir. It would have been somewhere nearby."

Forsyth studied the muddle of impressions in the mud, shoes, bare feet and animals. Nothing useful.

"But there is one thing, sir."

The Inspector looked up.

"There were seven incisions across her abdomen."

Forsyth frowned. "That's very unlikely, constable."

"Yes, sir."

Barbara was in the study writing a letter when Maliha found her. The morning sun had already made the heat barely tolerable and the little *punkha* engine was throbbing away beneath the floorboards. Maliha wondered whether it might not be more effective for the engine to drive, say, a rotor to provide a more pronounced wind effect.

"I'm sorry to interrupt you, Barbara."

The older woman glanced around and smiled. "Just a moment." She finished a line and put down her pen. "Is this to do with the girl in the summer house?"

Maliha was not surprised the staff had informed their mistress, since Maliha was only a guest, albeit an almost permanent addition to the household. She nodded.

"Who is she?"

"A Balinese princess named Ngurah."

"Well, I am pleased she is a member of the aristocracy. How did you come to make her acquaintance?"

"She is under the guardianship of a woman, it seems, from my old school. She has gone missing."

"I was under the impression there was no love lost between you and that place."

"The girl herself currently has no one to look after her."

"Is she a danger?"

"I believe she is quite dangerous." Barbara raised her eyebrows at this. "However I do not think she is a threat to this household."

Barbara waited. Maliha was aware that her hostess could be as acute with her perceptions as Maliha herself. Mrs Makepeace-Flynn was waiting for the rest.

"There are those who would wish her ill."

Barbara considered this for a few moments. "The Dutch?"

Maliha nodded again.

"Very well. She can stay in the summer house for now. I will instruct the staff to remain silent."

She picked up her pen which Maliha took as her dismissal. She turned and headed for the door.

"Maliha, please deal with this matter as quickly as you may."

v

Ngurah did not look pleased with her new clothes. She picked at them, pulling them away from her skin as if trying to prevent any of it from touching her. "These are servants' clothes. They are not silk."

"They are not. However no one will notice you. Did you sleep well?"

Ngurah's expression took on a note of disdain as she glanced at the sheet lying across the wooden frame of a summer swing. It was in need of a good clean, as was the rest of the place. Complete redecoration might be in order. There was an indistinct and unpleasant smell lurking in the still air.

"I sleeped."

"Slept," Maliha said. Ngurah frowned but said nothing. "A disguise is important. You will walk a pace behind me, slightly to my right."

"No!"

"Then you must stay here."

"Why walk behind you? You are not white."

And there it was.

"No, but my skin is not as dark as yours, is it? I am Brahmin."

Or was she simply British? She did not know anymore. For the British she was too Indian and to the Indians she was too British. Only people like Barbara or Mr Crier did not seem to care, and considering his recent behaviour it was possible she had been wrong about him. Even she could not see into their hearts.

"You are Brahmin?"

Maliha chose not to add that her father had been a Glaswegian engineer. Ngurah turned and faced her, pressing her palms together again and bowing. "I did not know."

"If it helps you with your disguise to keep that in mind then please do so. We must be going."

Maliha glanced around quickly and frowned. She studied the young girl thoughtfully, assessing the clothes. "You have your *kris* at your back?"

Ngurah reached back over her shoulder and touched the hilt of the hidden weapon. Maliha pursed her lips but knew that separating the girl from the knife would be almost impossible.

She led the way from the summer house and walked back up the gently sloping lawn. She did not make directly for the house but went around. The trap was prepared and waiting at the side of the house, out of view of the road and nearby homes. One of the Makepeace-Flynn's old chestnuts was harnessed and stood quietly in the shade flicking its tail while the houseboy, Anand, held the bridle.

They climbed into the back, Ngurah lent Maliha her hand so she could step up. Maliha acknowledged her assistance with a nod when they were seated opposite one another. Anand climbed onto the driver's bench and with a slap of the reins they moved out of the shade, along the short drive and onto the road lined with trees and electric lamps.

"Where were you and Mary staying?" Maliha asked, as Anand urged the horse into a slow trot.

"I do not know its name," she replied. "My teacher feared to become lost, the streets have no names."

"We need to find it."

The trap moved rapidly along the street, passing residences with plenty of land between them. They turned on to a broader thoroughfare lined with shops. There were several carriages of different types on the road and people going about their business before the day's heat became insufferable.

Maliha considered that she might have brought one of Barbara's parasols to hide herself. However no one even glanced in their direction.

"There was mosque," said Ngurah.

"Well, that's a start." Maliha leaned forward. "And which entrance through the wall did you use?"

"I not use gate."

Maliha could not imagine how she had succeeded in scaling the wall. The British may not have been able to prevent people from living outside but they did stop them from constructing their homes too close to the wall. It was, after all, a defence against potential rebellion.

"Anand, will you stop at the park, please?"

"Yes, *sahiba*."

The trap came over a rise, ahead was the commercial air-dock. Its grassy deck sprinkled with flying ships of different designs and vintages. The "ice buckets" of the Bainbridge import business, with their distinctive scarlet livery, were grouped around a cluster of warehouses.

Passenger vessels, including Captain Voss's Zeppelin with its huge gas envelope, were drawn up at the nearer fence and immigration buildings. Even as she watched another vessel swung overhead. It was constructed from brightly painted wood and had Chinese characters across the bottom of its hull. Probably an independent ice trader. Smoke poured from the stack at its rear and each of its seven buoyancy bags appeared to be open at the bottom. A hot-air balloon with a Faraday device, thought Maliha, very unusual.

They passed the final shops and drew up at the entrance to the Albert Memorial Park. Their elevated position permitted them to look left across the buildings of the unnamed city outside the wall, while the monolith of *Sigiriya* filled the view to the right. The sunlight gleamed from the glass and steel making it difficult to look at directly.

With Ngurah's assistance Maliha climbed down from the trap, and strode into the park leaning heavily on her stick at every other step. Ngurah followed dutifully behind. The park was almost empty at this time of day. It was enjoyed more in the evenings after the heat of the day had passed.

The grass was maintained as green as possible by constant watering from the irrigation network. The achievements of the ancients never ceased to impress her: the Egyptian pyramids, the Parthenon in Athens, the great *dagobah* at Anuradhapura and the tremendous irrigation system that covered Ceylon. How they had managed to construct such things she had no idea.

When she was sure they could not be easily overlooked Maliha scratched a rough circle into the grit of the path with her walking stick. She marked the centre.

"This is *Sigiriya*. That—" she indicated the circle. "—is the wall."

She looked Ngurah in the eye, the girl nodded. She placed the stick outside the wall and pointed in the same relative direction. "North."

Ngurah nodded again.

"Where you were staying, could you see *Sigiriya?*"

Ngurah stared at the armoured rock to their right for a long moment then down at the circle. She pointed her toe at a point in the North-East quarter. Her toe-nails were painted blue and she wore open sandals of exquisite workmanship; delicate filigree of a metal that may have been gold intertwined the leatherwork. Maliha had failed to suggest replacement sandals.

"Here."

Maliha looked up and across the city. Beyond the wall there was a partly constructed minaret near the location.

"Is that the mosque?"

"Yes."

"Then let us be on our way."

vi

The morgue was a depressing modern brick-built structure lacking the ornament. Almost as if the architect did not wish to celebrate death. And perhaps in a place like this that would be so, thought Inspector Forsyth.

Now the old Queen had been gone a few years, the popular desire to wallow in the grief of death had passed. Good King Bertie might be old but he had always been one for celebrating life, unlike his mother. And then there were the customs that prevailed in this place. No one higher than an untouchable wanted to go near a corpse let alone touch one.

Must be hard for the constable.

Well, policing was a necessity and if he couldn't deal with it he could use the door. But he wouldn't. Choudhary was one of the first of his people to make it to detective constable and he was a good CID copper. He'd make sergeant easily, maybe even inspector.

Forsyth shivered. Damn it but the place was cold even out here in the foyer. The constable had his arms wrapped around him in a vain effort to keep warm. Forsyth grinned.

"You think this is cold, lad?"

"Yes, sir."

"You should try the Govan mid-winter."

"Was it colder than this, sir?"

"It was."

"Then I am happy to have missed it. No disrespect intended."

A morgue attendant, a Sinhalese, appeared at the door. His white lab coat, none too clean, was padded underneath with what appeared to be blankets. He said nothing but held the door for them. Forsyth took care not to brush against him as he passed him in the tight open doorway. Some of these lower caste could be strange. If they made you unclean, by speaking to you or the slightest touch, they would seek punishment for the crime.

Beyond the door was a flight of steps going down, Forsyth made sure to hold the rail as he descended, it was even colder here—the lower floors were walled with ice blocks—and it would be easy to take a tumble on the icy steps. His breath steamed.

The corridor was dimly lit despite the electric bulbs hanging from the ceiling every couple of yards. He and Choudhary made their careful way down the passage towards a set of doors. One of them stood open, and a rough voice exploded from it.

"Hurry up, Forsyth, it's bloody freezing in here and I haven't got all day. Still got my rounds to make."

They entered the much better lit room. It was large enough to hold six examination slabs but only two were occupied with bodies. Dr Bristow stood beside the one farthest from the door as if he were expecting the rest of the tables to be filled. He still wore his bloodstained whites and was wiping his hands on a rag that looked like it might make stains worse rather than better.

The corpse in front of him was still covered.

"You want to come at it slowly or shall I get straight to the meat?" He laughed at his own joke. Forsyth smiled humourlessly. Medics were all the same.

"Whatever you like."

"Is your constable ill?"

Forsyth turned. Choudhary has shivering violently. "He's fine. Just get on with it."

Bristow pulled back the sheet and uncovered the naked woman's body to the hips. Her skin was so pale as to be almost white except for the lividity of the face and the dark red of the cuts and tears in the skin. But it was the seven precisely cut lines in her abdomen that held him.

"Thought you'd like those."

"I don't like them at all," Forsyth said. "They can't be on this body."

"Well they are, and I'm afraid that means our very own ripper has struck again."

"She's not a man by any chance?"

Bristow raised his eyebrows. "Police humour, is it?" He lifted the sheet the rest of way. "Definitely female."

Forsyth shook himself. "What about the rest of the damage?"

"Atypical for our ripper. The attack on the face is normal, of course, he really doesn't like faces. But everything else is wrong. See here—" he lifted the woman's right forearm "—these are burn marks, could be a poker or cigar, no way of telling the difference after her being in the water for a few hours. Oh and several of her fingers are dislocated or broken."

Forsyth turned to Choudhary. "Your report didn't say anything about burns or dislocations."

"No, sir." Choudhary clamped his mouth together, perhaps to stop his teeth from chattering.

"Was there any sexual attack?"

"Not that I could find, though I can't be completely certain, of course. But I am confident she was still a virgin."

"Alright. When can I have your report?"

"Later today."

It took the constable several minutes to warm up sufficiently to be coherent once they got back outside and on to the street. Forsyth noted how all the foot traffic was somehow on the other side of the road.

"Alright, Choudhary. So tell me what you gathered from that?"

"The person who's killed and mutilated five young men in the last year has changed to killing women."

"And how likely is that, constable?"

"I don't think it's very likely at all, sir."

Forsyth took his pipe from his pocket and knocked it against the wall. He rummaged in another pocket and pulled out a pouch of tobacco. Absently he filled the pipe and put it into his mouth without lighting it. He stared unseeing into the distance.

"You're right about that, lad."

CHAPTER 3

i

Maliha had Anand stop a short distance from the gate. They would not be following the main road once they were out of the Compound so there was little point taking the trap outside the wall.

"You can return home, but we will be back in no more than three hours."

Maliha watched him pull the trap around and trot away. She frowned. A vague thought nagged at her, something she had missed. She looked around to see if the distraction was in the immediate vicinity. Nothing. Ngurah waited patiently. They had best be getting on.

The streets around the gate were not busy, primarily taken up with the homes of the middle classes and military barracks charged with the protection of the walls. The opening in the wall was wide enough to take four elephants abreast and was three stories high. Each of the double gates ran in four concentric tracks to carry their terrific weight.

Situated facing the gate was a massive vehicle, as big as a house, with half a dozen independent artillery guns and machine gun stations mounted around it. It sat upon pneumatic wheels that stood taller than she did, eight on each side. It was painted in mottled khaki and on the body just above the rear wheels was the insignia of the Royal Field Artillery.

If the machine had been quiescent it might have made an interesting study. However, smoke poured from the stack and it growled with suppressed energy. Its front-facing weapons were trained on the gate. Unlike *Sigiriya* this was more than a symbol of the Empire's power, it was a threat. The Empire was maintained through strength of arms, regardless of any good it did.

She steered a course around the vehicle and could not help the cold shiver that ran down her back as she stepped in line with its barrels. If there were an uprising the colour of her skin could easily make her an enemy.

The soldiers at the gate were alert but she did not look at them. The intense pressure of the crowds going in and out, the thronging of so many people made Maliha uncomfortable. Her years in England had indoctrinated her into the British sensibilities of space, though she was fairly sure she had always felt that way. She knew it was foolish but found herself holding her breath.

They reached the other side of the thick wall where the pressure of the crowd diminished allowing her to breathe again. A new problem presented itself: now they were on foot, and relatively close to their destination, she could not see the proper direction to take.

"Stop a moment," she said to Ngurah.

Maliha turned and faced *Sigiriya*. She closed her eyes and brought the view from the park to mind, located her current position in that memory and opened her eyes with a smile.

She examined the haphazard jumble of buildings to the right. There was a relatively wide roadway leading in the direction they desired.

"This way."

ii

Inspector Forsyth sat at his desk and studied the report from Dr Bristow. There were additional details but nothing that aided in discovering who the dead woman might be.

Apparently she had not eaten properly recently, though she was not suffering from long-term malnutrition. The skin of her fingers was not calloused except for a hardening on the thumb pad and the side of the index finger of her left hand. So she was left-handed and sewed. Her feet indicated the use of solid European boots and the remnants of her clothes suggested good quality.

All of which made her well-to-do.

He sighed to himself, it still did not mean anyone would come forward to claim her. There was no scarcity of wives who had become a burden to their husbands for one reason or another. The asylums were favourite for disposal but permanent removal was not uncommon.

Except: Why the burns and the broken fingers? And how could a woman bear the marks of that killer?

There was a rushed knock on the door followed by a thump. The door burst open and Choudhary almost fell in, carrying a large, and presumably heavy, box.

"Sorry, sir."

Forsyth waved him in and Choudhary deposited the box on a chair at the side of the room.

"The case files for the other murders, sir."

"Did you serve on any of those cases, Choudhary?"

"No, sir. I had only just been transferred to CID when the last one was found."

"That might be a good thing. Fewer preconceived ideas."

Forsyth took a drink from his cup. The coffee was cold but it was liquid. The heat in Ceylon was drier than Bombay, but there was a lot more of it. Maybe he could visit the morgue and use some of their ice or, better, get Choudhary to do it.

"You do know we're exactly nowhere with this, Choudhary?"

"Yes, sir."

"Pass me the first file, you take the next, then we'll swap. We're going to read every single one of them. Every word. It'll pass the time to the next murder."

"Yes, sir."

Choudhary lifted the lid from the box and handed the topmost file, over an inch thick, to the Inspector. Then took a similar one for himself and sat, unbidden, in the chair opposite.

*   *   *

The Inspector had only managed half a dozen pages from his file before he received his summons from the Chief Superintendent.

Choudhary watched him drain the dregs of his coffee and head out, shutting the door carefully behind him. Choudhary leaned forward in his chair and tried to decipher Dr Bristow's handwritten report on the second murder. The boy had been fifteen according to his parents and was a worker at the air-dock. It was a good job and paid relatively well.

The report described the battered face and the seven abdominal cuts. Death itself had apparently been suffocation caused by obstruction of the trachea with blood and tissue from the facial damage. Did that mean he hadn't meant to kill him?

Of course they were making an assumption that the murderer was a man but the idea of a woman committing a crime of this type seemed ... unlikely.

Choudhary stood up and walked away from the file. It soiled his mind and made him feel dirty. The contamination that the untouchables carried with them. He shook his head, that was old thinking. He was a policeman, this was his job. The job he had chosen and he was good at it. But he felt tainted, he might as well be an untouchable himself.

He sat back down. Picked up the file and continued to read.

Maliha had been long enough away from India and so inculcated into British attitudes she found the squalor outside the wall repugnant. Yet she had grown up with it even if she had not lived in it.

They made their way through makeshift buildings catching occasional sight of the half-built minaret. Maliha had told herself they would be stared at, and she was not wrong. Though her skin was the same shade as many of the occupants her European clothes made her stand out as she picked her way carefully through the open sewers that passed for streets.

In some places enterprising individuals had laid planks on bricks to lift them above the unpleasantness but such places were rare. Surely some enterprising Empire do-gooder could raise money to pave all the streets. Perhaps she would mention it to Barbara, who would mention it to her circle. Some busy-body would certainly take up the idea.

The passageways were not crowded but nor were they empty. Men lounging on corners, beggars blind or crippled—they were not permitted in the Compound—sellers of fruit, water and other foods in baskets carried on their heads or slung in loops around their shoulders. And the man with the red material tied around his wrist who was following them.

"Here," said Ngurah. Maliha turned and saw her pointing off to the side, along a smaller alleyway.

"You go first," she said. Ngurah led the way between two wooden constructions. From one doorway three young children watched them pass with impassive eyes. Maliha almost flinched as the smallest, a girl, reached out and let the material of Maliha's dress brush her fingers.

The alley opened out into a wider space flanked on one side by a two-storey wooden building. Ngurah went inside without a pause but

Maliha paused for a moment, as if in hesitation. She caught a glimpse of red at the other end of the alley before she too allowed herself to be engulfed by the dark.

There was an old and wrinkled woman sitting on a wooden chair just inside the door. The chair was missing a leg and was propped up with a pile of stones. Ngurah was already on the stairs but Maliha did not follow. She turned to the woman and pressed her palms together at waist height.

"*Namaste, mata-ji.*"

The old woman looked up as if she had not been aware of their presence. She touched her hands together. "*Namaste.*"

"Is this your place?"

"It is the place of my son."

"This girl, she had a friend, a white woman. Have you seen her?"

"The girl's mistress went away two days ago. She has not returned."

"I seek her now. Do you know where she might be?"

She shook her head. "I do not know."

Maliha nodded. "*Namaste.*"

She turned back to the waiting Ngurah, and followed her up the creaking steps. The air temperature increased as they reached the upper floor.

"That was your language?"

"It was Hindi."

The door leading to the room Ngurah and Mary shared was constructed from mismatched woods. But it was solid and fitted the frame. Maliha took in the room, the two wooden pallet beds, empty window frame covered with a curtain so thin that the roofs outside were clearly visible. The floor was covered with old newspapers, and one sheet lay on the bed with the picture of Barbara with her at the General's funeral.

There was an empty basket that stank of rotten fish.

"Is there anything here you want to keep?"

"No."

The something that had nagged her before came back to prey on her mind. She stared around the room, what else was here? Ngurah said she had written letters. "Where are the pen and paper?"

"No more paper. Teacher took pen."

"Ngurah. Who did she write to first?"

The girl had been standing near the door, Maliha turned to see why she did not answer, but Ngurah had retreated into the corner. The door was moving though there was not the slightest breath of wind.

A dozen plans flashed through Maliha's mind, she rejected them all except one. Purposefully she looked out of the window, away from the door, and then turned back to the pallet bed to examine the basket as if it held some secret.

The knowledge that she had turned her back on danger sent a shiver through her. There were several possibilities and in increasing order of likelihood: Mary had returned; someone wanted to speak with them; or someone hoped to kill or capture Ngurah.

Given that they had been followed, the final option far outweighed the alternatives and presented the greatest risk to her own safety. So she turned her back to make the man with the red scarf, as she knew without doubt it was he, believe he had the upper hand.

She gave him sufficient time to enter the room then hefted her walking stick and turned abruptly to face him.

He had a black cloth wrapped around his face and a *kukri* in his hand, a very appropriate weapon for the limited space in the room, though the shape of his eyes did not suggest he was Nepalese. There was the red scarf around his wrist.

She brandished her walking stick. She imagined he might be smiling beneath his mask and in truth she was likely to lose her balance without the stick. But that was hardly the point.

"If you kill me I will not be able to tell you anything."

He took another step towards her to a position just beyond the tip of her stick. She lunged at him using it like a sword. He swung the *kukri*, the flat of the blade knocking her stick away. Maliha stumbled as her right leg failed to support her. He lifted the *kukri* for a killing blow. Then grunted as the point of the *kris* burst through the front his chest.

It withdrew and a stain of red spread around the hole. He stumbled forward trying to carry out his last attack but collapsed. Ngurah stood behind him, her face rigid, both hands gripping the hilt of her red-stained *kris*.

Ngurah stared down at the body. "He is dead?"

Maliha watched the pool of blood spreading from the body, soaking into the newspapers and dripping between the floorboards. She sat back on the bed, a sudden weakness flooding through her as the tension faded.

"Without doubt," she said. "A pity, I would have liked the chance to question him."

"He would not answer."

"Sometimes a lack of answers can reveal the shape of the truth."

Ngurah frowned. "You do not make sense."

"This is also quite inconvenient. I will have to report this to the police."

"We have not found my teacher."

Maliha sighed. "She is probably dead, Ngurah."

"Perhaps she is prisoner. She has no *kris*, she not kill herself." There was a note of desperation in the girl's voice. Maliha could feel the girl's desperation. No one wanted to be alone.

"You are right. It is possible." She clambered to her feet. "Let us see what we can make of this. He may tell us things without the need for words."

She stood over the body, avoiding the blood. The red scarf was coarse silk. His clothes cheap but hard wearing, and worn through on the elbows and knees. As she previously surmised from his complexion he was Sinhalese, but his blade was definitely of Nepalese origin.

She estimated he was in his thirties but with very weathered skin. His hands were heavily calloused indicating a lot of hard labour. It meant nothing; physical and outdoor activity was the commonest form of work.

But the scars meant something, she ran her fingers across his palm and stretched the skin revealing wide areas of scarring in patches rather than the lines one might expect from a cut or tear. She felt frustrated, she could not unravel their puzzle.

"Help me turn him over, Ngurah."

Maliha grabbed his arm and stood up. She looked at Ngurah who had not moved but was watching her with a frown creasing her forehead.

"I not touch."

Maliha chose not to express her annoyance. She manhandled the body awkwardly and finally managed to get the leverage to roll him onto his back. She examined his feet, there was similar scarring on the side of his right foot. And both knees. Perhaps it was a corrosive liquid.

Ngurah took several steps backwards, Maliha glanced up and saw her pointing towards the door again. Moments later the old woman peeked around the corner. Her hand went to her mouth as she took in the dead body, Maliha and then Ngurah with the blood-drenched *kris*.

Maliha pushed herself to her feet.

"Do you know this fellow, *mata-ji*?"

She shook her head. Maliha knew there was little point in castigating her for not warning them. No one wants to die.

"Send a boy for a constable."

The old woman did not move, just stared.

"Has the room been paid for, for the last two nights?"

The woman shook her head.

"I will pay for those, and for tonight."

She nodded and turned away.

iv

"Who did you say, Choudhary?"

"Maliha Anderson," he said from his chair. "Apparently she's killed someone."

Forsyth closed the folder and dropped it on his desk. "I wouldn't put it past her. We'll take that one."

"But the murder, sir?" said Choudhary staring at the box of yet-to-be-examined folders.

"Do you have any new ideas, Constable?"

"Not yet, sir."

"That's why we'll take this one."

He put on his jacket and headed for the door. "Come on, Choudhary."

"Sir."

Choudhary left a marker in the folder and closed it. Forsyth was already in the corridor and had intercepted Inspector Smythe-Johnson.

"You've already got a murder." Smythe-Johnson glared at Forsyth.

"Do you really want to go outside the wall?"

Smythe-Johnson's eyes narrowed. "What do I get in return?"

"What do you want?"

"Give me the Liversedge case."

"But that's solved."

"You haven't submitted the case files yet, have you?"

An unpleasant smile twitched at the corners of Smythe-Johnson's mouth. Forsyth put out his hand and they shook. "So how do we find the place?"

"There's a boy waiting for you outside."

The police station was located on the edge of a cluster of judicial and legislative buildings nestling near the wall and bordering the Army ground. Convenient for both justice and brute force. The boy was a local about fifteen years old, and thin as a rake. He waited in the shade of a tree.

Forsyth took out his pocket watch and flipped it open. They were going to miss luncheon. A policeman's lot. A steam whistle pierced the air as Choudhary drove the one and only police carriage on to the street. It had three pairs of wheels of which the front and middle turned when he adjusted the horizontal steering wheel, the middle pair turning less than the front pair. Its smoke stack generated a trail that hung in the midday heat and slowly dissipated. Apart from the rear area for the driver and stoker (Choudhary performed both functions) there was seating for four at the front.

As the machine trundled past Forsyth swung up into the front section so Choudhary didn't need to slow down. The boy climbed into the back and grinned, his white teeth gleaming.

Forsyth shouted above the noise of the pistons and rhythmically hissing steam. "Find out what he knows about the crime."

"Yes, sir."

The noise increased as the machine picked up speed. Forsyth hoped Choudhary was concentrating. They took the next turn to the right that had them cutting across the residential district towards the northern gate.

The great and good who were out walking or shopping paused to see what machine was clattering by, but lost interest the moment they realised it was a police vehicle.

Forsyth mulled over the case for a while but ultimately there was nothing they could do. The interviews being conducted by the uniformed men might yield some evidence. Beyond that they had a murdered white woman who had suffered torture and been killed by someone who, up to now, had only been interested in killing boys like the one in the driver's cab.

Choudhary leaned over the barrier between the driving station and luxury leather seats.

"Well?" said Forsyth, craning his head round and looking up.

"Imran, that's his name, was sent by his grandmother. His uncle owns a place where they rent rooms. His grandmother says this Maliha Anderson told her to fetch the police as there was a dead body in a room."

"Did she say who killed the victim?"

"Only what I've told you, sir."

Forsyth blinked twice. "Who's steering this thing?" There was the slightest trace of panic in his voice.

Choudhary smiled. "Imran. He's good at it, we could employ him as driver."

"You stay there with him."

The soldiers eyed the carriage as it passed through the gate. Forsyth waved his warrant card at them. One of them nodded. There was little love lost between the civilian and military forces.

The carriage came to a halt a minute after passing through the gate. Forsyth climbed out to join Choudhary who was in the process of putting on his jacket. His shirt was dusted with soot.

"We go in there," said Choudhary, indicating the maze with a glance.

"Who's going to look after the carriage?"

"Imran has a cousin."

"Alright, well, let's get him here and find Miss Anderson."

v

Maliha walked restlessly up and down the passageway outside while Ngurah sat on the stairs. Maliha had insisted she clean her *kris* and put it away. Now she sat with her own thoughts.

The heat had become even more intense as the day wore on and there was a constant buzz from the other room where the body lay gathering flies. The acrid stench of corrupting flesh flowed out of the room.

The old woman had brought bottled lemonade a while earlier but it had not lasted long.

"Who did she write to first, Ngurah?"

The girl jumped and brushed the back of her hand across her cheek leaving a trail of wetness. She'd been crying. "What say?"

"You said Mary had written to someone else. Who did she write to?" And where is the letter she sent to me?

"Young man. She did not want write. Did not trust. But he have money."

"Did he have a name?"

"Teacher not say his name."

Maliha frowned in frustration, the girl was very obtuse.

"But Teacher say always to practice reading. I read his name. His name is Jack."

"Jack Bainbridge?"

Ngurah nodded. Maliha smiled grimly. So Mary was the one who had been engaged to him and broke it off. There were only a handful of reasons that might happen, and none of them reflected well on Jack. So, Mary arrives on the run and penniless, she contacts the only person she knows for money, they arrange a meeting and she disappears. Meanwhile the Dutch have succeeded in tracking down Ngurah and sent someone to kill her. She shook her head. No, far too simple.

Where were those policemen? Time was slipping by and she needed to talk to Jack Bainbridge.

They did not arrive precisely on cue, however it was only ten minutes later she heard a familiar voice at the door below and heavy footsteps on the stair. Ngurah fled the stairs and stood behind Maliha as a bowler-hatted head emerged from the stairwell.

"Inspector Forsyth."

"Miss Anderson." He spoke before he turned at the top of the flight, his face was as grim as she remembered. Their first meeting had been just after she had learned of her parent's death, and their second after she'd almost been murdered herself.

Another plain-clothes policeman followed Forsyth, a Sinhalese in European clothes, late twenties.

"I was aware you had transferred."

"I believe I should thank you for that."

"If you consider it to be a good thing."

Forsyth nodded. "This is Constable Choudhary."

She smiled a greeting. "*Namaste*, constable." He nodded in return, looking a little uncomfortable.

Forsyth frowned and stepped forward. "I understand you've got a body."

"In there. Can we conclude this quickly, Inspector?"

"You have somewhere to be?"

"Yes."

"Take a look at the body, Choudhary." The constable went into the room. "Alright, Miss Anderson, perhaps you'd like to tell me what happened."

Maliha related the bare bones of the story. She included the search for Mary Carnforth but left out Jack Bainbridge and Ngurah's royal heritage. She was forced, however, to admit that Ngurah had killed their assailant which led to the *kris*. Fortunately Forsyth seemed unaware of its significance.

"I will have to take the young lady into custody," said Forsyth finally.

"Is there any way we can avoid that? It was self-defence."

Forsyth considered the question. Maliha glanced at her watch, it was already three in the afternoon.

"Will you be responsible for her?"

"Yes."

"She must remain at the Fortress."

"Of course."

"And not kill anyone else."

"I cannot promise that, after all, we were attacked."

"So you say, but the fatal blow is in his back."

Maliha said nothing. She and the Inspector regarded one another for a few moments. "Very well."

*   *   *

Choudhary emerged from the room and watched Maliha and Ngurah disappear down the stairs.

"You did not mention the murdered woman."

"No, she'll find out soon enough without my help," Forsyth said. "But I'll lay good odds that our murdered woman is this Mary Carnforth."

"You're using Miss Anderson as bait?"

"I'm not sure bait could ever be the right word for her. She's more like a beater flushing the game out of the bushes."

"And the girl?"

"She's done a good job acting as bodyguard so far. We'll let her continue in that role."

"Yes, sir."

"Oh and get after them, will you? I want to know where she wanted to be in such a hurry."

CHAPTER 4

i

Anand was where they had left him, just inside the gate. He was asleep on the bench of the trap and Maliha poked him awake with her stick. She was angry with Forsyth, he was clearly keeping something back and had permitted her to leave with Ngurah far too easily. It was not that he had attempted to deceive her that she found annoying, it was the fact he thought she was so easily fooled. It was insulting.

She knew she ought to return home and change into a more suitable dress for visiting but time was of the essence, and the customs of the British were sometimes ridiculous.

Anand drove the coach through the wide gates of the Bainbridge mansion and up the long gravel drive lined with orange trees. The house came into view, it was a three-storey structure of stone constructed in the Georgian style even though it was only seven years old. She had heard Cecil Bainbridge boasting it was an exact replica of their estate in Buckinghamshire.

Maliha presented her card to doorman and they waited in the cool interior. Cecil Bainbridge clearly had pretensions, the ostentatious house, the extensive staff all bought with new money. The family itself had no history, Bainbridge had built it all himself in the age of the entrepreneur. His wife however was from an older family with lineage but no money.

They were guided into a room predominantly yellow in colour, with heavy and dark furnishings favoured by the old Queen that clashed with the colour scheme and the delicate ceiling mouldings. Maliha took a place at the window with Ngurah standing behind her.

A woman in her fifties entered. She was thin and pale enough to be suffering from consumption, yet she moved without hesitation. She did not smile.

"Miss Anderson?"

Maliha stepped forward and gave a brief curtsy. "I am sorry to disturb you, Mrs Bainbridge."

"What can I do for you?"

"I wondered whether I could speak to your son?"

The look on Edith Bainbridge's face was that of a person trying to decide whether to be horrified or merely shocked.

"I am sorry, Mrs Bainbridge. We have no time for etiquette. Your son is most likely implicated in a serious scandal and I must speak with him before the police realise he is involved."

The woman sighed and sat. "How much do you want?"

Maliha took a moment to comprehend her question. "I do not want money, madam. This is not something money can mend." Though this would clearly not bode well for Jack Bainbridge if there were previous affairs that had been hushed up, they were very likely to come to light.

"Then why are you here?"

"Only to speak with him. It is about Mary Carnforth."

The ramrod stiffness of Mrs Bainbridge's stance weakened and she seemed to gain ten years in age. She nodded.

* * *

It took half an hour for Jack Bainbridge to appear in the room. Maliha had been served tea and had declined to let Ngurah be taken to the staff quarters. Instead she stood in the shadows like an unspoken threat. Maliha instructed her to say nothing.

Jack looked as if he had not slept but did not appear to be drunk. He slumped into a chair opposite Maliha while his mother took up a place between them as if she were an umpire in a tennis match.

"What do you want, Miss Anderson?"

"Did you kill Mary Carnforth?"

Jack was aghast, but Edith recovered herself first. "Mary's dead?" She looked at her son with an uncertainty that suggested she considered it entirely possible he could have committed such an act.

"I haven't killed anyone, Mother."

Maliha kept up the attack. "When did you last see her?"

"I haven't seen her since she broke off the engagement last year."

Maliha could sense Ngurah stirring behind her. "That is a lie. You have corresponded over the last couple of days and you met with her yesterday morning."

Edith placed her teacup on the saucer.

Maliha pressed home. "You met with her and she hasn't been seen since."

Jack stared down at his hands. "I don't remember. I didn't kill her, I couldn't, I love her."

Maliha persisted. "But you met with her?"

He nodded. "I arranged to meet her, yes, but—" he looked up with sad puppy dog eyes. "—I don't remember going there."

"Where did you meet?"

"Outside the House of Blissful Sleep."

Edith broke in. "You arranged to meet her at an opium den?"

ii

The arrest of Jack Bainbridge for the murder of his ex-fiancée was on the front page of *The Times of India* the very next day along more lurid details of his victim found in the lake. Maliha absorbed the story in a few moments, there were very few facts and nothing she did not know. She tried to read the rest but her extraordinary skill had deserted her: it usually took her less than ten minutes to read every word but her annoyance at Inspector Forsyth distracted her and she faltered halfway through.

She attacked another slice of toast.

"That is your fourth, Maliha." Barbara admonished her. "And I was expecting to do the crossword at some point today."

Maliha folded the paper and placed it on the table by Barbara's elbow. "Sorry."

"Annoyed the police solved it before you?"

"They haven't solved anything. They've taken the route of least resistance, as usual." Memories of arguing with her mother floated into Maliha's mind, why could others not see what was so obvious? "Even assuming the body they found is Mary—"

"Isn't she?"

"Yes, probably." Maliha took a deep breath. "Even so, Jack Bainbridge said he arranged to meet her outside the Wall, but she was found inside. And if he had done it he was so drunk he doesn't recall committing the crime, he wouldn't have moved the body."

"Perhaps he wasn't drunk. He might be lying."

"Have you met him when he's not drunk?"

"Once or twice."

"And what was your assessment of him in that state?"

"He seemed a decent enough fellow, I suppose. As much as any one of these youngsters can be considered decent. Too smart for their own good in my opinion," said Barbara. "And you have seen him when he is worse for drink. Only the other night, his aggression towards Captain Voss was entirely uncalled-for."

"Exactly. If he were sufficiently drunk and with the right provocation, yes I believe he might be capable of murder perhaps even the woman he loved. But if he was that drunk he wouldn't have moved the body."

Barbara opened the newspaper and read the headline. "So, what are you going to do about it?"

Maliha pushed back her chair, wiped her hands on the napkin.

"I believe I will send some letters. What I need is information."

*   *   *

The morgue was not considered a place of interest for tourists. Maliha and Ngurah waited in the foyer. Maliha watched as Ngurah watched her breath condense in the cold air, at least until the cold bit through her light clothing and she began to shiver. Maliha's message to Inspector Forsyth had been short and to the point. She suggested that since Mary had been Ngurah's *de facto* guardian she should be given the opportunity to view and identify the body. His letter, by return, requested their presence at the morgue at two in the afternoon.

It was now two fifteen. The doors swung back and the Inspector arrived with his constable . The constable was weighed down with two large suitcases which he placed on the ground and unlatched.

"You are late, Inspector."

"We stopped off to pick up some coats. Thought you might appreciate it."

The constable stood holding two army greatcoats by the collar.

Maliha eyed them suspiciously. "Where did you find them?"

"I assure you they have been freshly cleaned." Forsyth reached down and pulled up a third coat and put it on. "You think it's cold here? It's far worse down there."

Maliha took one of the coats from the constable, and Ngurah followed her lead. The coats were so large the hem of the one Maliha wore brushed the ground. Ngurah was slightly better off as she was taller. Even the constable put one on.

"I'm going to suggest they have a wardrobe of them put in," Forsyth said. "Follow me."

He led the way through the inner door and down the ice-walled stairs and passage into the back room. An attendant stood by the wall behind the body. Forsyth walked through to the back.

"I should warn you, her face was severely battered. She's not a pleasant sight and may not be recognisable."

The attendant took hold of the top of the sheet, but Maliha put her hand out preventing him from pulling it back. "Ngurah, this will be very bad. You do not have to do this."

Ngurah looked her in the eye. "I see her."

Maliha nodded and withdrew her hand. The attendant pulled the sheet back to reveal the bruised and contorted features. The face was not recognisable as Mary Carnforth's but then it would not have been recognisable as anyone in particular. Maliha looked up at Ngurah. Her face was stoic and her eyes glistened with tears that had yet to fall.

"Is it Mary Carnforth?" asked Forsyth.

"I cannot tell," said Maliha.

"It is my teacher," said Ngurah, still staring.

Maliha frowned. "How can you be sure, Ngurah?"

"The hair. It is her hair."

Maliha turned to the Inspector. "Was there any indication she was right-handed?"

It was Forsyth's turn to frown. "She was left-handed."

"Yes, she was," replied Maliha. "I think we are as sure as we can be, Inspector."

"There's some paperwork to be signed."

"Can we have a few moments?"

The inspector turned away and headed from the room accompanied by the constable. Maliha heard only one set of footfalls retreating up the corridor which meant the constable had been left just outside. Quickly she took the top of the sheet and pulled it back exposing the arms and abdomen. Ngurah drew a sharp breath. Maliha scanned the injuries, she noted the circular marks on the forearms, the bruising, the odd angles of the fingers and the seven precise incisions across the abdomen. She threw the sheet back into position and glanced at the attendant, he stood impassively.

"You must find the one who did this," muttered Ngurah to Maliha. "I kill him."

iii

Constable Choudhary heard the half-caste woman approaching the door and stepped away from the wall. The coat helped but it could not keep the cold from penetrating to his marrow. He found Maliha Anderson quite fascinating, so young and yet she lived with an intensity he had never before encountered in either a man or a woman. It was simultaneously alluring and frightening.

"Constable?"

"Yes, Miss Anderson?"

"She was found floating in an irrigation tank?"

The younger girl, Miss Anderson had suggested she was Javanese, emerged like a cat from the examination room.

"She was found in the large north-west tank at Avudangawa, Miss."

"Near the wall or the residencies?"

The constable hesitated but Forsyth had been quite clear in his order to answer any questions she might have. "The wall."

"Have they been able to establish the time of death?"

"Dr Bristow's best estimate was the small hours of the last night."

"But she went missing early in the morning of the previous day."

"According to your associate."

"Indeed, and Jack Bainbridge told you he had arranged to meet her."

Choudhary could not do it, he simply could not bring himself to reveal what the prime suspect had said under questioning. "I'm sorry."

Maliha had noted the way he had stared at her, and recalled a trick she had seen played. With an effort she forced a smile on to her face. It felt out of place. She twisted her voice into something less hard, less forthright, almost soft.

"That's quite alright, constable. You have been very helpful." She reached out and touched her hand to his arm. "But there is one question, I hope you don't mind, about the man who attacked us yesterday. He had a red scarf tied about his forearm. I was curious to know if it had any particular meaning."

"That is no secret, Miss. There is a gang, they call themselves the Blood Sky. It is their sign." The constable flapped his arms and banged them against his sides a few times.

"Oh, I'm sorry. Shall we go up?"

The constable lead the way with Maliha and Ngurah trailing behind.

"I assume this gang has some reason for existing? Some purpose?"

"They're declared intent is to throw the British out of Ceylon."

Maliha recalled the armoured monstrosity that crouched at the gates of the Compound. They reached the stairs and climbed towards warmth.

"Is that even possible?" Maliha asked.

"British or Dutch they are not your lands," Ngurah said.

Maliha hesitated. What could she say? That she was not British, though her every move, her clothing, her position in relation to the native peoples said otherwise? Or that she agreed that all colonial powers should leave, and sound like a rebel herself? Whatever she thought it would be unwise to say such a thing in the hearing of a representative of that authority.

Too British for the Indians and Sinhalese, too foreign for the British.

They came out into the noticeably warmer foyer where Forsyth stood at a small table, fountain pen in his hand while the fingers of his other hand pressed down on a few sheets of paper.

Maliha shed the coat and handed it to the constable then stepped across to the table. She took the ebony pen from him. She glanced at the nib, it was gold with its place of manufacture inscribed in a tight arc: *Birmingham*. A good quality instrument.

She took in the words of the sheet in a moment and prepared to sign.

"Don't you think you should read it?" Forsyth said.

"I already have." Without waiting for his response she inscribed her initials and surname. "You'll be informing her family?"

"I'll send a telegram when I get back to the office." Forsyth gathered up the sheets folded them and placed them into an inside pocket of his jacket.

Maliha faced him squarely. "Why would a member of the Blood Sky rebels make an attempt on my life?"

Forsyth shrugged as if indifferent. "They are just criminals who hate the British. You were females alone in a dangerous place, your clothes alone would make decent money. Why wouldn't he?"

"You think it was petty theft?"

"Any reason to think it would be anything else?"

"What do your investigations say?"

"They say it was petty theft until I have a reason to the contrary."

iv

Maliha took time to return to the house, write a letter to Captain Voss, and change into a proper visiting dress. These traditions were archaic but when you dealt with the people who had lived with them for so long it was wise to play by their rules. She also found a quantity of correspondence had been delivered in her absence, it took a few minutes to read and absorb.

She came down the stairs into the hall. Ngurah stood waiting but she turned away as Maliha approached.

"Do you want time to grieve?" Maliha asked. She understood how important it was. When Maliha had first heard about her parents' death from a newspaper she had been aboard the *RMS Macedonia* a few hours out from Ceylon. She had not had time to digest the information before Inspector Forsyth had questioned her over the deaths. And shortly after she had been attacked by the murderer.

It was not until she had arrived back at the burned-out husk that had been her family home that she had reached that cathartic moment.

Ngurah looked up, her eyes were dry.

She had been on the run since her parents had been killed, had she had time to grieve for them before losing her one true friend? It was doubtful. She could not avenge herself on those who had killed her family so she transferred that vengeance to those who had harmed the only remaining person she cared for.

Sathi came through from the domestic areas carrying her parasol. Maliha exchanged it for the letter and instructed the maid to send it immediately.

"We must visit Mrs Bainbridge once more."

*　*　*

Maliha was immune to the insult when Mrs Bainbridge came down to meet her in the hall instead of in a reception room. She was almost surprised the woman had agreed to see her at all.

The older woman wore a typically inappropriate heavily boned dress in the heat of the day. The new free-flowing French fashions, designed without restraints, would be far more appropriate in this climate. But since Maliha herself was not dressed that way she could hardly criticise. What was surprising was the hand-rolled cigarette held casually between two fingers, it was unusual to see an older woman smoking, particularly one from such a distinguished line.

"Please understand I do not welcome you into my house, Miss Anderson."

"I appreciate you giving me your time."

"What is it you want?" She took a long pull on the cigarette and allowed the smoke to remain in her lungs before finally exhaling. Maliha found it quite disconcerting.

"I believe your son to be innocent."

"Of course, he's innocent!"

Maliha leaned forward propping herself up on her stick. "However proving it to the satisfaction of the police is another matter."

"I have some influence."

"I'm afraid you will find Inspector Forsyth quite immune to influence." Maliha had no idea whether that was indeed true, however she thought it likely.

Edith Bainbridge looked away, her eyes never still, glancing one way and another, but never directly at Maliha. The woman took another lungful of cigarette smoke and the smell of fresh-cut grass wafted across the room.

"I am endeavouring to find the real murderer—"

"You? What could you possibly achieve?"

"Your son has little chance of escaping a guilty charge. He may escape the gallows if the jury can be persuaded he was not in his right mind at the time of the murder."

"He is innocent!"

"He will hang."

Mrs Bainbridge's bravado lasted barely another ten seconds but its collapse was considerably more dramatic than Maliha had predicted. Mrs Bainbridge tumbled the last few steps and lay unmoving.

Maliha summoned a maid to fetch smelling salts and the butler to find the lady's physician. With Ngurah's assistance, they moved the unconscious woman to the nearest room and loosened her stays. It was not an operation that could be carried out delicately but only the maid returned while they were about it and she did not raise any objections.

Maliha took the opportunity to examine the woman in more detail. Her teeth were quite discoloured and her lips had several sores. She sniffed the woman's hair and found only lavender and scented oils there. There were however one or two burns on her fingers.

With Mrs Bainbridge resting quietly with the maid at her side Maliha went back into the hall and recovered the remains of the cigarette which had landed on the open wooden edge of the hallway and gone out. She sniffed it thoroughly, the scent of the cannabis plant was unmistakable. She placed the remains in the pot of a large aspidistra.

She returned to the unconscious woman, turned to the maid and pursed her lips. "Mrs Bainbridge is terribly unwell."

The maid nodded.

"Do you think she will even see Christmas?"

The girl shook her head.

"What is your name?"

"Evans, miss."

"Have you been with the family long?"

"But two years, miss."

"Did you ever see, Mary Carnforth?"

"I did, miss," the girl drew a deep breath and it was as if the flood-gates had been opened. "She cut the family to the quick when she threw over the young master. His heart was broken, course, he moped for weeks and months. But it was the lady who suffered the worst, she already knew about—you know—and she had so hoped to see a grandson before—."

Maliha nodded at each of her points. Behind her she could see Ngurah clenching her fists at the accusations against her teacher.

"—And the master was not happy either." The maid ended breathlessly.

Maliha glanced down to ensure Mrs Bainbridge remained unaware, noting that colour had returned to her drawn cheeks. There was a commotion at the front door.

"But the young Mr Bainbridge, hasn't he got in with a bad crowd?"

The door was pushed open by the butler and an older man she did not recognise bustled in carrying a black medical bag. Evans looked Maliha in the eye and nodded.

"Everybody except Evans, out."

v

Inspector Forsyth sat in his office. The sun was sinking and unfortunately, as the most recent addition to the team he had been granted the room with a southerly aspect. The blinds were drawn but heat radiated off them.

The police did not have the budget for *punkha* engines, instead they made do with muscle power which was utterly insufficient to the task. He took a swig of boiled water flavoured with lemon. It was an insipid drink but it held thirst at bay.

He looked through the information he'd received on Mary Carnforth. Educated at Roedean and supposed to have been in Bali—wherever the hell that was—teaching the children of some king or other. A thought occurred to him.

"Choudhary!"

It took a few moments but his door opened and the constable poked his head through. "Sir?"

"That girl who was with Anderson."

Choudhary said nothing just looked expectant.

"Well?"

"What about her, sir?"

Forsyth had the decency to feel slightly embarrassed about the question he was trying to pose. "Look, Choudhary, I've not been out here very long. I'm not good at recognising local differences."

"Are you saying you cannot tell us apart, sir?"

"That's close to insubordination, Choudhary."

"Yes, sir. Sorry, sir."

"Well?"

"I'd guess she's from the islands, sir, somewhere like Java."

"Bali?"

"That's one of them."

"Very well. Get me information on recent vessels arriving from Bali and newspapers from the last two weeks."

The constable withdrew and Forsyth allowed himself a confident smile. The cuts on her abdomen were a distraction. They may or may not have been done by their mass murderer, but it didn't matter. All he had to do right now was solve this case, if it lead them to the same killer as the boys that was good, if not they'd still have the murderer of Mary Carnforth.

And as long as the murderer believed that they thought Jack Bainbridge was the killer, he wouldn't be on his guard.

Forsyth took a long, self-congratulatory swig of the disgusting drink.

vi

Maliha had not visited the air-dock since her arrival on the *RMS Macedonia* and even then she had not been out on to the field. The carriages of first-class and second-class passengers came aboard the vessel to pick up their owners.

Anand swung the carriage around the last of a line of warehouses and out into sunlight. There were five large ships docked, the largest were two Zeppelins resting solidly on the ground with their helium bags bobbing above. It was an advantage of the Faraday effect that when it was disengaged there was no chance a zeppelin could be blown away.

Of the other three ships one was Dutch, another helium balloon ship, there was a small American vessel built in the British style using rotors for lift, with wings to assist when travelling horizontally. But the last one was something she did not recognise at all. She directed Anand to drive closer.

It was quite small and resembled some of the early designs from the 1870s. It appeared to have no lifting mechanism at all, but four over-long wings jutting from its sides, so long they drooped. Rather than sitting directly on the ground it was raised up by sets of wheels at strategic locations. There was no smoke stack, but a set of pipes suggested it employed one of the *Herr* Diesel's engines and this appeared to drive the single rotor at the rear.

It had a simplicity of design but it was not elegant. The enclosed crew bay seemed suitable for no more than two people and it had no insignia. But whatever nation it belonged to must be English-speaking since painted in small letters below the canopy was the word "Alice".

They moved past it and Maliha looked ahead towards the *Hansa*. She saw Captain Voss descending the set of steps from the lower deck of the gondola.

"Miss Anderson, I am very pleased to see you again." He clicked his heels, took her hand and bowed over it. His Germanic gallantry made her smile though she made sure it was gone when he stood straight. He turned and swept his arm towards the steps. "Please to come aboard."

She saw him glance at Ngurah and pause for a moment as if he recognised her, or perhaps he was wondering whether it was better manners to let her up the steps first. Ngurah took the moment of indecision as an invitation and followed Maliha up the steps.

The tour of the vessel occupied the next hour as they visited the main engine room with a diesel engine on a scale she found breathtaking. Even the smaller thrusters—where the engine was mounted with the rotors outside the gondola—were much larger than they looked.

The passenger accommodations were sumptuous though naturally not as extensive as those aboard the *Macedonia*. This vessel could take only one hundred and fifty passengers compared to the four hundred of the British ship. But comparisons seemed churlish, the Captain was proud of his ship.

They took some refreshments in the officer's lounge. At length Maliha decided she had indulged her interests enough and it was time to make some progress.

"Do you read the newspapers, Captain?"

He took a sip of his coffee and nodded.

"The woman who was murdered—" she paused for effect, "—you carried her here."

"And this is her maid. I recognised her but I was not sure." He turned and studied Ngurah who has seated on a hardback chair nearer the door. "I am most sorry for your mistress."

"She was teacher," Ngurah corrected. Voss looked at Maliha for clarification.

"I cannot go into detail at this time, Captain. It is a complicated affair and I do not want to drag you into a potential international situation."

"But you want something, Miss Anderson, and I believed you only wanted to admire my *Hansa*."

"Please understand I am very happy to have seen your beautiful vessel, but perhaps I would have come another time if not for this."

He nodded. "What is it you want?"

"I would like a list of all the passengers for whom Ceylon was the end of their journey. And if you have any knowledge of who they are I would be most interested."

A short time later Maliha and Ngurah took their leave of Captain Voss and his ship, with a list of five names tucked neatly into her reticule but from the Captain's description of his passengers she knew which of them was of most interest.

CHAPTER 5

i

Maliha was grateful for the return to the house. She had been on her feet nearly all day and her leg ached. They took dinner with Barbara in a strained atmosphere where little was said.

They withdrew and sat in the warm air circulated by the *punkha* engine. She and Barbara drank tea, while Ngurah had lemonade. The light faded outside. Unlike Britain with its long twilights, here in Ceylon so close to the equator night came with the abruptness of someone extinguishing a candle.

Maliha closed her eyes. She needed to think.

That Mary had been murdered by the serial killer, a fact which delighted the newspapers, was quite incidental to the whole affair. It was the additional injuries she had suffered that were important. She had been tortured and there was only one fact a simple tutor from England could possibly have that was of interest: the location of Ngurah. And the only people who would have an interest in that were the Dutch—just as she had originally surmised.

The Blood Sky member who had attacked them must therefore be working for the Dutch. This was entirely possible, there was no doubt all interested nations had networks operating in each others' countries and territories. And they were not going to stop now.

She suddenly sat bolt upright with her eyes wide. "I have been a fool."

Barbara put down her book and removed her *pince nez*. "What is the problem, my dear?"

Maliha pushed herself up and leaned on her stick. "Barbara, I do apologise for the inconvenience but I think it would be as well if you call the staff, have them lock the doors and extinguish all the lights in the house."

"I see." Barbara rang the bell and went to the door where she switched off the room lights. She spoke briefly to Sathi when she appeared. Sathi went off at a run and Barbara disappeared into the hall.

Maliha turned to Ngurah. "You have your *kris*?"

The girl reached into the folds of the sari she had been lent for the meal and drew it out. Maliha nodded and went to the window.

With her body protected by the column between the windows she peered out. Barbara returned carrying a shotgun, broken across her forearm, and a leather sack. She had two revolvers pushed into the sash around her waist.

"Which do you shoot better with, Maliha?"

"I was never invited to any shoots, Barbara, you know how they felt about me."

The older woman harrumphed but said nothing more. Maliha knew she had been reminded of the time not so long ago when she would have behaved in precisely the same manner towards Maliha. *Had* behaved that way, at least for a while, allowing Maliha to stay in her home was partly as recompense for that.

"There are two characters loitering in the road. I imagine there will be others approaching through the garden," Maliha said.

At that moment, Sathi and Old Vidu arrived. Barbara set them to moving the furniture as a barricade for the door.

"How much ammunition do you have, Barbara?"

"Twenty cartridges or so, at least the same again for the others."

"If you would be so kind as to commence shooting at the fellows out front. I think that would be best."

Barbara moved up and looked out. Seeing the range she pulled out one of the revolvers.

"Use the shotgun, please."

If Barbara frowned Maliha could not tell in the darkness, however that seemed the most likely response. "Please, the shotgun will be most useful in this situation."

Maliha moved away from the window as Barbara loaded the shotgun. The two servants had managed to push the heavy cabinet across the door. "Vidu, please use the fruit bowl to smash the glass so Mrs Makepeace-Flynn can shoot out of it."

He looked at her in surprise then across at his mistress, Barbara nodded. He picked up the lead crystal bowl in both hands, walked across the room and flung it through.

"Please take cover—" Maliha's final word was obliterated by the shotgun going off. There was a burst of bird and animal noises from beyond the room.

Barbara fired the second barrel and pulled back to stand behind the pillar. Several more windows shattered as bullets whined through, embedding themselves in the walls and ceiling mouldings.

"Are you alright, Barbara?" shouted Maliha.

"I'm fine. But I'm not sure I dare another shot."

Maliha glanced across at Ngurah, she could only see her eyes, reflecting the small amount of light coming through the window and the flashes as guns went off.

Old Vidu and Sathi hid in the corner. They jumped as someone slammed into the door trying to open it. The solid oak cabinet shuddered but didn't move. Thank heaven for the twenty-four piece dinner service and solid silver cutlery.

Whoever had been frustrated by the door now fired on it. Maliha estimated there were at least three of them. The explosions of guns going off and splintering wood was tremendous. But the door was solid and there was no sign of anything getting through it.

There was a well-oiled click as Barbara finished reloading the shotgun and snapped it back together. The shots through the window had stopped but the door was splintering on this side.

"They'll be trying to come through the window," Maliha shouted.

Barbara stood up unprotected at the window and fired out. Another fusillade erupted into the room. Barbara threw herself to the floor. "That'll teach me," she muttered.

A dark and hooded figure crashed through the window but seemed no more than a rag doll as it slumped, dead before it even reached the ground. Someone on the outside was assisting them. Ngurah was on her feet and pierced the body's abdomen with the *kris.* "Ngurah, get down!"

A second figure struck the window frame. This one did not even make it into the room, it fell limp half in and half out the room. Maliha allowed herself a smile.

Barbara glanced at the two dead bodies and noted the lack of gunfire from any direction. She pulled herself to her feet. The door now sported a number of holes, there was a solid thud and splinters flew as one of the holes grew in size. Barbara stood carefully, walked to the door and fired both barrels through the gap.

There was a scream and a gurgle from the other side. Then four gunshots at evenly spaced intervals. And silence.

ii

With the four of them pushing the door was clear in moments. Barbara had the shotgun ready as Maliha yanked open the door.

"Please don't shoot, Mrs Makepeace-Flynn," called a male voice from beyond the door.

Four bodies lay in the hall, one on its back with features blasted away. The other three were face down with bullet wounds in their backs. Behind them, beside a shattered window, was Mr Crier, a pistol in his hand.

"Mr Crier, I wasn't expecting to see you until Saturday," said Barbara. She broke the shotgun and hooked it casually across her arm.

Maliha switched on the lights, Mr Crier was dressed in a casual suit and even climbing in through the window had not dirtied him in the slightest. She inspected his handiwork, they had been shot cleanly through the upper abdomen. As had the two that had tried to enter the other room.

"You have consistent aim, Mr Crier," she said.

"A misspent youth, I'm afraid."

"And you are very timely in your arrival."

"I was in the area and heard a shotgun."

Maliha glanced to confirm that each of the bodies had the red silk scarf tied around their right forearm. Barbara gave some instructions to Sathi and Old Vidu, who hurried out the back way. No doubt glad to be away from the devastation.

"So you're not familiar with the Blood Sky?"

He shrugged. "I've seen their names in the newspaper," he looked at Barbara. "Good shooting, by the way, though next time I would suggest not wasting cartridges when they are so far away."

Barbara did not enjoy such familiarity and opened her mouth for what Maliha expected to be a sharp retort. So Maliha interrupted. "I assure you it was quite deliberate."

Both of them stared at her, she felt awkward and looked down. "Better to start an offence before they had a chance to get into position. And I felt it prudent to attract as much attention as possible." She finished looking pointedly at him. "It drew you, did it not?"

He bowed his head in acknowledgement.

"Speaking of attracting attention," said Barbara. "I'd best deal with my neighbours."

Outside the window they could see shadows of people, some holding lights. She went to the front door, unbolted it and stepped outside. Maliha crouched down to examine the bodies. One of the ones Mr Crier had shot caught her attention.

"Have you seen this before?" she asked him and held up the assassin's hand for him to study.

He took the hand from her, his fingers brushing hers. He studied the palm. "You mean these scars?"

"They are like burns, but not quite."

"Ice."

"Of course."

She stood up.

"Let's go into the other room, shall we?" She indicated the room across the hall. "It is less public and we have matters to discuss."

*   *   *

Though he could not imagine what those matters might be—his mind was still rather stuck on the way her fingers had touched his— he turned and went to the door. He pushed it open and held it there. Rather than come immediately she called behind her.

"Come on, Ngurah." A dark-skinned young girl emerged. At first he could not quite appreciate what his eyes were telling him. The girl was wiping blood from an ornate short sword—a *kris*, popular in the island states.

Maliha went past him, her stick clicking on the tiles, as he held the door open. He had never known her to wear perfume but had always appreciated the way she gave the sense of being clean. However the hall stank with cordite so on this occasion he simply imagined it. The native girl stalked past him without looking. She gave an aura of being quite dangerous and it wasn't just the sword.

Maliha sat and the girl stood a few steps behind her, as if she were a bodyguard. There was most certainly a story there which he really should enquire about though she might completely blank him. He made to sit on a sofa opposite Maliha with a small table between them when he noticed the set of decanters on the sideboard.

"Do you think, Mrs Makepeace-Flynn would mind if I had a drink?"

"I do not think that would be appropriate, Mr Crier."

He sighed. "You do not change, Miss Anderson."

"I should certainly hope not."

He sat down, leaning forward with his hands clasped on his knees. She really could be quite infuriating, yet he was sure it was not intentional.

"Do you think we have known each other long enough to dispense with formalities?" he asked.

"I think that entirely depends on which formalities you wish to dispense with."

Was she laughing at him? Almost certainly. "I wondered whether we might use our Christian names, if you don't think that's too familiar."

The way she turned her eyes in his direction and *considered* him made him feel like he was an insect under a magnifying glass.

"So which of your Christian names do you prefer? William, Albert or Valentine?"

For heaven's sake, she already knew his entire set? "Most of my close friends call me Bill."

She turned her nose up. "I will call you Valentine."

He groaned inwardly but put a smile on his face. "Should I call you Alice?"

"I prefer not to be known by my *Christian* name, Valentine. You may call me Maliha, but not in company. In company we will continue to refer to one another appropriately."

He felt as if he had gone three rounds with a tiger. "Thank you, Maliha. I completely understand."

He settled back into the sofa. He was glad he had arrived in time because no matter how infuriating she might be, he would have been very upset if she had been hurt. He did not take that thought any further as all by itself it had an unpleasant effect on his stomach.

"I must admit to being curious as to why were you being attacked by this Red Blood gang?"

"Blood Sky."

"Indeed."

"You don't think they were after Barbara?"

Now she was playing with him, which surprised, pleased and annoyed him all at once.

"I can imagine Mrs Makepeace-Flynn being sufficiently rude to annoy almost anyone," except apparently Maliha, "but I find it hard to imagine a murderous gang attacking in force to extract an apology."

"I think that might be the only way you could extract an apology from my hostess." Now Maliha really was smiling. He could not recall if he had seen her smile properly before. She was usually so stern and this smile transformed her features.

"But seriously?"

She eyed him, the smile was gone from her lips as if it had never been. "They want to kill Ngurah here." She gestured at the girl who stood behind her like a menacing shadow. He looked at her unable to divine why she might be so important.

"But a Sinhalese nationalist group?"

"Oh they are working for the Dutch."

"Do you have proof?"

She sighed. "I do not and, if truth be told, I doubt I ever will."

"I'm sure you are perfectly capable of resolving the case."

She frowned, an expression he was so accustomed to that it was almost a friend. "Of course I am. I did not say I would not resolve the case, I quite clearly stated that I did not think I would have proof."

He swallowed. She had a knack of making him feel an inch high.

"Do you want to find somewhere else to stay?"

"For me? No. I have been British long enough not to be driven out by a violent gang. Especially considering we won."

"With my help."

She raised an eyebrow. "There were only five of them."

He smiled. Indeed, Barbara Makepeace-Flynn wife of a General and veteran of the Sudan and South Africa; this dangerous girl; and the leadership of perhaps the most intelligent woman he'd ever had the pleasure to meet. No, their assailants had not stood a chance. His intervention had merely shortened the encounter and reduced the risk, which was what he intended.

"Alright, is there any way in which I can help? It seems they are likely to try again."

"That is a certainty and they will use more force next time." She pursed her lips and stared at him in silence for a few moments. "I believe you are well connected, Valentine?"

It was strange, when she used that name he did not mind it half as much as he ought. "I don't know where you got that idea, Maliha."

Maliha stood and he jumped to his feet.

"Can you take Ngurah somewhere safe?"

He grinned. "How about inside the military camp? I do know a few of the chaps."

She turned on him. "I am trusting you, Valentine. She is Balinese aristocracy, she must have privacy and a female attendant."

He looked at the girl again, with fresh appraisal, then turned back to Maliha. "I do understand. I'm sure that can arranged."

He waited in the hall while Maliha spoke to the girl, Ngurah. Their voices were raised at one point and there seemed to be negotiation going on. Finally they both emerged just as Barbara returned from outside, somewhere along the line she had gained a cup of tea. It looked incongruous with the shotgun that she still carried.

He took his leave of them and went out trailing the unhappy looking Ngurah, with Sathi in attendance, at least until a replacement could be found.

iii

Choudhary had handed him the *Hansa*'s passenger list with a hint of repressed excitement almost before he had had a chance to sit and sip his first coffee of the day. Choudhary always started early, in some distant way Forsyth felt that perhaps he ought not to be outdone by a junior. Then the thoughts of all the extra hours he put in when the job demanded came to him and he rejected the notion of the starting earlier. Let Choudhary have his glory.

He scanned the passenger list, most of them were continuing on but there were a small number who had the Fortress as their final destination. Choudhary had underlined one of them: a certain Raymond Franks, senior accountant in the firm Bainbridge Ice Imports. An address had been written in Choudhary's neat hand below.

"Get your coat, constable."

It was something Forsyth said from habit, and Choudhary went along with it.

"Yes, sir."

One got one's amusement where one could as a policeman.

The journey to Franks' bachelor apartment located near to the homes of the exceedingly wealthy was quick and simple. Forsyth persuaded the doorman and then the concierge, on production of his warrant card, to let them in and not to alert Mr Franks of their arrival.

The trip in the hydraulic lift to the fourth floor continued the normal and uneventful trip. The lift and corridors were as spotless as you would expect from upper middle class apartments. They no doubt maintained an extensive and efficient staff, including a kitchen if a resident required such service.

There appeared to be twelve apartments on each floor. Each corridor was carpeted with a good quality but durable material which helped to muffle the sounds of neighbours moving to and from their rooms. The walls were plain but an enterprising manager had placed framed photographic prints at intervals, most depicted sporting events.

The fact that the door to apartment nine stood ajar was the first sign of trouble. Forsyth checked his gun, then had Choudhary push the door further open. It was dark inside though sunlight leaked around one of the closed doors.

They moved through quickly, opening doors on to well-furnished but otherwise empty rooms. They reached the bedroom door, Forsyth went through first.

Raymond Franks had died in his sleep, for that one could be grateful. There was a bullet wound in his head, it looked like a fairly large calibre. It was a neat wound, but the exit had caused a great deal of damage. His life blood, and brain no doubt, drenched the sheets and pillows.

"Mr Franks!"

A young man's voice pierced the quiet from behind them. "Oh my Lord!"

Forsyth turned in time to see the fellow's look of horror, the breakfast tray crashing to the ground and the man take to his heels.

"Get after him, Choudhary."

The constable leapt over the smashed crockery and made off down the dark corridor.

"And make sure you tell him you're a policeman!"

Forsyth was about to return his attention to the corpse when the headline on the fallen newspaper hit him. He spun back and grabbed it up from the ground. REBELS ATTACK was all he had read but when he unfolded it he saw the rest INSIDE THE COMPOUND.

He scanned the article quickly gathering the facts such as they were. Assassins attacking the home of Barbara Makepeace-Flynn in the night. Gun battle with Blood Sky gang. Five assassins dead, unknown number flee. And Maliha Anderson was in the middle of it. Damn her.

He let the newspaper fall and stared out of the window across the city. Serious trouble was brewing and that trouble wouldn't come from some group of natives. The real trouble would come from the people he was supposed to protect who would now panic that it was a return to the days of the Indian Mutiny with the British being slaughtered in their beds.

It was going to make solving the murder—two murders—quite difficult. He recovered the newspaper and re-read the article. Apparently none except the attackers had died. Just as well otherwise they'd be calling out the army.

For now he should just investigate the crime in front of him and try to understand how it fitted with the death of Mary Carnforth. One thing was clear, this one had not been mutilated which meant the only reason for his death was to keep his mouth shut.

Forsyth took a mental step backwards. Assuming it was connected. It could be a coincidence.

He looked down at the dead man, the one who had recognised Mary on the Zeppelin and informed his employer of the return of the woman who had spurned his son, and somehow brought about her death, and his own.

No, not a coincidence.

iv

There were not many things that made her angry, Maliha thought, but one of them was standing directly opposite her barring her entrance to the Vishnu Gentlemen's Club. If only Vishnu would take offence and deal with him.

Still it had not been unexpected. She glanced at her watch. She had sent the letter to Mr Crier almost as soon as he had left the house the previous evening detailing her plans and arrival time. He should have received it. On cue the double doors behind her banged open and he arrived.

"Good morning, Miss Anderson."

"This idiot won't even tell Cecil Bainbridge I want to speak with him."

"I'll do what I can."

Her frustration reached a pitch as she allowed Mr Crier to step past her and up to the doorman, a man in his mid-fifties sporting medals from Afghanistan and South Africa. He stood ramrod and unmovable, he had his orders and he would not bend for anyone. To Maliha the idea she needed to have a man do something for her grated.

She moved away and stood near the front door. It was ornately carved and the Victorian stained glass portrayed an image of Vishnu against the cross of St George.

"Miss Anderson?"

She turned back, her anger bubbling at a lower level.

He was smiling while the doorman was speaking to a young Sinhalese boy in uniform who ran off through one of the doors on the far side.

"This way," he paused by the doorman's cubby-hole. "I just need to sign the visitor's book."

It was a large book, with dates and names of visitors and who they were guests of. She reached for the pen after he had signed. He hesitated before passing it over.

"I imagine lady visitors don't normally sign."

"I doubt it," she replied.

"Well let it be their first." She carefully dated and signed under Mr Crier's name. She glanced at the list. Visitors were quite common, she turned back a page and then another. Five days worth. Among the names she did not recognise she spotted Captain Voss and Wim Brouwer. Not entirely surprising.

Mr Crier led her to a door close to the front that opened into a sumptuously furnished, though quite small, room that smelled of dust and old oak.

"Ladies Room. We won't be disturbed."

She did not quite trust herself to speak yet and went round the room examining the ornaments and ornamentation. She reached the window that looked out on to a side street. There was a breeze on her cheek, turning she noted the *punkha* had begun to sway. If there was an engine driving it it was too far away to hear, but in a place like this they would still use a *punkhawallah* just because they could.

She glanced up at Mr Crier standing by the fireplace. He was watching her.

"Thank you for coming," she said.

"It is my pleasure, Maliha."

She frowned at him.

He smiled. "I believe you do that far too much."

"What do I do far too much?"

"Frown and look stern."

"I do not believe that is any of your business."

He looked as if he had a retort ready to be delivered but he held it back. The moment was broken by the door opening. Cecil Bainbridge did not sport the imposing moustache popular among the military, instead he opted for something more restrained and business-like. His casual suit was of the highest quality tailoring, his tie was in an immaculate knot and not a single hair was out of place.

He closed the door with precision. They took their places on the settees, Maliha sat and the gentlemen after her.

"I imagined it was you who wanted to talk to me, Miss Anderson," he said. He was sitting back with one leg over the other but his hands were restless, rubbing one against the other.

"Your wife is recovered?"

"As best she may," he glanced down at his hands as if only just realising what they were doing and laid them out flat on the cushions on each side. "Let us not prevaricate, Miss Anderson, you have questions to ask I imagine."

His forthrightness was so rare she distrusted it immediately. "Perhaps just some clarifications, if you don't mind."

He nodded.

"It was Raymond Franks who told you that Mary Carnforth had returned to Ceylon?"

"Yes. He was concerned that she might cause more trouble and as a dutiful employee thought it best to warn me."

"You didn't tell your wife or son."

He sighed. "What good would that do? I killed her."

Maliha blinked twice, and Mr Crier positively jumped at the revelation.

She knew he was lying. "But you did tell someone."

"I killed her."

"How?"

"I beg your pardon?"

"How did you kill her?"

A shadow passed over his face, he lifted his hands and stared at them as if trying to imagine them causing a woman's death. He raised his head and looked her in the eye. "I beat her, flayed her, and burned her. I took all my hate for all the harm she had caused to my wife and my son, and I made her pay. Then I marked her so they would think the serial killer had done it."

Maliha frowned, then thought of Mr Crier's admonition about frowning and chose to ignore it. Could Cecil Bainbridge really have done it? Could the attack in Mary's room truly be a coincidence? Had someone else on the Zeppelin recognised her or Ngurah?

She heard him say "Miss Anderson." And realised it was the second time. She focused on him.

"Do you have anything else you want to ask?" he repeated.

She shook her head absently and stood.

"Then, if you don't mind, the club really doesn't like women visiting."

Her confusion over his confession even prevented the anger from boiling up against this bastion of maleness once more. Mr Crier was at her elbow and gently guided her to the door.

"Good morning, Mr Bainbridge."

"Good-bye, Mr Crier, Miss Anderson."

They reached the door just as Inspector Forsyth and Constable Choudhary burst through. Choudhary looked surprised.

"Miss Anderson," he growled. "There is something inevitable about you."

"You found out about Raymond Franks."

"The *late* Raymond Franks."

She absorbed the information. Forsyth continued. "So, do you have anything to add?"

"Someone's covering their tracks."

The sound of the gunshot was muffled by the closed door behind them. Mr Crier leapt for the door and flung it open, with Forsyth and Choudhary right behind him.

"Get out, Mr Crier," shouted Forsyth. "Choudhary call a doctor, there's probably one in residence here."

Maliha drew back and stood by the wall. She watched the running back and forth with only half her attention. From the depths of the club came Dr Bristow, the police consultant, and went into the room to examine the body. At which point Maliha smiled.

After a short while, Mr Crier came and stood with her almost protectively.

"Let's leave before the Inspector decides he wants to interview us," she said quietly and slipped out the door with Mr Crier behind her.

CHAPTER 6

i

Wooden boards had been placed across the broken windows of the bungalow giving the house an abandoned look. There were gouges in the brickwork where bullets had struck. The front of the house would require almost complete renovation. She hoped Barbara would accept some financial help.

Inside the hall, rugs had been laid to hide the bloodstains until they could be properly removed and the smashed door had been replaced by another from elsewhere in the house. Maliha allowed Sathi to take her hat and asked her to bring some lemonade.

Barbara was in the front room writing letters, the lights were on since the windows were less able to transmit daylight. She did not look up as Maliha entered and sat on the sofa. Maliha was tired and felt a strong urge to remove her shoes. It was not the sort of thought she would normally have and it quite surprised her. She closed her eyes instead.

"Miriam Scarborough is a suitable busy-body, don't you think?"

Maliha opened her eyes again, she did not think she had slept and yet lemonade sat at her right hand, and Barbara had turned around in her chair. She must have been out like a light. Barbara's comment confused her for a moment until she recollected a discussion they had had at breakfast.

"Do you think she will be able to make it happen?"

"I suggested that having such appalling squalor on the doorstep of the Empire's jewel was an insult to the crown," Barbara said. "And she is a terrible snob."

"What about fears of rebellion, after last evening and this morning's murder, I would imagine that all right-minded patriots are quivering with fear. Helping the Sinhalese may not seem such a good move."

Barbara shrugged, pressed her palms against her knees and pushed herself to her feet. "There are always rebels."

And always there are women like you that hold the Empire together, Maliha thought.

The puffing of a steam engine grew, and crescendoed immediately outside, the volume and strain in its sound dropped but it continued to pump regularly.

Maliha sighed inwardly. That would be the Inspector having finally caught up with her. There was a harsh rapping on the front door, and Maliha listened as Sathi allowed the Inspector and his constable to enter. Barbara spoke with them briefly, Maliha heard tones of sympathy and then questions being asked.

"If you would care to come through, Inspector."

Barbara returned to the room ahead of the two policemen. Maliha was really not in the mood to speak with them, she had had enough of people to last her several weeks. Unfortunately, this story was not yet done. If she had deduced correctly there was one more act to be played out. She grabbed her stick and pushed herself to a standing position.

"Inspector. Constable Choudhary."

Barbara picked up a book and went to an armchair near the window. It would have been improper to leave them alone with Maliha, even if they were officers of the law. Maliha sat, the Inspector placed himself in the hard-backed chair by the writing desk, which gave him some additional height. The constable remained at the door.

"Miss Anderson, you left the scene without permission."

It wasn't a question, it did not require a reply.

"I have two more dead bodies."

"I imagine you'll find that Mr Franks was murdered with a gun similar to the one Mr Bainbridge used to kill himself."

There was the hint of a gasp from Barbara.

"So Bainbridge killed Franks to shut him up and then killed himself out of guilt."

"That is certainly how it looks."

"Don't play games with me, Miss Anderson."

"How else is one to think of it, Inspector?" she said with more energy than she had intended. Being tired resulted in less control.

Forsyth seemed to gather himself together and when he spoke again he had lost the aggressive tone. "Where's your young companion?"

"Safe."

Forsyth stood up and examined a painting on the wall. A still life of flowers in a basket.

"D'you know what's really odd, Miss Anderson?"

Rhetorical questions also did not require answers. Forsyth let the silence continue for a few moments then turned. He looked over at Barbara. "Perhaps you can shed some light on something that's concerning me, Mrs Makepeace-Flynn." She looked up in surprise.

"It seems no one is investigating the attack that took place on this house."

Maliha suppressed her genuine surprise at his comment. She was strangely pleased that something unexpected had happened.

"I got back to the station and we had been told, in no uncertain terms, by someone very high up that this attack was not to be investigated at all." He glanced from one woman to the other. "Would you have any idea why that might be?"

Barbara shook her head. "I have no idea."

"Would you not be breaking that order by even asking the question?" said Maliha.

"The attack on this house has something to do with that girl, and that girl is something to do with Mary Carnforth and that's the murder I want to solve. I said neither of you were to leave the Fortress; and I told you that you were responsible for her." With each phrase he had taken a step towards Maliha until he was looming over her.

She had to crane her neck to maintain eye contact. "She hasn't left the Fortress and I have been quite responsible in ensuring her safety. I could not have done so if she had stayed with me."

She raised her glass of lemonade, and sipped from it. He backed away.

"Aye, well, perhaps you can tell me where she is." He sat back down on the chair.

"I don't think that would be a good idea."

"I need to interview her!"

"Which is precisely why I will not tell you. However—" Maliha eyed him. "—I'm sure the Club has all the information you need."

*　*　*

Maliha sat on a chair on the verandah looking south across the city, the wall and the rock. News of Ngurah's relocation would no doubt have filtered out by now. Tonight would be dark with a new moon.

That fact, along with the reports she had been receiving from her friends, made her certain it would happen tonight.

ii

When he arrived at Barbara Makepeace-Flynn's house at ten o'clock in the evening, William Albert Valentine Crier found Maliha waiting for him in the hall. She must be eager for the off, though she exhibited no sense of enthusiasm. Either way it would not have been considered proper, but by now he was entirely used to her behaving in a surprising manner. He was not certain whether it was because she had no time for the niceties, or because she took pleasure in upsetting people's expectations. Or perhaps both, they were not mutually exclusive.

Her letter had arrived in the late afternoon post with a number of explicit instructions which included wearing a dark suit, bringing an electric torch, along with the largest telescope he could conveniently carry and arriving in the late evening, she had suggested the time.

Tracking down a telescope at that time had not been easy and he wasn't sure the one he had managed to acquire would be of sufficient power. Not that she had specified that particular factor.

So there he was, on the doorstep of the Makepeace-Flynn household and he felt quite uncomfortable. The maid—was her name Sathi?—seemed to be smiling, not that she had the expression on her lips, but it was in her eyes. And why wouldn't she, to all external appearances he and Maliha would be stepping out together.

Maliha had said nothing of being outside, however the clothes she had recommended—nay insisted upon—made it clear they would be walking out. It was not that it was entirely improper in this day and age, though she was not yet twenty-one she was most certainly her own woman. It wasn't that, it was something else.

But he wasn't sure what.

No one but the most reactionary British wore coats unless it was actually raining, and even then an umbrella was of more use. But Maliha did have a shawl wrapped around her shoulders, and while he was not one to study women's fashions it seemed that the dress she wore was less "big" than was common and it moved slightly in the breeze, which implied the material was lighter than the usual.

And her hair was up, revealing an elegant throat. The effect was very striking.

"When you have quite finished examining me, Mr Crier." She stepped forward, her stick tapping on the tiles. "Did you bring your gun?"

He lifted the leather satchel, its strap fell from his shoulder. "Everything you specified."

Sathi reappeared from the direction of the kitchen carrying a small picnic hamper.

"And I have brought a light repast."

"Picnicking at night? Why, Miss Anderson, that is quite Bohemian."

She frowned. "I wonder if I should reassess your invitation."

"Since you have not deigned to explain the purpose of this outing—" which clearly had no romantic element "—I cannot assist."

"Levity is not called for."

A retort to the effect that he had always found levity to be called for reached the tip of his tongue but he considered uttering it might be cause enough for her to rescind the invitation. So instead he offered to take the picnic basket, which she handed to him.

She paused at the door, rifled through her reticule and withdrew an envelope. She checked the address then dropped it on to the small table by the door. She looked back.

"Sathi, we will probably not return this night. But if you can bear it, perhaps you or Old Vidu would remain awake?"

"Yes, Miss." Sathi dipped in a brief curtsy.

"Namaste."

"*Namaste*, Miss."

For some reason their exchange filled him with dread.

* * *

The night air was warm and the streets, while not busy, still carried traffic on foot, horseback, and in carriages both horse-drawn and mechanical. Maliha breathed deep smelling the heavy scent of night flowering plants along with the stink of coal smoke.

As they stepped out of the bungalow's drive on to the road proper Mr Crier, Valentine, moved to her side and offered his arm. She slid her hand under his and rested it lightly on his forearm.

"I trust the picnic basket is not too heavy?"

"It is no burden, Maliha."

She steered their course on the same route Anand had driven the carriage. They ambled along as if in no great hurry, as indeed they were not. The events of the evening were unlikely to begin for at least an hour.

After ten minutes they approached the main shopping thoroughfare and had already attracted some comments of surprise from others out in the cooling evening: the shock of seeing a native woman, albeit in western dress, on the arm of a white man.

"Would you prefer it if I walked apart?" she asked.

She felt the muscles of his arm stiffen. "What kind of man would I be to want that?" he said, it was almost a growl.

"A very typical man in my experience."

"I am sorry your experience has been so unkind."

She smiled sadly, he could probably not imagine the kind of treatment she had received. Nor perhaps would she want him to. He would feel male outrage and the need to defend her honour.

Even so, perhaps she should protect him and she lifted her hand from his arm.

"I would miss your hand very much if you were to withdraw it," he said quietly. "I might be forced to remonstrate with you. Loudly."

He was so infuriating with his perpetual insouciance. She knew he was grinning. She sighed and placed her hand back on his arm, perhaps more firmly than before just to be sure he was aware it was there.

"If our skin colours were reversed you would be flogged," she said. "Do you consider that to be fair?"

"Not in the least," he said. "Let us be glad of the current arrangement."

They came out on to the more brightly lit market street and walked along the stone slabbed pavement that ran along the tarmacadamed roadway—a recent invention that made streets suitable for the much heavier mechanical carriages, and resisted rain so much better, vital during the monsoon.

Many of the shops remained open in the evening to provide services to those who choose to take the air as it cooled. But by silent agreement, perhaps not to cause too much outrage, neither of them stopped nor spent any time more than glancing in at the shop windows. Not that much of it was of much interest to Maliha.

Soon they left the shops behind and climbed towards the park. There were more people here, mostly courting couples stepping out together without a chaperone. Things had changed so much since the old Queen had died.

It was darker here and Maliha pulled her shawl up over her hair. She pulled in closer to him as a group of young men approached, laughing and chatting. She knew there was no threat, but to be among so many strangers made her uncomfortable. She felt foolish, even more so as they passed and one of them laughed loudly. She jumped at the sound.

Didn't they realise what was going to happen?

No, of course, they didn't. Only she—and the perpetrators—knew.

* * *

He and Maliha sat on the linen cloth extracted from the picnic basket. They were not the only couple. The hill was dotted with courting pairs, one or two of them kissed. In public. He caught himself imagining what it might be like to kiss Maliha though, for some reason, the thought worried him. She would not be the first woman he had kissed and he had had no complaints, however he did fear he might come in for criticism.

She still had not told him why they were here. Why she had dragged him out to watch the stars and the Fortress. She had chosen the location with some precision, he would have been happy to have stopped earlier but she insisted on coming round to this side so they could see the great steel, glass and stone of *Sigiriya*.

"Can you see the time?" she asked.

She did not ask every minute but it had been barely twenty minutes since the last occasion. "Nearly half-past eleven."

Against the backdrop of lights from the city streets far below he watched her turn her head towards him. Yes, he would brave criticism if he could have the chance to press his lips against hers. Perhaps hold her in his arms. Feel the coolness of her skin. He cut short his train of thought. Best not to follow that particular line.

"You have not asked me," she said, and for one crazy instant he imagined she was referring to being kissed.

"Why we're here?" he said and she nodded in the dark. "I imagine you'll tell me when you think I should know."

"Am I really so condescending, Valentine?"

He opened his mouth to speak, yet there was nothing to say. All he wanted to do was kiss her but she was too far away. And then the silence had drawn too long. And she turned away.

Her face, her clothes and the entire hillside lit up. He blinked. And everything was dark again. Maliha pushed herself to her feet.

He looked out across the city trying to determine the cause of the light. Beyond the wall to the north and east huge clouds of smoke roiled up from the buildings, lit from below with a bloody red light.

The sound of multiple explosions rolled across the buildings. Women screamed, everyone was on their feet. More flashes of light in the city with no name, more smoke rising. Flames climbed into the air as dilapidated buildings burned, the light grew in intensity tinting the rising clouds with their red glow.

Maliha watched it happen without expression, she barely seemed to breathe.

iii

The grassy hillside cleared within minutes, the couples and their escorts stumbling up and away. The fires on the other side of the city took hold, flames licked up from burning buildings. From this distance, there was no sound.

In the streets below, within the wall, traffic had increased. Fire engines, their bells tinny and small, rattled through the streets towards the wall. Troop transport vehicles left the Army compound, like a tap being turned on slowly—just one or two at first then rapidly increasing as they became more organised.

Small Royal Navy ships rose from the inner air-dock and floated effortlessly in the direction of the burning city. It was like watching toys.

"You knew this was going to happen," his voice cracked in accusation.

She did not deny it. She watched the city burn knowing innocent men and women, and children, died there.

"How could you know?"

For a moment, a flame flared high above the wall as it consumed something more to its taste. It subsided and joined its fellows feeding on the wooden buildings.

"It was bound to happen."

"But how did you know it was going to be tonight?"

"Because there was no other time it could be."

"I don't understand you."

"I know."

She waited expectantly. There were events still to be played out. The Army had finished moving out and some of the larger Navy vessels were now in the air. And moving to strategic points around the blazing landscape.

The Residences had come alive with activity. Lights were burned in every home. Many carriages were already on the move, these ones heading to the gates furthest from the conflagration. She wondered momentarily how the guards would react to the escaping British. Would they let them pass unhindered?

Chaos had been achieved with very little effort. She turned her attention to the quiet darkness of the non-military air-docks. She identified the ice warehouses, she could not see the Chinese vessel she had spotted a couple of days before. It could be gone already, but that was not what she was looking for. She thought she caught a glimpse of light.

Maliha watched the conflagration a few minutes more. She hoped not too many would be hurt but there were other matters which required her attention.

"Do you have the telescope?" she asked without turning. She held out her hand and waited as he rummaged in his bag. He placed the heavy tube in her palm. She could feel the smooth wood with its brass binding.

Carefully she extended it to its full length, the fact that she had to rest her weight on her stick made it awkward as she brought the lens to her eye. It was a good telescope, and the view of the ice docks sprang into view. She was right, there was activity around one of the helium-balloon ships, a couple of people with lanterns and other men.

"What do you make of that, Mr Crier?"

She held out the telescope. He took it almost aggressively.

"What am I looking at?"

"The ice docks."

There was a long pause as first he located the place, focused and examined it in more detail.

"One of the ships is readying itself to take off."

She held out her hand again. "If I may?"

She guessed that he relinquished the telescope reluctantly since there was a notable delay before he gave it back. She located the ship again, smoke blacker than the night poured from its exhaust ports and the vehicle slid to one side as its Faraday device engaged. It gained the air with an effort but stopped as soon as it had enough height to clear the buildings around it.

As she watched it turned toward the Army barracks, the smoke redoubled from its exhausts and it leapt forward. In less than thirty seconds it had traversed the distance and hopped the fence into the inner compound. The pilot must have cut the Faraday device because the ship abruptly fell from the sky, its balloons insufficient to give it full buoyancy against gravity.

She let the telescope drop from her eye, holding it in one hand was very tiring. She passed it back to Mr Crier. And spent a few more minutes watching the flames licking the wall of the Compound.

Finally she turned away from the devastation. She knelt awkwardly, the strain of it making her old injury ache. She gathered the picnic items and placed them carefully into the basket, noting how it seemed to occupy more space than before, despite them having eaten.

"What are you doing?"

"Packing up." She glanced up at him. "We must be getting on."

"Where are we going?"

"The Dutch Quarter."

iv

The last time he had looked at his watch it had been a quarter past twelve. So he guessed it must be half-past by now. The roads remained busy with carriages loaded up with families and their luggage on their way out of the city. Most vehicles, whether mechanical or horse-drawn, sported electric lanterns that lit the streets dazzlingly bright as they passed and then plunged them into even deeper darkness.

Maliha was single-minded and seemed disinterested in any conversation. She strode the streets with a clear knowledge of their route and eventual destination. Which she seemed in no hurry to share. He did not find it too troubling, certainly no more troubling than the horror they had witnessed.

He had older brothers who served in both Army and Royal Navy. They did not discuss what they had seen and he had learned not to ask. He had his own nightmares. He tried not to dwell on it yet that seemed counterproductive, the more he tried not to think of it, the more imaginary images of suffering came to mind. He may not have known anyone who lived outside the wall but they were people regardless of their status.

Maliha came to a stop and pulled herself into the shadows of a large gate. He followed suit and stood beside her.

"I would like you to give me your gun." The first words she had spoken since the hilltop. It gave him pause, she had phrased the request oddly. He looked down at her, standing only inches from him. Her eyes reflected starlight. She was asking him to trust her.

He removed the gun from the bag, checked it and then passed it to her. She turned away from him, facing into the dark shadow. When she turned back the gun was no longer in her hand.

"For later," was all she said.

He looked around, not entirely sure where they were. The buildings looked somehow non-British. Maliha was watching the house diagonally opposite their current position. He studied it, light filtered through the thin curtains and matting that covered the windows. Then he knew.

They stood for another twenty minutes. Not speaking and barely moving. The frequency of vehicles on the road decreased. It was so quiet one might believe that nothing untoward had happened all evening. But there was a slight breeze and with it the smell of burning wood.

A low droning impinged upon his consciousness, he looked up and down the street but couldn't see a mechanical. He frowned as it grew in volume but still no vehicle. Maliha tugged his arm, he looked down at her as she pointed her finger at the sky. Of course.

In the black of the night a wide and flat ice bucket skimmed above the tops of the buildings, following the road. He imagined navigation could not be easy. The engine drone cut out and, from the building across the way, three hooded figures emerged. Ropes were thrown down and the figures caught hold. Helium must have been vented as the flying machine settled, crushing bushes and trees. A door opened in the side and half a dozen similarly garbed figures left the ship, one of them carrying a large bag.

Which was the moment a gun clicked in his ear as it was cocked.

* * *

Being threatened by someone with a gun was quite unnerving. It was not that death scared her, the cycle of existence stretched out into an infinity of time; it was the prospect of pain that provoked a reaction, and the tortured body of Mary Carnforth.

She was glad she had relieved Mr Crier of his weapon, but was still concerned he might do something foolishly heroic while there was only one gun trained on them. She hoped his fear of her being injured would hold him back. She was relieved when two more hooded members of the Blood Sky emerged from the shadows with guns aimed at them.

As she and Mr Crier were shoved across the road by their hooded captors, the airship lifted from the ground and floated up, drifting on the slight breeze. The engine coughed into life, its roar filling the street, the driving rotors spun up to speed and the vessel gained speed rapidly. It was out of sight in less than a minute, its drone subsiding into silence.

They were guided into the house. She had never visited and was impressed with the collection of native artefacts from all across the East Indies. Though at what price had they been gathered? The Dutch may have been another empire but at least the British did not seek to enslave their subjects. Not anymore. Usually. She sighed, it was never simple.

They were forced along a corridor to the back of the house where two more hooded members of the Blood Sky stood outside a door. They were relieved of the picnic basket and Mr Crier's bag. They searched him for weapons but, as she expected, did not touch her. Then they were pushed forward into the room, only one of their three captors entered the room behind them but there was another standing near the window.

The room was an office and, unlike the rest of the building, quite devoid of art. Wim Brouwer sat behind the desk, leafing through a set of technical drawings. The bag she had seen brought in lay discarded. A second white man waited while Brouwer examined the documents.

He seemed satisfied, stuffed them roughly back inside the bag and handed them to the other man who left in a hurry.

Brouwer turned his attention to them and smiled. It had all the friendliness of a snake.

"Miss Anderson, I am not surprised to see you."

"You're not?" said Valentine.

"I think you do not have respect for your companion. You British have much to learn about women." He grinned and took a drink from a lead crystal goblet. "Miss Anderson has been like the British bulldog."

"You got your plans then?" she said.

"Your government's secret is not a secret any longer." He wiped his lips with his sleeve, the smile stayed on his lips as if glued there.

"And your man will leave the city through the gates opened for escaping residents, to rendezvous with a fast airship."

"You see, Mr Crier. She is very clever," he said. "Cleverer than you, I think. But—" he paused for effect "—not clever enough."

Brouwer became serious. "What are you good for, Mr Crier, eh? You and your British Secret Intelligence Service."

Maliha accepted his revelation as fact, it was what she had suspected anyway, but they were getting off the point. "And what of Ngurah?"

"Dead." He waved at the members of the Blood Sky. "My friends killed her when they stole the plans. Putting her in the protection of the British Army made my tasks simpler."

"How many of the Blood Sky realise you will betray them as soon as it is convenient for you?"

"I help their cause, they help mine, it is good for both."

"You had them abduct Mary Carnforth, then tortured her to find out where Ngurah was hiding."

"She was not helpful."

"But you're not the one who killed those boys?"

He laughed out loud. "I am not a pervert, Miss Anderson. This is a matter of state. No, of course not, but Dr Bristow was at the club and happy to talk about the latest horrors he had examined.

"The club has been useful, I hoped to blackmail Cecil Bainbridge, but I had nothing. Then he told me about the girl, so I promised to deal with it and killed her for him. He was not happy about that but then I had him. I did not expect his suicide, your British honour is very strange."

"But you killed the accountant."

"I did not murder anyone."

"Except Mary."

"Except her, yes." He became introspective for a moment. "It was interesting."

The Blood Sky member at the window took half a step forwards, staring into Maliha's eyes intently.

Maliha sighed. "Enough of this."

She turned away from them as if overcome by the horror.

"Yes," said Brouwer. "Enough of this, I'm afraid it is time for you both to die."

Maliha turned back and nodded to the Blood Sky member behind Brouwer and at the same time thrust the gun into Valentine's hand.

The Blood Sky member stepped up to Brouwer, pulled back her hood and drew out her *kris*. Maliha appreciated the fact it took Valentine only the merest hesitation to grasp the situation. He twisted round, the gun fired just once and the attacking figure behind them went down. Three more shots rang out in the house and another figure fell through the doorway.

The falling bodies gripped Brouwer's attention and for a moment he did not notice the movement beside him, then the glint of the *kris* caught his eye and he whipped round. The tip of the blade dipped and pressed against his neck.

"Wait," called Maliha.

Ngurah turned and frowned. "He is mine. You promise."

"I promised, but he should know the extent of his failure first."

Brouwer's confidence and humour had drained away along with the colour in his cheeks. His awareness focused only on the metal of the sword. His eyes flicked to the bodies on the floor and the gun held casually but steadily in Valentine's hand.

"Mr Brouwer—" his eyes snapped to her face "—you are no less arrogant than the British. You think you can come into our lands and do whatever you wish. You cannot. You tried to kill thousands of people this night merely as a diversion. You believed you had killed Ngurah. You have attempted to steal plans that would give your miserable empire even more power."

"I succeeded." His voice came out as a strangled whisper as he tried not to push against the blade.

"No. In all those things you failed utterly," Maliha said icily. "The Blood Sky will have killed almost no one despite their bombs, there will be no uprising against the British. Ngurah stands before you. And the plans you stole were not the ones you wanted."

"They were genuine."

"I imagine they were, I doubt they could produce effective fakes in so short a time. But they were not the designs for the complete nullification of gravity. You failed."

Before he had a chance to reply she turned and walked from the room. "Valentine, please," she said, quietly. He followed her out.

They were not quite out of earshot when there was a short cry cut-off by a gurgle.

v

They were standing on the gravelled drive outside Brouwer's house when a pumping engine heralded the arrival of Inspector Forsyth and

Choudhary. He climbed down while his constable mounted an electric light on the side of the machine and switched it on, bathing them in white light. Maliha had shielded her eyes before the light came on. Mr Crier and the British Army soldiers, masquerading as Blood Sky members, squinted as they flung their hands in front of their eyes.

Forsyth strode up the path but Mr Crier stood forward, still rubbing the tears from his eyes, and blocked his way.

"Out of my way, Crier."

"I'm sorry, Inspector, I'm afraid I can't allow you inside."

"Says who?"

"His Majesty, or at least a duly authorised representative."

"I am a representative of the King, Mr Crier. You'll have to do better than that."

"Unfortunately, I outrank you." Mr Crier reached into his jacket pocket and brought out a small wallet. Inspector Forsyth had no difficulty reading it in the light the vehicle provided. "This is a matter between governments."

"Brouwer's a murderer."

"He was also a spy and that is more important."

"I beg to differ—"

Tired of the petty game of one-upmanship, Maliha broke in. "This is moot since you, Inspector, cannot arrest him, and you, Mr Crier, cannot interrogate a dead man."

"He's dead?"

"Not before he confessed to the murder of Mary Carnforth."

"You heard his confession?"

"She engineered it," put in Mr Crier. He almost sounded proud. "And apparently ensured he did not get the plans he was after."

Maliha frowned at Mr Crier's praise. "I really am most weary, and would like to go home, gentlemen. You can ask Mr Crier about the details, Inspector, he saw it all. You really don't need me."

Forsyth regarded her for a few moments. "Aye, very well, Miss Anderson. Constable Choudhary will drive you back."

On a different day she might have been interested in riding in the driver's compartment but she was truly exhausted and her leg ached with too much use. It was the same as when she had exposed the murderer on the ship, and after the Taliesin Affair. A feeling of utter exhaustion as if all her energy had been spent.

The vehicle rumbled through the otherwise quiet residential district. Ngurah sat facing her, she had not said a word since Brouwer's office.

It was only fifteen minutes later that they trundled up the driveway to the Makepeace-Flynn bungalow. There were lights still on. Sathi came to the door. The constable set the engine to a low throb and climbed down to assist Maliha and Ngurah from the carriage. Sathi looked relieved to see them.

The constable escorted them to the door but did not leave once the door had been opened.

"Miss Anderson?"

She turned to look at him. "Constable?"

"How do you do it?"

"Do what?"

He looked embarrassed. She could almost see his traditional upbringing about women battling new ideas. It seemed the need for guidance won out. "How do you reconcile being on both sides?"

She saw no reason to make it easy for him. "What sides?"

"India. Empire."

"Why do you want to know?"

"They have invaded our countries," he glanced at Ngurah as he said it. "But we work with them. Is that right?"

"We can only play the cards we are given, Constable Choudhary," she said. "Or choose not to play them. I can't tell you how to reconcile Ceylon and Britain because I don't reconcile India and the Empire. I am both but they are separate. People are not their nationality, they are just people."

He nodded and turned away.

She had reached the door when he called out. "They will never accept you."

She glanced back, he had climbed into the carriage and was preparing to engage the engine. "There is no 'they', constable, there are only individuals who make choices."

It took a week for the Fortress and the Compound to return to some semblance of normality but after the rebellion there was a sense of foreboding and nervousness that permeated the British. The Army was more overt in its operations and there were patrols in the streets. The death of the Dutch trade attaché was reported in the newspapers as an accident with an unspecified cause.

A third of the makeshift city had been destroyed in the fire. But, by a miracle, very few had been killed. The details in the newspaper were sketchy but it seemed those who lived in the areas where the explosives had been set had been warned in advance; most had evacuated. As to the identity of those who had given the warning, no one was entirely clear, beyond the fact they were women.

As a result there was little increased resentment towards the British and that was offset by the charitable patrons who had already stepped forward with a plan to rebuild the city with proper sewerage, brick buildings, perhaps bring back the concept of ragged schools.

There was a part of Maliha's mind that tried to insist the deaths that had occurred had been her fault. But she knew the bombings and fire had always been part of Brouwer's scheme to acquire the details of the total gravity nullification. If she had not intervened, with the assistance of the Guru Shahin and her family, the deaths could have numbered in the tens of thousands.

"I don't know how you did it," declared Mr Crier. "How did you get those people out?"

"I have no idea what you're talking about," she replied then narrowed her eyes. "It is your arrogance that brought this about. Launching those vessels the way you do, you are rubbing it in the faces of your rivals. Anyone with the slightest understanding of science would recognise it for what it is."

She swung around, turning her back on the view, and strode away across the park. She heard his footsteps running after her. "I really cannot make a comment, Maliha. It's not my decision."

"You will not indulge in familiarity in public, if you recall our agreement." She smiled inwardly. He was easily distracted.

"I'm sorry."

She allowed him a few moments to stew. "There is something you could do for me, however."

"Name it."

"I would not offer so recklessly if I were you."

"For heaven's sake, Maliha, you are without doubt the most infuriating person I have ever met. What do you want?"

She dropped her head so he would not see her smile. "I want you to take Ngurah to the United States of America."

His silence was lengthy. They reached the gate of the park and stepped out on to the main road. Traffic moved back and forth, a preponderance of horse-drawn carriages.

"I can take her to Britain," he said finally.

"She will not be safe from either the Dutch or the British. She will become a pawn, and when they see the opportunity they will sell her to the Dutch."

He became silent again, he was no fool, he knew she was right.

"In the USA she will have a better opportunity to build her own life," she said. "You know people there?"

"Yes."

"Then it is settled, Valentine," she said. "You can take her in your air-plane machine."

"Yes, of course."

She picked up her pace, walking stick clicking on the paving slabs. It took him a few moments.

"How do you know about that?"

She turned back and smiled at his astonished face.

He appreciated her smile, she thought, and it was not an unpleasant thing to do, within limits.

HALO ROUND THE MOON

BOOK 3

He groaned, more in annoyance than pain, though there was that as well. The horse had leapt the fallen tree trunk without a problem. There had been no pace adjustment but something had gone wrong. His stomach had been left behind as the saddle slipped and he flew sideways.

The muddy ground had struck him on the cheek and there had been a sharp pain as something cut into his lip. Then the rest of his body hit the sodden ground, splashing into water, mud and leaf mould. He tasted blood and earth.

"Alex?" His sister's voice seemed distant. Perhaps it was; he'd drawn well ahead of her as they raced through the trees. He cursed himself for choosing to jump—she'd never let him live it down. Something moist snuffled his face and he opened his eyes. Badger's muzzle blocked the light of the overcast sky.

"Get off me, stupid."

He still had the reins in his hand. He heard something behind him and a whispered word. Pain shattered his thoughts and his head felt as if it would explode—and when the pain came again, it did.

CHAPTER 1

i

"You need to get a maid of your own." Barbara Makepeace-Flynn folded the newspaper and laid it neatly beside her breakfast plate. She raised her morning coffee and eyed Maliha as she sipped.

Rain tumbled from the sky outside the window making a constant and insistent drumming on the verandah of the large bungalow.

The younger woman glanced at the newspaper. The fact Barbara had not passed it across to her emphasised her desire to resolve the issue. Maliha was somewhat non-plussed, Barbara had not been confrontational, at least with Maliha, for a long time now. They had a working understanding. Or so she'd thought.

"I don't think I make excessive demands on Sathi's time. Do I?"

She found discussions of her personal affairs quite awkward. She could happily interrogate someone on their business, regardless of the subject matter. She could examine a dead body with relative equanimity, and had done so on more than one occasion. She could even put her own life at risk in pursuit of the truth. However, when it came to her private requirements it was quite a different matter.

"If you are going to be stepping out with Mr Crier more often, you will need someone."

"I hardly think that is likely, Barbara." The events surrounding the attack on the Compound had been unique. Their evening out on that occasion had had no romantic aspect whatsoever. But even she could not prevent herself from glancing across at the sideboard, where the silver platter contained yet another letter from him.

He had recently returned from the USA, where he had taken the Balinese princess they had rescued while investigating the death of her teacher—an old school acquaintance of Maliha. Thankfully this was one escapade completely ignored by the newspapers; the attack on the Compound was far more newsworthy and Valentine Crier's position in the Civil Service ensured that even if they had got wind of the event it would have been silenced.

"It's quite ridiculous," said Maliha. "We have nothing in common at all." Valentine might think he could ignore their racial difference, but no one else would. Except perhaps Barbara, and her conversion to a more liberal viewpoint was quite recent.

Barbara smiled as she prepared to butter another slice of toast.

Maliha frowned. "This is not some romance novel."

The older woman made no comment.

"I cannot *marry* him." She almost choked as the words came out of her mouth. The mere idea that anyone would want to marry her, that she would be a suitable mate for any male. Ridiculous.

"You know best, my dear," said Barbara, but Maliha knew she was the butt of a joke. She focused her attention on her toast and coffee, and they ate in silence for a few moments.

"Have you finished with the newspaper?"

Barbara picked it up as if she were going to pass it across but did not.

"Shall we resolve the matter of your maid?"

Maliha sat back in her chair and placed her hands in her lap. Just as she had when she was a young girl being admonished by her mother.

"I do not wish to be difficult, Maliha, however if I must I will tell Sathi she should not deal with your particulars."

Maliha felt as if she was ten again, and had to suppress a petulant retort to the effect that she would do her own washing. It was all part of society's demands. There came a point where a person of a certain class became unable to deal with everything in their lives and this demanded they weighed themselves down with staff. And each new addition was another bar that imprisoned them in their social position, another limit on the freedoms she wanted.

"I cannot employ an Indian or Sinhalese."

"Why not?"

"Because they are my people."

"So is Sathi and you have no problem with her."

Maliha could not decide whether she was more angry with Barbara for pointing out the obvious or with herself for failing to think rationally. It was disturbing to find herself in such a position when she prided herself on her logical thought.

"Besides—" continued Barbara, "—a white girl might have difficulty working alongside Sathi and Old Vidu."

"Perhaps you could just get a housekeeper?"

It was Barbara's turn to frown. "You are trying my patience, Miss Anderson."

"Very well. I will place an advert."

Her train of thought was interrupted by a thumping on the front door.

ii

William Albert Valentine Crier—known to his close friends as Bill, and to Maliha as Valentine—stood and dripped in the hall standing on the polished floorboards near the wall to avoid damaging the rugs.

Maliha emerged from the morning room and stood in the doorway with her arms crossed. She was wearing one of the new lighter fashions that did not constrain a body. It looked good on her, and completely different from how she had been when he first met her on the flight from London.

"You have no manners, Valentine," she said and then, into the room behind her, she said. "Mr Crier. Uninvited and unannounced."

Sathi relieved him of his dripping coat and umbrella, placing the latter in the stand and the former she took with her into the back, for drying.

He brushed himself down to take out the wrinkles in his suit. "Sorry, Maliha. I'm afraid it's important. Can we talk?"

Maliha glanced back into the morning room, nodded to something spoken and then limped across the hall. She was not using her stick. If it had been any other woman he would have offered his arm, but Maliha would have been insulted by his presumption.

"You really have no sense of propriety, do you?" she said. "Demanding we are alone together as if I am a woman with no shame."

She was smiling when she said it. Or perhaps it was his imagination.

"In my experience, Maliha, you are the one who likes to shock." Each sway of her body revealed a small and perfectly formed foot between the straps of an open sandal.

He followed her through to what passed for a library in the bungalow, and a withdrawing room as needed. Barbara Makepeace-Flynn was not poor—her late husband, the General, had not had money but her family was not short a penny or two; nevertheless she lived modestly. The furniture was of a taste many years past but she was not a young woman and lived with what made her comfortable.

Maliha sat in a settee on the far side of a small table; Valentine placed himself diagonally opposite on a matching settee. The table hid his view of her toes. The monsoon rains teemed down outside as if they were going to wash away every trace of civilisation.

"Have you read the papers?" he asked.

"I have not had an opportunity this morning," she said testily. He assumed she was criticising his unexpected arrival.

"I'm sorry I arrived so early."

She frowned, which was not as attractive an expression as the rare smile she permitted. "Not everything is about you, Valentine. Barbara and I were having a discussion."

The admonition was alleviated by her willingness to call him by his first name—well, his third and least favourite name. Still, it was a familiarity she was willing to provide and that was enough.

"Seriously, Valentine, if you are going to sit there and moon over me I may as well fetch a photographic portrait and leave that here instead. I thought you had something important to discuss."

He shook himself mentally. "Yes, I need you to come to a funeral with me."

"Why? Who's died?"

"Alexander Mawdsley."

She leaned forwards, resting her arms on her legs and clasping her hands together, the dark brown of her eyes focused on him. "Mawdsley? The City and Cornwall Mining Company?"

"Randolf Mawdsley owns it and his son is heir apparent as it were. Was."

"You think there's foul play?"

He sighed. "Frankly, according to the reports, it's unlikely." Was there a hint of disappointment in her eyes? Probably. "He was killed by his horse while out riding with his sister."

The reaction he got was not what he expected. Maliha rose quickly and, with a more pronounced limp, went to the window. "Horses are dangerous." She was clenching and unclenching her fists as she spoke.

"Sometimes," said Valentine.

He watched as she stared down at her own hands and brought them under control, forcing one to grip the other. "Why do you think the death is suspicious?" Her voice wavered. He fought the urge to go to her.

"His sister Selina, she's expected to marry a German, Herman Stines."

"Stines, the mining family?"

"Yes."

"I see the problem." She seemed to have overcome whatever difficulty she had encountered. "It's your masters who are concerned about this, isn't it?" She limped back to the settee and sat on its arm. He wasn't sure how Mrs Makepeace-Flynn might feel about her perched on the end like that.

"It's their job to be concerned," he said. "Which makes it mine. Besides, Alex was a friend."

She took a moment and then replied. "Very well, I will accompany you." She stood up, hiding her ankles. "When is the funeral? Can I see his body?"

"I don't know about the body but we can have the police report. We will be spending a couple of days there. We'll be travelling into Kerala by atmospheric."

A look of horror crossed her face. "You seriously expect me to accompany you for *several days?*"

"You can travel separately if you prefer. Alex's father knows who you are. I won't do anything to sully your reputation."

The expression on her face was something new: a strange mix of anger and pity, and he had no idea what it meant. She stalked from the room without a word.

iii

Maliha's walking stick clicked on the stone slabs as she followed the porter trundling her bags across the station concourse towards platform five. Above them the great arched ceiling of glass and steel rattled with the continuing downpour. During the years she had been at school in England her memories of the incessant deluge—her mother used to call it Elephant Rain—had diminished but they had returned as wet days continued.

Behind her, wearing a practical sari, walked Amita. Valentine's deadline and the requirement to stay for several days had forced Maliha to take radical steps in acquiring a personal maid. Letters had been written and by the end of the day Amita had arrived on the doorstep, only fifteen years old but recommended. And, most importantly, Barbara seemed content with her selection.

Maliha had found it odd to be able to leave tasks, such as laying out her clothes, to someone else. These were activities she had done for herself all through school since even if someone else had offered—which they never had—they could not be trusted. In the two mornings since Amita's arrival, Maliha had yet to become used to the decadence of having someone else brush her hair. But she could not deny she found it pleasant. Amita did not presume to speak much, which was all to the good.

There were perhaps two hundred people on the concourse, but the space was so wide it was not crowded. There was a distinct drift towards the same platform. There were business men, families, with the servants in tow. She could not help but notice the occasional glance in her direction. She knew the thoughts that went with those glances: first they took in her relaxed European dress, and then her darker skin tone which conflicted with their initial thoughts; followed by a study of her features to determine whether she were of Mediterranean origin and the final realisation she was a native. Sometimes there would be further study: her walking stick and her limp suggested a woman of a certain age, then closer inspection showed her to be quite young.

Where their thoughts went after that she could not say but her experience told her that most resolved not to speak to her unless absolutely necessary. It was of no concern to her, or so she told herself.

Along the length of each of the eight platforms ran the pneumatic tube that carried the engine and its carriages. The doors of the carriages and the enclosing tube matched up exactly so the opening mechanism operated on both simultaneously. That was simple engineering, but what fascinated Maliha was the end of the tube where massive pipes introduced the pressurised air that pushed the train.

They passed on to the platform proper where the huge pipes and their associated gauges and valves were manned by three pneumatic engineers climbing across the mechanism. Maliha was pleased to note all three were either Sinhalese or Indian. She stopped.

"*Namaste*, gentlemen." She nodded her head to them. The porter turned at the sound of her voice and came to a halt. The men were taken aback at having been addressed directly by a passenger and exchanged quick glances. The older of the three slid from the machine and bowed back as he pulled a rag from his pocket and wiped his fingers.

"*Namaste, sahiba.* How can I help you?"

"I wondered whether this device uses an Anderson valve?"

The engineer frowned. "For the main high pressure inlet, *sahiba*. Yes."

She smiled. "Thank you. *Namaste.*" She pressed her palms together.

There was an immortality in names, she thought. Her father might be dead, but the work he had done, the reason he was brought out to India, how he had come to meet her mother, they lived on in the very metal of the Empire.

The porter seemed grateful the interruption was short-lived and guided her to the entrance to the first class compartments. As the train was only traveling to Kerala there was no need for sleeping berths. At over 150 miles per hour it would be at its destination before dark.

Valentine had arranged the tickets and had not booked a private compartment. The porter carried her baggage onboard and Maliha received a receipt from the baggage manager—in case of loss. With Amita she took a seat in an empty compartment. The maid could read and Maliha had lent her *Much Ado About Nothing* to improve her. Having ensured her mistress did not require anything, Amita applied herself to the book.

The three-minute warning bell jangled through the carriages.

Maliha looked forward to the off; when the Faraday device was engaged it took the strain from her leg and she could walk normally without her stick. The trip from England on the *RMS Macedonia* had been delightful in that respect, if unpleasant in most others.

There was a suppressed commotion of muffled voices and movement in the walkway outside the door. It was flung open. A man in his late fifties entered, carefully placing his feet with the precision of someone who hadn't actually been able to see them for many years. He wore a suit that fitted his bulk so well it declared its owner to be someone who knew how to use the wealth he clearly possessed, but the cut was local so he was not a recent incomer.

The woman who followed was in her early twenties. A gold wedding band glinted on her left hand.

Maliha nodded as the woman's eyes met hers but received no acknowledgment in return. The man did not even glance in their direction. The wife passed a travelling case to the porter who came in after them, he placed it on the shelf above their heads and withdrew. The husband unfolded a copy of *The Times*—only four days old, Maliha noted—and buried himself in it.

The final warning bell jangled. There was a distant powerful hiss of steam and the oiled grumble of gears followed by a clang as the doors were closed and sealed.

"*Aieee!*" Three pairs of eyes focused on Amita, who had grabbed at the window frame with one hand and at her throat with the other. The book floated to the floor of the carriage in no particular hurry.

Maliha sat forward, her movement pulled Amita's eyes to her, and spoke quickly in Hindi. "*It's all right. It's just the train. You will feel light while we travel. It's the* Faraday effect."

"*I was falling.*"

"*Be calm. It will not harm you.*"

"I am sorry, *Sahiba.*"

Amita sat back. Maliha reached down, retrieved the book and handed it to her, then glanced at the husband and wife. He was resolutely ignoring them after the initial outburst. "My apologies. My maid has not travelled by atmospheric before."

The woman's eyes flicked towards her husband for a moment. She allowed Maliha a brief smile then sat back.

iv

By the time Amita settled, the train had left the station and was just passing over the wall of the Compound. The organised streets of the interior gave way to the haphazard slums of the city that had no name as yet. Part of the reconstruction project after the fires earlier in the year was the selection of a name, by popular vote. By this time next year it would be a real place.

The train picked up speed. Every half mile there was another pumping station pouring smoke from its chimney, the steam engine at its heart ready to push air into the tunnel after the train had passed the pressure valve. Though there were windows at frequent and regular intervals in the tube itself—allowing passengers the impression of an uninterrupted view as they sped through the landscape—every minute there was a short period of dark as they passed through the pumping station and the valve, accompanied by a low-pitched scraping sound that travelled the length of the train from front to rear.

The first stop on the journey was Anuradhapura, barely thirty miles from the Fortress. The city was so close the train did not get up to full speed and in less than half an hour it was slowing again. The pumping stations no longer pumped and only the momentum of the mighty engine carried it in to the station. The train jerked as it changed tube, coming in to the platform, and the brakes engaged. There was a small amount of jerking adjustment as it lined up with the external doors.

Full gravity returned and there was a whoosh of escaping air as the doors opened and the internal pressure equalised with the outside.

Their two travelling companions did not move and no one entered.

The train moved off again. From here it was two hours to Madurai, crossing the Gulf of Mannar from Ceylon to mainland India, from there the same time again to Kochi in Kerala province. The train was far faster than flying.

The Mannar railway bridge was a miracle of British engineering. Between the two land masses was twenty miles of shallow sea. Using cranes, ships and flying machines all aided by the Faraday effect, an atmospheric tube had been constructed connecting the two parts of the Empire.

And through that narrow tube, across those miles of sea lashed by the monsoon winds, with a high swell developed across the entire Indian Ocean, flashed the line of carriages. Pumping stations were separated by two miles but were enormous. Their coal supplies were constantly replenished, so they could maintain the pressure. Though Maliha assumed the train's momentum would doubtless carry them all the way across even if the pumping failed.

Whatever else she might think of the Empire, their railway engineers were—as her father had been—second to none.

Luncheon was announced as they crossed into India. Maliha made her way to the dining carriage. She was not invited to eat with the husband and wife but found a table initially set for two. The waiter removed the other place setting and she ate alone. A well-to-do native was not denied any rights that they could pay for, but that did not make them welcome.

She found the experience of being out in the world again slightly strange. Over the months she had lived at the Fortress she had become accustomed to the way Barbara and Valentine treated her as an equal. Even Detective Inspector Forsyth's bad humour was not due to her colour, or even her sex, as he was rude to everybody. But now she was relearning how cold it could be.

She finished her meal quickly and returned to the compartment. Amita was not there, she would be with the other servants, but Maliha did not begrudge her some time to herself—as long as she did not take advantage.

Despite British rule, the city of Madurai had a curious autonomy, an inner strength. She had visited once or twice with her mother when she was young, and had been inside the vast red temple. The British were a presence here as everywhere else but somehow subdued, less than they were elsewhere.

The train spent half an hour in Madurai, during which time the wife reappeared but was not joined by her husband. She took her seat, with a fleeting smile in Maliha's direction, then took up her own book. Shortly before the train was due to leave, Amita returned and asked Maliha whether she would like some *chai*. It had been a long time since she had had any, so she took a few coins from her purse and passed them to the girl.

"Would you care for some?" Maliha asked the wife.

The woman glanced at her watch, a delicate silver affair, and seemed to be calculating.

"Thank you, that would be nice."

"Without milk, Amita." The girl nodded and left.

The woman held out her gloved hand. "Margaret Henley."

"Maliha Anderson."

"Oh, the detective."

Maliha resisted the temptation to frown, Valentine wouldn't approve, besides she was attempting to be sociable. So she put a smile on her lips, even though she did not feel it. "I think that is rather overstated."

"You must be terribly clever."

Maliha put more effort into the smile and sat back. Such celebrity was not a thing she had courted, but apparently it was unavoidable.

Mrs Henley did not seem to notice her discomfort. "And you're going to Kerala? Are you investigating a murder?"

"Not at all," Maliha replied. "I am accompanying an acquaintance to a funeral."

"Alexander Mawdsley?" Her eyes were bright with excitement.

Maliha's heart sank. "I'm afraid so."

"You think Alex was murdered?"

Not at all. "Really, I'm just accompanying a friend."

Thankfully Amita chose this moment to return with the *chai*. Maliha rose and opened the door for her as the train shuddered into motion. The smell of herbs filled the compartment.

Amita handed the first cup to Mrs Henley, and the other to Maliha. She picked up her book, sat down and opened it at the bookmark.

"What line of business is your husband in, Mrs Henley?"

"Eric? Oh, he's in trains." She smiled at her little joke. "Freight. That sort of thing."

Maliha nodded, She knew of the uninspiringly named Empire Bulk Shipping Company from the financial pages. The business specialised in the transport of heavy items such as ores and stone both by atmospheric and by sea. Even with the Faraday effect there were some things it was impracticable to transport by air.

"He has been married before?"

Mrs Henley took a sip of *chai* before replying. "Twice."

No doubt a match made on the stock market floor.

It was then Mrs Henley gave her a sly look over the cup of *chai*. "Do you have a gentleman friend?"

The necessity of a response to the outrageous question was pre-empted by the appearance of Mr Henley at the compartment door, working the handle awkwardly. Mrs Henley looked in horror at the cup of *chai* in her hand. Maliha moved swiftly. She reached across and took the cup from Margaret's hand then passed it to Amita who placed it between her leg and the outer wall of the carriage. She adjusted her sari to hide it from view.

Maliha sipped from her cup and looked out of the window. The smell of alcohol entered the compartment with Eric Henley. He sat opposite his wife with a grunt and a sigh. He rested his head against the cushioned support, closed his eyes and was snoring within moments.

Amita offered Mrs Henley her *chai* but she declined.

v

After an hour passing through the mountains—with one tunnel so long the train began to lose speed before reaching the pumping station at the far end—they descended towards the coastal city of Kochi.

It was not raining this side of the mountains but clouds still rolled across the sky, hiding the sun. Through the window the hazy horizon resolved into a coastline threaded with rivers, and speckled with towns and villages.

The port of Kerala boasted the usual selection of temples, churches, and government buildings amidst low residences and shops. They flew past as the tube ran around the south of the city centre and into the station.

Once the train had arrived Maliha reclaimed her luggage, and another porter guided them across the smaller concourse to a private waiting area. Mr and Mrs Henley were there as well, along with one or two others who had also been on the train and heading for the funeral.

Maliha kept herself to the side of the room near one of the frosted-glass windows. Amita served her with British tea and some fancies. Not the usual fare of a station and no doubt laid on by the Mawdsley family for their guests.

After about half an hour one of the station staff came through to announce that their transport to the estate was ready, their luggage had already been loaded and, if they would be so kind as to follow him, he would show them the way.

The short walk led them from the station and across the street to a fenced-off grassy area. Maliha had been expecting a steam charabanc, they approached instead a medium-sized dirigible.

The vessel's balloon envelope rippled in the light wind, while the gondola sat firmly on the ground waiting for its Faraday device to be engaged. It was a German-made Zeppelin with diesel engines but nothing on the scale of the *Hansa*, commanded by Captain Voss. This was a short-range passenger vehicle without the elaborate cabins.

But it was not spartan. The interior was carpeted, the wooden structural supports were covered in gold leaf and the passenger seating resembled a gentleman's club more than an omnibus, even a luxury one. Several of the men were already acquainted and had a number of settees and armchairs pulled together for themselves.

The ladies congregated in another part of the salon. In this instance the ladies consisted of Mrs Henley, Maliha and another woman. Their previous conversation had confirmed Maliha as an acquaintance so, despite the suspicious look from the new woman, she was invited to sit with them.

Margaret smiled and said in low tones, conspiratorially to the other woman. "This is Maliha Anderson."

The second woman appeared to be a little older than Margaret with pale complexion and red hair. "*The* Maliha Anderson? I am so delighted to make your acquaintance."

"You're from the United States?"

"Constance Mayberry, Connecticut," she replied. Now that names had been exchanged they sat. Maliha relaxed back into the comfort of the chair. Constance leaned forward.

"So, you're investigating the mysterious death of Alexander Mawdsley."

"I already explained to Mrs Henley—"

"Margaret."

"—I'm accompanying a friend. It was just a tragic accident, was it not?"

Maliha let the question hang, as the Faraday device was engaged and most of her weight left her body. Constance was holding her cup at that moment but expertly compensated for its sudden reduction in weight without spilling a drop. An experienced traveller without doubt.

"Why, Miss Anderson, you are quite disingenuous," Constance said without rancour. "You deny any involvement then interview us for details."

"Besides," said Margaret. "Maliha has a gentleman friend and I'm much more interested in him."

Maliha frowned. "He is no more than an acquaintance." And then felt some confusion as to how she had come to admit it. It did not matter, they would have known soon enough. She was not, however, used to being the target of such feminine banter and enquiry—at least not to her face, and not without malice.

She took a sip from her cup to hide her embarrassment.

Constance reached across and patted her knee. "Not to worry. You have to understand that we wives have so little to concern us in our daily lives that we make it our business to know everyone else's and discuss it at length. Otherwise—" she sat back and relaxed into the softness of the chair. "—I believe we would simply die of boredom."

"Or frustration," said Margaret with slightly more intensity than Maliha thought necessary. She glanced up and noticed Margaret's eyes focused with undisguised animosity on the men and her husband in particular, who was holding forth on some subject with a whiskey in his hand.

Outside, the sky darkened under thickening clouds. Maliha had thought she might ask whether she could go up to the bridge but, with the weather closing in, the crew would be ensuring the vessel did not founder. She made do with taking a walk to the windows that displayed the landscape in panoramic view. She took her stick even though she did not require it in reduced gravity.

They had not risen far, only a few hundred feet, and were heading north with the sea on their left and the mountains to the right. The clouds were low and threatened more than just rain. The vessel swung unpredictably in the gusting winds. She dug her stick into the carpet as a third anchor point.

Constance appeared at her elbow. "Margaret means no harm."

"I don't think she is satisfied with her husband," said Maliha.

Constance hesitated before replying. "She is not satisfied *by* her husband."

Maliha felt as if her muscles had seized—she had not meant *that*. This was not an area in which she was either experienced or, truth be told, interested. Of course the girls in school had discussed men interminably but Alice Anderson, as she had been then, was not permitted to join any conversation of that sort.

She had read many books—her appetite for knowledge was insatiable and the speed with which she could consume them meant she knew more of the science between men and women than most. But it was all theoretical, had been written by men and, to her certain knowledge, some details were quite inaccurate.

"I'm sorry, I have embarrassed you."

Maliha was saved from having to reply by a steward who asked them to take their seats as they would be landing directly.

She looked out through the window and saw a large building in classical late Georgian style with windows shining with electric lighting. And to one side the landing field, criss-crossed with beacon lights.

She took a seat with Margaret and Constance, wondering how she would survive even one day in this world of gossip and innuendo.

vi

Maliha had come down to dinner with considerable trepidation. She had delayed as long as possible, since dining with people she did not know was not appealing. Amita had worked on Maliha's hair, and had applied a minimum of make-up to complement the restrained blacks and purple in her dress.

Amita fussed and told her she was elegant and beautiful. But, thought Maliha, how could one be elegant when one had to walk with a stick, like an old woman? The doctors had told her there was a possibility her injury might mend in time, but that she should not hope, so as not to be disappointed. Strangely she was not sure how she felt about that. Her injury allowed her to take liberties and make excuses when it suited her. If it were gone, she would have less freedom.

She timed her arrival well enough, but her lateness meant that all eyes were on her when she entered the reception room. There was time for her to greet Constance and Margaret—much as she might not entirely enjoy their company, they were preferable to people who she did not know at all. At least they had got over the fuss of her being *the* Maliha Anderson.

The party went into dinner and she found herself on the same table as Catherine Mawdsley, their hostess, and between Constance and a very precise young man. The cut of his suit identified him as German and he was introduced as Herman Stine. Selina Mawdsley was on his other side. He focused his attentions on Selina and seemed oblivious to the fact his comments elicited no response. Perhaps the two were well suited.

The sounds of conversation from the rest of the room stayed muted, as was appropriate given the solemnity of the event. It was almost as it were a feast to give Alexander Mawdsley a send-off. He was the guest of honour, present only in the memories of those who knew him.

"Where is your mystery man?" asked Constance.

"Not arrived yet."

"How rude of him. He will not see how very striking you look this evening."

Maliha was not sure how to respond to such an undisguised compliment, it made her quite uncomfortable. She threw Constance a weak smile and paid more attention to her food.

"I'm sorry for not greeting you appropriately on your arrival, Miss Anderson."

It was Catherine Mawdsley. Maliha looked up from her food. "You have a delightful house, Mrs Mawdsley."

"Am I right in thinking your mother was a Brahmin?"

The question has asked in such a casual tone Maliha could only surmise it was genuine. She fumbled for a suitable response that would deflect the attention. But could think of nothing.

"Yes, she was."

"Oh, I'm so sorry, has she moved on to the next cycle?"

Next cycle? Surely not. "I'm not sure—"

"*Samsara*," Catherine interrupted as if to be sure that Maliha did not mistake her.

"Oh, yes." Maliha felt lost. Whenever she felt she was on firm ground among these people, one of them would say something that pulled her certainty away from her.

"Like poor Alex," she said. "He will do better in his next life."

She lapsed into silence, for which Maliha was grateful.

"I think I will have to steal your maid," said Constance. "She has a real touch."

Maliha did not think Constance would be quite so keen if she knew everything about Amita's background. Though she did wonder momentarily how loyal Amita might be now she could claim a proper employment history.

"It's kind of you to say so."

Constance leaned over conspiratorially. "Does she choose your dresses too?"

Maliha blinked.

Constance smiled. "Yes, mine too. In your case I'm sure you'd got more important things to think about. But in my case, well, I guess it's just laziness."

The meal continued with more of the same, and Maliha fielded comments as best she could. She listened with half an ear to Herbert Stine, his accent was refined and his English excellent—speaking with the careful precision non-natives use. His conversation seemed to revolve around battles and battlefields as he engaged with Constance's husband Leonard Mayberry, across the table.

"The Imperial Navy is, of course, the most powerful military force we possess, much as is your Royal Navy, but it seems to me you have ignored your Army."

"I am not English, Mr Stine. And I can assure you *we* have not ignored our ground-based troops. We have individual field armour that makes every infantryman into a walking artillery piece."

"But their range, Mr Mayberry, how soon before they run out of steam? How long before their weapons are exhausted? In Germany we have perfected the mobile fortress. A battleship on wheels, carrying a thousand infantry."

"Do you ride, Mr Mayberry?" Selina's voice cut through them both, they fell silent as if they had been admonished though Maliha was not sure whether it was intended as such or merely that the girl had not been listening.

* * *

The women withdrew at the end of the meal. Maliha would have preferred to retire but lacking the presence of Valentine she felt she ought to make an effort. Selina was not there and Maliha commented on it to Constance.

"She's probably gone to tuck her precious horses in bed and sing them a lullaby."

Maliha's face must have shown her incredulity.

"Well, maybe not bed and a lullaby, but she spends more time in the stables than in the house as far as I know. Randolf—Mr Mawdsley—blames his wife's fancies."

"Fancies?"

"You heard her. Anyone would think she'd gone native," Constance hesitated apparently realising what she'd just said.

Maliha smiled to put her mind at rest. "I was very surprised. Is it just a fancy, really?"

"If she lived in England or America I think she'd be the sort of woman who consulted astrologers before she decided what to wear. Here she follows the Hindu Astrologers. She's convinced herself Selina is some sort of goddess—" Constance dropped her voice "—uses it to explain why she's not all there. Claims she's above it all. Above us, anyway."

Maliha excused herself as soon as it was polite and returned to her room to let Amita undo all the good works she had achieved in the evening.

CHAPTER 2

i

Valentine tightened his grip on the controls as the air-plane shuddered and sank through the cloud layer. The wind buffeted it from all directions, sometimes from more than one at a time.

Dawn's light had been creeping up from the horizon, turning the sky from night-time black sprinkled with stars to deepest blue. And the brightest star in the sky had been the Queen Victoria Void-station that hung unmoving above the equator just south of Ceylon. As he began his descent the sky had ranged from white in the east through the entire spectrum to the dark of night.

He loved to fly. He had been born in the year a Royal Navy crew had made the first journey into space in a vessel bigger than this but with a similar fixed-wing design. However, theirs had been equipped with rockets lashed to the outside to drive them higher and higher. Now the trip to the station could be done in five hours and was performed regularly.

But not in a ship like his. The *Alice* was strictly an atmosphere craft, but one of the fastest in the Navy, and it was all his. Well, not strictly true, not his in terms of property and ownership, but for his exclusive use, a perk of being an operative of the Special Intelligence Service, serving King, Country and Empire.

At a velocity of over two hundred and thirty miles per hour the trip from the Fortress to Kochi was considerably shorter than by train. Not only did he not have to make station stops, he could fly direct. Less than an hour.

The main difficulty with the *Alice* was that it could only take off and land on a strip. It could not ascend or descend vertically like the bigger ships—but it could outrun an atmospheric. Alexander Mawdsley's father was a shrewd, forward-thinking entrepreneur and had had a strip built at his country home. Sometimes he too needed to travel quickly.

Much as he did like flying, Valentine did not like clouds, particularly when traveling along routes frequented by passenger flyers. But it was Thursday, and the P&O ships did not cross Kerala on Thursdays.

He burst out into rain. He did not like rain either.

He throttled back the diesel engine, and its roar reduced to a loud grumble. It was not practical to have a steam engine on such a small ship, nor a Babbage machine. He flew by the stars, by the sun and by the landscape—he leaned forward to peer through the glass with streaming water flowing across it—if he could see the landscape, otherwise he must simply estimate.

He took the *Alice* down to a couple of hundred feet and reduced speed to a mere fifty miles per hour. The terrain looked familiar. He rocketed past the buildings of Kochi and smiled to himself, he had always been good at estimating distance. Less good with people, and one person in particular. She was good with almost everything, except people. They had that in common if nothing else.

Others would consider their relationship to be quite strange. *Relationship, Valentine? I assure you we have no relationship.* She didn't have to be present for him to hear her caustic commentary. They had spent most of their time together dealing with dead bodies and murderers.

He smiled and banked the air-plane, opened up the throttle heading north once more. He located and followed the road he knew led towards the Mawdsley estate. He let the ship climb to five hundred feet to avoid scaring too many animals.

But the fact was that he enjoyed her company despite her frowns and criticisms. And while Valentine might be his least favourite name, he found it quite pleasant when she used it. However, she would want him to call her "Miss Anderson" and it was entirely unlikely she would call him anything but "Mr Crier" through this entire trip.

Chances were this was nothing at all. A riding accident. There was no reason to suppose otherwise.

Less than twenty minutes later the house came into view. He flew over the landing strip at low speed to alert the ground crew of his intention to land. He made a wide circle around the house. Close to the main building the grounds were manicured in lawns, orchards and flower beds.

Farther out, to the north, were acres of woodland, planted by the original owners a hundred years ago. Riding tracks and paths ran through the woods. The stable block was separate from the house and, while not on the scale of some houses, could hold up to fifty horses. A stream came down from hills to the west of the house, crossed the lawns to the south and headed off towards the coast in the east.

Perhaps he would get a chance to ride with Maliha. Not that he was here for pleasure. Alex had been as good a friend as you might expect from someone you only saw every few months. The loss was sad but, truth be told, would not seriously impact on his own life. Not the way that losing Maliha would.

He had known her less than six months and in that time she had faced death twice. She moved towards threat instead of away from it. She was the most courageous woman he had ever known, braver than most men.

He passed over the landing strip again, and saw four men in gardener's uniforms, stationed two at each end. They were ready for him. He took a tighter turn away from the house and came in for the final time. He cut the engine to idling speed and the air-plane's velocity dropped to the speed of a fast horse. It also became a devil to control. He pumped the hydraulics to lower the undercarriage and moments later the wheels touched grass.

He cut the engine completely. At fifteen miles per hour he switched off the Faraday device. The whole vehicle drooped as gravity took its full effect, the wings curved downward at their ends and, with the increased weight, the wheels dug into the ground, bringing the plane to an abrupt halt.

The ground crew ran across to him and assisted him in climbing out. It wasn't raining but the air was heavy with humidity. One of the crew opened a hatch in the side of the ship and pulled out his baggage.

He shook out the kinks in his legs. The constant vibration of the air-plane had a detrimental effect on his muscles. He looked up towards the house and saw a figure heading his way. He smiled as he saw the limp.

He went back to the ship one final time and pulled his leather case from the cockpit. Then he strode through the moist air towards her. Within a few moments he was close enough to see the familiar frown.

"I think you should know that I am not enjoying this."

ii

They found their way back to the house and the now empty breakfast room. He piled his plate with cold meats, fresh rolls and kedgeree then took his place at a table near the window. Maliha sat on the chair opposite, both hands on the walking stick.

"Has anyone been rude?" he asked between mouthfuls.

She pursed her lips. "They have not."

"Locked you in a room, beaten you?"

"Of course not. Don't be facetious, Valentine."

"Then what have they done?"

She hesitated. "They insist on talking to me."

He knew that laughing at this point would be counterproductive. Despite everything she was quite delicate. "Perhaps they just want to be friends?"

"I am not in their circle."

"Perhaps they don't care."

She paused again. "It is not something I am comfortable with."

He cut a roll in two, buttered each piece and lay sliced ham between them. She watched in silence, he half expected some critical comment but none came. He picked up his sandwich then put it down again. "I have something for you."

He rummaged through his case and pulled out a well-used but unlabelled manila folder. He passed it across and returned to his sandwich.

Her eyes barely moved from left to right, but they followed her finger as she ran it down the first page of the police report of Alex's death. Her reading speed was astonishing yet he knew from experience she took in every word. She flipped to the next page and gave it the same treatment.

"Is that all?"

"That's it."

"Died from a blow to the head from a horse's hoof."

He took another mouthful.

"Which horse was it?" she asked into the air.

He was chewing so merely raised his eyebrows. He had noticed the same point.

He swallowed. "What do you need?"

"I need to see the body; and the place Alexander Mawdsley died."

"I doubt there'll be anything left to see, considering the weather."

She eyed him. "I am aware of that. But if we don't look we'll never know, will we?"

* * *

Maliha looked back at the almost useless police report. Even Forsyth wouldn't have been so lackadaisical. He was suspicious and cynical, ideal traits in a policeman, though better intelligence would have been a bonus.

She was distracted by the door of the breakfast room being pushed open. An unhealthily thin young woman with wind-blown red hair, and wearing a black riding dress came in. The extremities of her clothing were discoloured with water and her cheeks showed the ruddiness of outdoor activity.

Valentine noticed the shift in her attention and turned. He jumped to his feet. "Selina."

Maliha watched him make his way round the main table. He stopped in front of the woman. In the light of day she had a better look at Selina Mawdsley. She was about twenty-four, though she looked a good deal younger. That she had been out riding so soon after her brother's death was curiously disrespectful, though typical of her apparent obsession. Maliha placed the police report on the table, picked up her walking stick and pushed herself to her feet. Her thigh ached in the damp.

"I am so sorry about Alex," said Valentine.

"Thank you, Bill," she replied.

Maliha tapped her way to an appropriate distance from them. Closer to, she noticed the girl's watery blue eyes and a nose that was too long for her face, quite distinctive. She possessed the romantic appeal of a pale consumptive. Selina glanced at her and then stared. It was not a piercing stare—it did not assess or judge—it was almost vacant and did not relent for long seconds. Maliha felt uncomfortable.

"Selina—" Valentine's voice broke the spell. "—this is my associate, Miss Maliha Anderson."

Maliha thought she might have to take him to task over the term *associate*, but Miss Mawdsley put out her hand. Maliha closed the gap and shook. There was no firmness in the other woman's grip, and she smelled of lavender and horses.

"Miss ... Anderson? Welcome to our home, I'm sorry it could not have been under better circumstances." The words emerged without emotion, a simple speech learned by rote.

Maliha did not release the hand, but looked into the eyes of the girl. "It must have been terrible finding him like that, Miss Mawdsley."

The hand was whipped away as if Maliha had become a snake.

"Yes, of course, it was." Miss Mawdsley recovered herself and gave an empty smile. "You're the detective Daddy hired, aren't you?"

Maliha responded with a smile of her own. The idea that she had been *hired* was quite insulting but clearly there had to be some way to justify her presence.

"A woman detective seems a very strange thing."

Maliha's smile became somewhat more genuine. "Not so, I do not believe there is anything a man can do that a woman cannot. You only need consider the scientist Madame Curie, or the mathematician Florence Nightingale."

Her speech was met with a blank look.

"Do you like horses, Miss Anderson?"

"I do not."

"There is no finer beast in all the world." Selina peered at Maliha. "Do you ride at all?"

"No."

"I can teach you."

"Thank you, that will not be necessary."

"If you want to see the place where it happened you may have to. It is not an easy walk."

iii

It was late morning before suitable transport was procured. Selina led the way riding a brown horse, while Valentine drove the trap. Amita had provided Maliha with an umbrella and equipped her with walking boots from somewhere. Her dress was going to become badly muddied. It could not be helped.

A gravel track led north from the house, past the landing field and the structured gardens. It twisted for half a mile through mature woodland, rising all the while. Looking behind, Maliha could see the rear of the house laid out in the valley. They crested a hill and the view was lost as they descended again through progressively wilder terrain. The gravel ended and the track became a trail of mud. However, the trap was light enough not to become bogged down, though the horse strained harder and the leather straps creaked.

They finally came to a stop where the track became too narrow to continue. Valentine hooked the reins on a branch, then came back to help Maliha. Her boots squelched into the leaf mould as she stepped down. She leaned hard on her walking stick to maintain her balance and it sank into the ground. She staggered. Valentine's hand encircled her upper arm and held it firmly so she did not fall. She pulled her stick out and found a root she could push against. Valentine loosened his grip.

Maliha looked up and saw Selina waiting for them a few yards off, deeper into the trees. Her expression was quite blank.

Valentine walked ahead. Selina coaxed her beast into a slow walk. Maliha brought up the rear, umbrella over her head and keeping her eyes down to ensure she had no further difficulty with the walking stick. The damp forest air was filled with the sound of birds, along with the muffled clump of hooves and the occasional snap of a breaking twig.

It took less than ten minutes of walking through the dripping trees for the damp atmosphere to penetrate her clothing and make every step a fight. The aching of her leg injury became a constant pressure, dragging her attention from the present to the moment when her thigh had been ripped open by the descending horse's hoof just a year before. The clatter of horseshoe on cobble … the cart wheel crushing her ankle…

"Miss Anderson?"

She shook herself and discovered they were no longer moving forwards. The path had widened but the way ahead was blocked by a fallen tree trunk. It had been there a long time judging from the thick layer of moss, fungi and plants growing from it.

Valentine was looking at her with some concern, while behind him, past the blockage, Selina sat serene on her mount. She seemed not to notice the water dripping from her hat, hair and clothes.

"Maliha?" he asked in a quieter tone. Her eyes snapped into focus and she frowned at him, she had made herself quite clear he was not to be familiar when they were in company. The concern in his face dissolved. "This is it, apparently."

She nodded and limped to the trunk. She looked across the surface, a section of the moss along the top had been gouged away, exposing the rotten wood below. She looked back along the path, then turned to Valentine.

"Mr Crier, would you be so good as to find the place where Mr Mawdsley's horse launched itself?"

He moved away from her, picked up a branch and broke off a shorter length. He squatted down a short distance away and began to scrape away the surface leaves. "What are you looking for?" he asked.

"I have no idea."

She made her way around the roots of the fallen tree, now a haven for insects that moved and buzzed around its dark spaces, and examined the trunk on the far side. A clear hoof mark was embedded in the trunk. She was not entirely sure what it meant. Her unfamiliarity with horses was a disadvantage in this instance. The ache in her leg suggested she had every reason to stay as far from horses as possible.

"Found it."

She glanced over at Valentine who was using his hands to clear a space. She went back around to examine the ground. Two hoofprints almost square to the trunk, a couple of feet apart, angled deeply into the ground. In her mind's eye she pictured the animal's rear legs thrusting hard to propel it up and over.

"Can you find the place it landed?" she asked without looking up. He did not reply but she heard him move away. She glanced back, imagining Alex Mawdsley on his horse travelling at speed along the path, encouraging his horse to jump what was, after all, not a great barrier, reaching barely two feet above the ground.

Yet it did not succeed. One of its hooves had scraped the top of the trunk, the other had struck it hard, perhaps to push off?

She turned to face Selina who had not moved, just watched. "Miss Mawdsley?"

Selina's eyes focused on Maliha's face. "Can you jump this?"

"Of course. We do it all the time."

"Would you do it now?" Valentine popped his head up and glanced at her. She knew he was silently admonishing her for ignoring Selina's feelings. Maliha was used to it, and she wondered how good a spy he could possibly be with such attitudes.

Selina pulled on the right rein and the horse walked round away from the trunk in a long turn. She seemed to be lining it up.

"Oh, I'm sorry, I meant from this side. If you could do it the way you normally would? The same speed as Alex would have?"

Selina walked the horse round the fallen tree and in front of Maliha. So close she could smell it, feel its heat, hear it breathing. Selina looked down on her. "How far away shall I start, Miss Anderson?"

Maliha held her gaze despite the sharp pain that shot through her leg. "From around the first corner, if you would be so kind." The horse clomped away. Its tail swished as it passed, the coarse hairs flicking Maliha's cheek. Her head ached and she realised she had no idea when that particular symptom had started.

She pulled herself together. There was no time for such weakness. She stumbled back round the tree trunk to where Valentine was uncovering the landing point. Four more hoof marks quite close together, one pair very deep, probably the ones to land first, the second pair slightly ahead but not so deep.

There was a muted drumming, Valentine stood up and stepped back as Selina appeared, urging her horse along the path at a fast pace. Maliha watched as the animal closed on it, pushed off and soared high over the trunk, landing on the other side.

Maliha limped over to the place where the original marks were now matched by the new set. She noted how the distance between Selina's horse's prints was smaller.

"Let's go back to the house," she said.

iv

It was getting on towards luncheon but Maliha needed to change. Amita had drawn a bath and laid out a complete change of clothes. Maliha was grateful for the attention, and the bath eased the aching in her leg.

Considerably refreshed she headed downstairs and found Valentine waiting for her. He guided her to the luncheon room where French windows opened on to a stone terrace. Beyond the terrace she could see one edge of the modern glass construction she had seen from the air. The room was already occupied by other guests. She spotted Constance and Margaret, who had a table to themselves. The men were once again in a corner deep in conversation.

Constance gestured for Maliha to join them, which meant she was unable to refuse. She fixed a smile on her face and, accompanied by Valentine, sat down at the table. Maliha noted that Margaret's décolletage verged on the inappropriate and she wore lipstick—an intense vermilion shade that did not sit well with her pale skin. Constance, on the other hand, was appropriately dressed with a high neckline.

"So your mysterious man is none other than the illustrious Mr Crier," said Constance with a smile.

"Mrs Mayberry, Mrs Henley." Valentine greeted them and took a seat next to Maliha.

"I guessed it was your air-plane circling this morning. You know how to make an entrance," said Constance.

"It's the fastest way to travel, Mrs Mayberry," he said as he prepared a sandwich for himself. "I had some business to attend to at the Fortress."

Margaret had a large glass that had already been drained. She nodded at one of the staff who came and refilled it. "So, Bill, you and Miss Anderson?"

Maliha could feel her cheeks heating up. She glanced at Valentine but his gaze was only on Mrs Henley.

"Not at all," he said with a relaxed smile. "We're just here on business, I'm afraid. Nothing worthy of gossip."

Margaret Henley smiled and sat straighter in the chair. "That's interesting."

Constance glanced across the room to where her husband held court with the other men. "So, Miss Anderson, have you made any progress? Was poor Alex murdered?"

Maliha paused between mouthfuls. "I'm sure it's too early to say anything about that."

"But you must have some ideas? You went to see where he died this morning. Did you learn anything?"

"Really, there is nothing to say," she replied, regretting their choice of table.

Mrs Henley looked up. "How's the scrambled egg, Bill?"

He was in the middle of a mouthful and swallowed hastily. "Very pleasant, Margaret."

"Would you fetch me some?"

Maliha frowned, and pursed her lips. Then caught herself, slightly confused as to why she felt Mrs Henley's request to be such an impertinence. She turned her attention to her own plate as Valentine climbed to his feet and headed for the serving tables.

"Excuse me," said Mrs Henley. "I think I want something else to go with it."

A flash of anger went through Maliha as the woman stood and went after Valentine. She attacked a slice of meat, cutting it into precise strips.

"How long have you known Bill?" asked Constance.

"Since April."

"You met on the ship that had the murder?"

She nodded and tried to head off further questions. "Excuse me for saying so, Constance, but you do seem to have a great deal of interest in Alex's death."

Constance Mayberry laughed out loud. "You are not entirely wrong about my interest, Miss Anderson. But I assure you, it is not personal."

Maliha took a sip of tea. "It is your husband who wants information?"

She did not deny it, but took a sip of tea.

"He knows where the Mawdsley fortune goes now that Alex is dead."

"Catherine and Selina, of course," said Constance. "If Randolf were to die."

"I doubt Selina has any interest in business. So it comes down to whomever she marries."

"Herman Stines."

Maliha smiled. "And your husband is not happy with that option?"

"The marriage was arranged to unify the families without control passing to the Stineses. So no, Miss Anderson, he is not happy with the situation. I daresay none of the gentlemen at that table are pleased." Constance turned her face full towards Maliha, leaned forward conspiratorially and lowered her voice. "You think the Stines might have killed him?"

"As I said before, I really cannot comment."

Constance fell silent. Maliha became aware that neither Valentine nor Mrs Henley had returned. She had to turn in order to see them. They were standing with their backs to her. Margaret Henley was standing very close to him, and his head was tilted down to her. As Maliha watched she placed her hand on his arm.

Maliha jerked back as if she had been struck and stared unseeing at the food in her plate. A rage burned through her thoughts and all she could see was that woman's hand resting on Valentine's arm.

"It's not my business, Miss Anderson, but maybe I can set your mind at rest."

Maliha blinked twice, the fact that Constance was speaking to her barely registered. She reached out and took her tea-cup, she went to drink but found it already empty.

"Miss Anderson?"

Maliha looked up. Constance's face was soft with concern. "You've got no cause to be concerned about Bill."

"I am not concerned. If he chooses to make a fool of himself with a married woman why should that matter to me?"

Constance smiled. "Of course. But you must understand, Margaret suffers from hysteria. I'm guessing she's due a treatment."

Maliha knew of it, how some women—particularly those of the middle and upper classes—were highly strung and suffered from their nerves. They needed a treatment every few weeks to alleviate the problem. She had never known a sufferer but then she did not have many acquaintances. She found the knowledge that the woman suffered from a condition did nothing to alleviate her feelings.

"She is under the doctor, then?"

"Not at all, she visits the Guru Nadesh." Constance glanced up and behind Maliha alerting her to the return of Valentine and Mrs Henley.

Maliha waited until they were sitting then announced to the shocked table. "Mr Crier, I would like to see Alex's body after lunch."

v

Valentine descended the main stairs, a pair of sweeping curves that led from an upper balcony round the entrance hall, meeting opposite the door and then continuing down to the tiled floor. He was glad to see he was early enough that Maliha had not yet arrived.

He was used to being treated as a slow student by Maliha, but this was something else. After dropping her "seeing the body" bombshell at luncheon she had left the table without another word. Constance had seemed privately amused at his discomfiture, while Margaret was particularly pleased about something.

He found Margaret's attentions awkward. After all, not only was she a married woman—which put her quite firmly in the forbidden category—but her husband was in the room. Though, to be fair, he seemed quite oblivious to anything apart from his own conversation.

Valentine was not completely unversed in the behaviour of women so knew he had committed some *faux pas*. However he was at a loss to know what crime he had perpetrated. On the other hand, it was almost gratifying that Maliha could, at least occasionally, behave like a normal woman.

He then warned himself to never *ever* make a comment like that to her in person.

"Mr Crier."

He looked up to watch her coming down the stairs. She had changed since lunch and wore another dress he had never seen before. He was aware she favoured the newer French fashions, but he had not expected her to wear them here, not when she was working. Yet, as she descended the carpeted stairs, the dress she wore seemed to float around her like a cloud. She quite took his breath away. Though she had to use her stick to maintain her posture he did not see it any more, or rather it was part of who she was.

"Miss Anderson." He wanted to tell her how well she looked, but she had forbidden personal comments and this was very definitely a public place.

She came up to him. He was not a great deal taller than her and what little she lacked in height she more than made up for in strength of will.

"Shall we examine the body?" she said as casually as though she were discussing the internals of a steam engine.

"Yes," he said. He did not offer his arm but set off at an easy pace along the passage that led towards the east wing of the building and the chapel. The windows on their right gave out on to the gravel drive and tended gardens.

They reached the east wing proper and turned left along its length. They passed reception rooms of various sizes, some with open doors, some closed, eventually reaching a place where the carpeting ended and they were faced with polished marble floors and an oaken door in a typical English church style.

But to the left was a smaller door. He opened it and cold air poured out, raising a mist that flowed across the floor. He allowed her to enter first, followed her in and closed the door. One wall had been lined with blocks of ice and a long wooden table supported the body, entirely covered by a white sheet.

Although he had been expecting a servant to be in attendance— and such there was standing at the far side of the small antechamber—he had not been expecting Catherine Mawdsley.

"Must you do this, Bill?" She addressed him directly, and did not even glance at Maliha.

"I'm sorry, Catherine," he replied. "I'm afraid I have my orders."

"But he's my son."

Maliha interrupted. "Do you not want justice for your son, Mrs Mawdsley?"

Catherine Mawdsley kept her eyes locked on him, almost as if he had spoken the words and not Maliha. "It was an accident." Her eyes moistened and she dabbed them with a kerchief.

Maliha looked at him, her expression unfathomable. She nodded.

"It probably was an accident, Catherine. We just have to be sure."

"And *she* is your way to be sure?"

"Miss Anderson is the most accomplished investigator it has been my good fortune to meet." He carefully did not look in Maliha's direction as he said it. It was the truth, of course, and he hoped she would accept the olive branch.

Catherine turned with an effort to face Maliha, her muscles rigid. "This is my son."

Maliha looked down for a moment then brought her gaze back to Catherine's face. "I will treat your son with the respect that recent events have taken from him, Mrs Mawdsley."

The older woman relaxed a little, turned away and headed for the door. But Maliha, it seemed, had not finished. "And if he has been murdered, I will find it out and I will see that he is avenged."

The door closed behind Catherine Mawdsley. Valentine glanced at the manservant standing by the far wall and then took the few steps to the body. He grabbed the sheet and threw it off. There was Alex, paper-white skin, pale lips, eyes closed and his hair tinged with frost.

"He's been cleaned," Maliha said in a resigned voice. "And his clothes changed."

"They are burying him in the morning."

Maliha examined the corpse's hands one at a time, rubbing the pads of his fingers. "Did he ride a lot?"

"Quite a lot, and he played polo."

"But he fell off his horse on an easy jump?"

She turned her attention to his scalp. Alex's hair had been trimmed to reveal the curve of the hoof print on the right side of his head, extending from above his ear, across his temple to the soft tissue of his neck below his ear. The skin had been stitched where it had been torn apart by the blow. Maliha pressed her fingers against the injury, and the bone below the skin moved unnaturally.

"Cracked his skull," she said.

"That takes a lot of force."

"Horses are dangerous," she said absently. She glanced at the servant and then turned to face him. "I need to see the rest of his skin, Valentine."

"Must you?" He already knew the answer, and that she had used his given name when another person was present to emphasise the point. He sighed.

"I'll wait outside while you undress him," she said.

With the assistance of the man-servant he stripped his friend. He noted the bruising on the left of his back where he had fallen, and around the joint of his right shoulder.

When Maliha returned, she took her time examining the bruises and damage. She too was interested in the right shoulder. She felt around the bones of the joint, digging her fingers into the cold skin.

"I'm sorry, Mr Crier, I wonder if you would mind removing your jacket and shirt. I need to compare the bones. I really don't know enough about how it's supposed to be composed to make a comparison."

So, in front of Maliha, and the servant, he took off his jacket, tie and shirt. It was not quite the circumstances he had imagined himself in a state of déshabillé with her. He caught himself. That was not something to be thinking about right now—he was not entirely convinced she could not mind-read.

He knew that he had a reasonable physique, he did not have excess fat and his job kept him well exercised. However, Maliha's apparent indifference as she pressed her fingers into his right shoulder joint left him empty.

"I think it might have been dislocated. The muscles don't seem to be in the right place," she said finally. "That wasn't in the police report either."

He watched her as she settled into a state of contemplation, her gaze encompassing Alex's body, but her eyes entirely unfocused. He shivered and reached for his shirt and jacket.

"Have we finished?" he asked.

"What? Oh, yes. We've finished," as if her mind were on other things. "Then we must go to the stables."

She left, her stick clicking on the tiles. Leaving him and the servant to redress his dead friend.

vi

Valentine was quite surprised when Maliha took his arm without any enquiry on his part, or comment on hers. Still, it was a practical move since walking was not easy for her on the uneven surface of the stable-yard. Even so she was quite unlike herself, putting considerable pressure on his arm, which also held the umbrella over the two of them.

"You know horses?" she asked. They entered the stables proper under a stone-built arch. The material appeared to have been recycled from an earlier much older building. The individual stables were laid out round the two-storey quadrangle.

"I'm not an expert."

"How could an expert rider fall off when the jump was not difficult?"

"Perhaps the horse didn't take the jump properly. It might have been scared by a snake, or anything. Horses can be strange beasts. I knew one that would take any jump but shied from cartwheels." There was a friendly looking chestnut with its head out looking at them in that way they did when they wanted attention. He steered Maliha in its direction.

"If you wish to pet that animal, I won't stop you but do not think I will come within three yards of it," she declared the moment she realised his intention. He sighed. "There was little difference between the relative positions of the hoof marks made by Alex's horse and those made by Selina's when she jumped."

She loosed his arm and leaned on her stick as he approached the horse, slowly so as not to give any alarm.

"You see," she said. "Even you are being careful."

"They can be nervy beasts," he replied. "In the wild they are prey, not predator."

He could have sworn she snorted at that comment. The horse welcomed his attention and Valentine regretted coming out without a treat.

"You, boy!"

He turned as Maliha accosted an Indian stablehand crossing the yard carrying a bridle. The boy came over, a look of concern on his face as if he were not sure whether he was about to be chastised by someone he'd never seen before.

Maliha launched into a stream of Hindi. Valentine could manage well enough in French and German but it had never occurred to him to learn an Indian language, but of course it *was* Maliha's native tongue. He tended to forget, to him she was simply Maliha.

The boy responded, usually promptly, but some of her questions had a slower response as if he did not want to answer.

"Give him something, Valentine," she said finally. He reached into his pocket and found a rupee and a shilling, he handed over both. The boy ran off with undisguised pleasure.

"Let us go. This place makes me uncomfortable."

She took his arm again and they headed back through the arch.

"Well, what did he say?"

"There was another omission from the police report. What's a breastplate?"

"It's a metal ring that connects the leather straps from the bridle and saddle."

"Apparently, it was broken but it's already back from the smith. Repaired."

"Probably snapped when he landed."

"Does that happen a lot?" Her tone was quite aggressive, the visit to the stable had certainly put her quite out of sorts.

"It's not unheard of," he said slowly. This time she definitely snorted. "Is that all he said?"

"Oh, well, he was full of praise for the young mistress and her skill with the animals. He was quite doe-eyed about her."

"Yes, Selina does love horses."

"To the exclusion of all else."

He sighed. "Yes, well, you've met her."

"Not unlike her mother in that respect, then."

* * *

The funeral was in the afternoon and it was raining, of course. Amita had supplied Maliha with a conventional black mourning dress with a high neck. The congregation had left the chapel after the interminable service and followed the coffin out to the private cemetery a short distance from the house.

There had been thirty people in the congregation, the businessmen and their wives, some of the senior servants, and the immediate family: Selina, Catherine and Randolf Mawdsley who, Maliha understood, had arrived late the previous evening. Though they were required to walk together, it was clear there was no affection between Catherine and Randolf as the gap between them as they walked was cavernous.

At the graveside Selina slipped her hand under her mother's arm, while her father stood aloof. The vicar from Kochi spoke the traditional words and the coffin was lowered carefully down into the grave.

She was pulled from her reverie by Valentine offering her his handkerchief. Her brow creased into a frown as she prepared a silent admonition, but in doing so she felt a tear drip from her eye. She took the handkerchief and dabbed her eyes with it. Valentine looked concerned, probably confused as to why she was crying. She was not entirely sure herself.

They made their way back to the house. Servants relieved the mourners of their umbrellas and coats. There was a light meal and tea prepared in one of the larger reception rooms.

The mourners remained subdued, as was appropriate. Their conversation was quiet and no more than a gentle susurration. She watched as Randolf Mawdsley carefully moved from group to group, saying a few words to each person before moving on. Selina and her mother stood near the empty fireplace, neither speaking and no one wanting to disturb them.

Finally, Mawdsley arrived at Maliha and Valentine. He shook Valentine's hand and nodded to Maliha.

"Thank you for coming, Bill."

"I am so sorry, Randolf."

Maliha caught the way the older man almost flinched as Valentine's words reminded him of his loss. The emotion was gone instantly, replaced by stoic reserve.

"Have you come to any conclusions, Miss Anderson?"

She hesitated. "I am sorry, Mr Mawdsley." She noted the increase in tension as she spoke. "I have not found anything decisive one way or the other."

Just as she had told Valentine earlier in the day.

"I see." The man seemed to shrink. Maliha wondered what answer he truly wanted. Did he want to know his son had been murdered? Did he want to know the most likely culprit was someone who had no motive? Or was it that he just wanted an answer?

She would not lie to him as there was no firm evidence one way or the other. She simply did not know. But she would find out.

CHAPTER 3

i

Valentine offered to fly her back to the Fortress in his air-plane while Amita traveled back with her luggage on the train. Since Maliha had first seen the *Alice* at the dock when she had visited the captain of the *Hansa* she had wanted to fly in it.

She was aware Valentine had named it after her, before he had learned she preferred not to use her first given name. That he had not changed it was, perhaps, a mild revenge on her for insisting on using his least favourite name. It was a game they played.

She found there was no delicate way of getting into the seat next to him—even with one of the gardeners helping her on one side and Valentine on the other. It was her leg that was the main trouble, failing to provide sufficient leverage and support. She would not have been particularly concerned but they had an audience. Constance and Margaret had insisted on coming down to the field to wave them off.

She had become more used to their solicitations but felt hurt by their friendly laughter and shouts as she clambered into the passenger seat. She knew that Constance meant no harm, but with Mrs Henley there was now that slight cutting edge to her words. There was little doubt that *she* would much rather be traveling in the plane with Valentine.

Amita had packed a small case with Maliha's essentials, even though they would meet again in the evening. She may not have known Amita more than a few days, but Maliha got the impression the girl was a romantic and expected Valentine to carry her mistress away to some exotic island, or some other such nonsense.

With a final pull she managed to get her legs and dress into place and seat herself firmly in the chair. She was once again in a less restrictive dress as it would have been quite impossible to fit wearing anything else except perhaps man's garb. Valentine had changed into a coverall.

He dropped into his seat next to her and strapped himself in. Maliha found her straps and inspected them to determine how they functioned. She had them clipped together before Valentine had a chance to decide she needed help. The canopy was closed into position over them. Valentine adjusted the dogs on his side to lock it in place then reached across to do the same on her side.

She watched carefully as he pumped the fuel and fired the engine. The roar ripped through the machine and she realised conversation was going to be quite impossible.

He looked across at her, with his finger hovering over a large switch labelled "Faraday". She nodded and, as he flipped it, the familiar lightness swept through her. He pushed the throttle to maximum and the *Alice* bounced across the grass. The air-plane picked up speed rapidly and, within moments, she felt her stomach left behind as the air-plane shot into the air.

She could see nothing but sky in front of her. She looked to the left and saw the ground rapidly disappearing below with the horizon at a sharp angle. She glanced at the controls in front of Valentine and saw the height scale increasing rapidly—they were already over one thousand feet.

She drew a sharp breath as they plunged into the cloud. It was not dark but they were surrounded by grey. Thirty seconds later they erupted from the mist into sunlight and clear blue sky. She was breathless and the cloud tops were beautiful, so unlike the dreary rain they created below.

She couldn't suppress the smile that filled her, from her very soul.

* * *

Valentine levelled the machine and throttled back. The roar from the engine diminished. He looked across at his passenger. He could not suppress his own joy when he saw the look on her face. He had never seen her so happy.

She felt as he did about flying.

There was no way they could converse over the noise of the engine and, without thinking, he reached out and placed his hand on her forearm. The skin of his fingers separated from hers by the thinnest wisp of material, and the movement of her muscles transmitted to him as clear as the movements of the *Alice*.

She turned her head towards him and for a moment he feared a rebuke—even though he wouldn't be able to hear it—but the smile did not leave her face and, wonder of wonders, she placed her other hand on his. And gave it a gentle squeeze.

His smile exploded into a grin just as a side wind buffeted them and he was forced to return his hand to the wheel.

* * *

The landing was terrifying but exciting. They had descended through the clouds over the north of Ceylon. She assumed that Valentine must calculate the distance travelled with an estimate of their air velocity. He had maintained the air-plane at a high altitude so they seemed to crawl across the clouds though their speed must have been in excess of two hundred miles per hour.

The steel and glass of the Fortress came into view. He reduced speed and flew across the landing field at the height of the towers of the Fortress itself. He then took the air-plane on a wide loop.

She studied the Fortress, the maze of buildings, hangars, landing platforms, walkways and offices that comprised the heart of the military might of the British Empire. It was a reminder—a warning to some, reassurance to others.

She had watched him land when he arrived at the house, and now she experienced it for herself. The ground rushed up at them, even though he had reduced to a pedestrian velocity. The air-plane bounced and she braced herself as he disengaged the Faraday device. Both she and the vessel drooped, and the ache returned to her leg.

Valentine unlatched the canopy and pushed it up. He climbed out stiffly and stretched. Maliha was uncertain how she should proceed: Undoing the straps was easy enough but she could not gain the purchase to lever herself into a position where she could step out. She felt her anger build, she was infuriated by her useless body.

"Hello," said a voice in her left ear.

She turned furiously and found Valentine's smiling face mere inches from hers.

"I cannot get out," she hissed and glanced behind him at the half-dozen Royal Navy ground crew standing a short distance away. Waiting. "It's embarrassing."

"It's the vibration of these things," he said. "Somehow they just pulverise one's muscles to jelly."

He looked at her carefully. "Now don't get all uppity, but I'm going to have to lift you out."

She was not a fool, she knew it was probably the only solution and it had more dignity than any efforts she might make to extricate herself on her own. She nodded. "Do they have to watch?"

"I think asking them to turn around would attract more attention than simply doing it. Are you ready?"

"Very well."

He leaned over the edge of the fuselage, she placed her right arm over his shoulder and leaned forward so he could put his arm behind her. Then the part she dreaded, she pulled her knees up and together, as he reached under them and lifted.

Once free of the air-plane he let her down and kept hold of her as she gained her balance. She brushed down her dress while he retrieved her walking stick and handed it to her.

"Thank you, Mr Crier," she said, holding her voice calm and unemotional. She knew what the watchers would be thinking: the cripple needs to be helped from the plane.

She made a point of walking away from the plane on her own. Leaving Valentine to catch up.

ii

Five days later the murder of Randolf Mawdsley was reported on the front page of *The Times of India*. Maliha absorbed the news item in a matter of moments. It was empty of useful facts and filled with speculation. He had been found dead by one of the cleaning staff in his apartment in the Compound.

"May I use the carriage?" she asked Barbara, who was going through the first post. Barbara glanced up.

"Randolf Mawdsley?" she asked. "I assume it's not a coincidence."

"Coincidences can happen," Maliha said.

"I was intending to visit with the girls this afternoon," she said, meaning a group of women of Barbara's age who interfered with the plans of bureaucracy and made things happen the way they felt was best.

"I can send Old Vidu back with it."

Barbara waved her hand, dismissing the idea. "I'll pop a letter to them and tell them to come here instead."

Maliha excused herself from the breakfast table, and rang the bell. She met Sathi in the hall and told her to have the carriage prepared, then made her way to her room. Amita had already tidied the room and made her bed. She was suitably efficient.

"I am going out, Amita."

Amita looked at her with her head tilted to one side. "This is for business, *sahiba?*"

"It is."

Maliha had surprised herself at how easy she had found it to slip into the position of a woman with a maid. It was true that when she had lived at home with her parents they had a retinue of ten servants. But after so many years away at school, having to do everything for herself, she thought she would find it difficult.

She went to the window as Amita bustled round the room collecting everything she would need. The monsoon continued unabated, the streets were awash and every pedestrian carried an umbrella aloft. Valentine would be at the murder scene as soon as he heard the news, so there was no need to contact him. She was glad as she had missed his company these few days. And that, in itself, was a novel feeling. She missed her parents but that was an emptiness that could never be filled; missing Valentine was spiced with the knowledge that she would see him again.

She allowed Amita to strip her of the light morning attire and encase her in the armour of a robust dress. Amita liked hats and had suggested she purchase several. They had visited a milliner the day before and acquired three. Maliha studied the effect of the small topper in the long mirror. She looked quite business-like and nodded her approval to her maid.

By the time Maliha reached the bottom of the stairs Amita had changed for the outdoors and caught up with her carrying her umbrella. Old Vidu stood beside the carriage and they assisted Maliha up the step and inside.

The newspaper had given the exact address. Maliha gave Old Vidu his instructions and the carriage clattered off through the drenched streets.

Of course it was no coincidence. Whoever was interested in the succession of ownership had ensured it was passed on immediately. But now it belonged to Catherine Mawdsley rather than Selina. That suggested Catherine would be at risk.

Another thought tickled her mind. What if the intention had been to bestow the inheritance on Catherine all along? Now that her husband was dead she could re-marry. It was certainly something to consider.

Before long the carriage passed into the business district and approached the apartments used by single and married gentlemen staying over at the Fortress. Most of the buildings were seven or eight stories tall, built in the neo-gothic style with perhaps a dozen apartments on each floor.

There was considerable traffic in the area. Apart from the usual business there were morbid sightseers hoping for some salacious news or even sight of the corpse. It was well known these apartments were also used for clandestine rendezvous with mistresses.

Old Vidu stopped the carriage a short distance from the building, and Amita handed her down to the pavement then raised the umbrella over Maliha's head. They crossed the street and pushed their way through the crowds to the entrance. There was a well-built policeman at the door, his truncheon hanging from his belt.

Maliha mounted the marble steps with Amita behind her. To her astonishment the policeman raised his hand and touched his fingers to his helmet as a salute. She was less surprised by his greeting.

"I'm sorry, Miss, you can't go in."

She reached the top step but he was still considerably taller than her. "Is Inspector Forsyth here?"

The policeman's eyebrow twitched almost into a frown. "Can I ask your name, Miss?"

Amita butted in. "This is Miss Maliha Anderson."

Maliha could see the orders the man had been given doing battle with his natural instinct to stop members of the general public from entering a crime scene.

"You have been instructed to let me through?"

He did not reply but stood back and held the door open for her. She paused at the door. "What floor, constable?"

"Seventh, Miss."

As they crossed the foyer—one man sat behind a desk watching them go, without comment—Maliha thought about the way the constable had saluted. It was odd. Thinking back she realised there had been similar instances of courtesy she had not previously received. It was not as if everyone knew who she was.

At the lift doors Amita looked confused. It was not as if lifts were a common-place. Maliha braced herself and pulled the handle sideways, the inner and outer concertina gates opened, running smoothly in their grooves. The cage swayed slightly as she entered with Amita behind her.

"Close the gates—hard," she told the girl. Amita grabbed the inner handle and applied more than enough force to slam the gates into position with a crash. Maliha pressed the button for the seventh floor. Amita lurched as a low-power Faraday effect switched on automatically, reducing their weight by perhaps a third, and moments later the cage slid silently upwards. A reduced-gravity lift, Maliha thought, a novel concept.

As they rose through the building, the scene through the gates revealed identically decorated corridors. Only the large number displayed opposite changed. The lift came to a smooth stop as they reached the seventh floor.

Maliha realised she had not asked which room, but another uniformed policeman waited at the top. He pointed to the right and she set off along the passageway with Amita in tow. There were no windows with the corridor running between apartments on both sides. Electric lights mounted in the ceiling illuminated the interior.

As she walked the corridors she noted cold air blowing through ventilation grilles. There must be a powerful system in the cellar pushing air through the halls and rooms. However, even that could not exclude the pervasive damp of the rainy season.

The passageway turned to the left and continued another hundred yards before she reached an open door with another constable standing guard just inside. He, too, saluted. This door opened directly into a living room. The walls were covered with a light flock-paper in a modern design. The chairs and sofas were buttoned leather.

One wall was given over to bookshelves, while a writing desk and small table occupied the far end, where a window looked out across the northern portions of the Compound and beyond the wall to the slums. She examined the books: dictionaries, a twenty-volume encyclopaedia, collections of maps, several atlases, including one of Mars, and not a single fiction work among them.

One shelf caught her eye. It held a set of thirteen brown leather-bound books with no title or publisher on the spine, instead dated by year and month, each spanning two or three years. She removed the most recent, which lacked an end date, and let it fall open in her hand. It was a journal written in a neat and confident hand. The page she read contained a dry summary of a day's meetings and events.

There were voices coming from farther into the apartment. The constable at the door left his station and went through to the back.

"Well, send her in then," came a loud and familiar voice with the Glaswegian accent that always reminded her of her father.

The constable emerged. "You better go in, Miss."

Maliha closed the book and replaced it on the shelf. She turned to Amita. "You should stay here."

The open door led through a short passage with closed doors to the left and right while a third, straight ahead, led into the bedroom. A simple wallpaper with pale blue stripes adorned this room; there was a double bed, its white linen splashed with dry blood and other discolorations. Maliha sniffed once and resolved not to breathe through her nose while in this room.

Inspector Forsyth stood at the end of the bed, and between the bed and the window was Doctor Bristow examining the body—she could only see a bare foot belonging to the victim raised awkwardly in the air. He must have fallen to the floor in his death throes.

"Miss Anderson. So kind of you to visit."

"How did you know I'd be coming?"

He almost sneered. "You're not the only one who keeps an eye on things. You and your government friend were at the funeral of Alex Mawdsley, looking into his death no doubt."

"Yes. And I should point out that the police reports were shockingly inadequate."

"Well, even those of us of lesser intellect can see when there's a coincidence that stinks," he smiled without much humour. "So, yes, I expected you. Where's your puppy dog?"

"I haven't seen Mr Crier in several days. Since you left word with your men that I should be admitted, I imagine you would like me to take a look."

Bristow stood up. "When you two have quite finished, perhaps we can get on?"

Maliha glanced round the room. There was an empty whiskey glass beside a burned-out cigar in a heavy glass ashtray on the cabinet by the window. The bedside lights on both sides were illuminated. The bed was in a state of disarray where the victim had fallen out, but the pillows on the near side had not been touched.

Maliha stepped closer and ran her fingers across the surface of the pillow, pressing gently. There was no depression in it where someone's head might have lain.

Forsyth watched. "Nobody slept on that side of the bed, as far as I can tell."

She leaned closer and sniffed at the pillow. There was no perfume but there was the smell of alcohol. She checked further, gently moving aside the bloody sheet. There was a faint stain on the bedsheet, she removed her glove and touched it. A slight dampness from the mattress seeped through the sheet. She sniffed her fingers. Whiskey.

"Poisoned, I assume," Maliha said. She wiped her fingers on a dry part of the sheet and put her glove back on.

"Either that or he suffered a spontaneous internal haemorrhage," said Bristow. "Do you want to take a look?"

"Any evidence of a mistress?" she asked Forsyth.

He nodded at the wardrobe near the door to the bathroom. She might be wrong, but she thought he smiled at the question, almost proud. She turned away and opened it, a pair of lady's overshoes lay at the bottom, and a silk dressing gown. She pulled it out. It was quite sheer and she couldn't see Catherine Mawdsley wearing it.

"Any evidence to say who his mistress was?"

"Nothing as yet."

Bristow popped his head up again. "Could have been suicide, y'know."

"We'll take your suggestion under advisement," growled Forsyth. Bristow harrumphed and turned his attention back to the body.

"The mistress is your prime suspect?" asked Maliha.

"The doorman confirms there was a lady visitor yesterday evening. I sent a message to the Kochi police to determine whether Mrs Mawdsley has an alibi."

"I'd check the daughter too."

Forsyth narrowed his eyes. "You think she might have done it?"

"Let's call it being thorough, shall we?"

"Have it your way. You know I didn't have to let you in on this investigation."

"You wouldn't have been able to stop me, Inspector."

She closed the wardrobe door and went through to the bathroom. There was a safety razor with a cup and brush for the shaving foam. A bath with plumbed hot water, and untouched towels. She opened the cabinet on the wall and found a set of lead crystal ware. One held a delicate rose perfume, another contained face powder.

Maliha returned to the bedroom. They had lifted Randolf Mawdsley onto the bed. His body was grotesquely rigid, his eyes were wide while his chin and clothing were stained with dried blood. Dark lividity showed he had died face down as he had been found: half-in and half-out of the bed.

"What time did his visitor arrive?"

"About eight thirty."

"And the time of death, Dr Bristow?"

The doctor frowned. "Considering the stage of rigor mortis, I would say no later than ten."

"So the mistress comes up to the room. He's in bed at a surprisingly early hour but she doesn't join him. Instead she gives him a poisoned drink. He spills some of it as he convulses then puts it neatly back on the cabinet before falling out of the bed and dying."

"That's about the size of it, Miss Anderson," said Forsyth with a smile.

And Maliha found herself smiling back.

Maliha went back into the living room. Amita stood by the window looking out. Maliha went to the writing desk and rolled up the cover. Everything was tidy but apart from basic stationery there was nothing of significance. She frowned and looked round.

Inspector Forsyth came through. "Who's this?"

"My maid. Have you removed his papers? His briefcase?"

"A maid, is it?" He gave Amita a long look. "So you're a woman of substance now?"

"Papers? Briefcase?"

"No papers and no briefcase, Miss Anderson."

"Then where are they?"

"That is an extremely good question."

The front door was pushed open and Valentine, dressed in a casual brown suit, rushed in. "Sorry, I'm late."

"Just in time," said Maliha. "We're going. Do you want to see the body?"

"Do I need to?"

"No. I can tell you everything you need to know."

Amita moved across the room and out into the corridor. Valentine looked slightly nonplussed as the Inspector stepped between her and the door.

"Just a moment, Miss Anderson," he said. "I have given you access to this crime, but it was not out of the goodness of my heart. If you have any information that might assist me in my enquiries I expect to hear it."

"Miss Anderson is not at liberty to reveal that information," said Valentine.

Maliha glared at him. "How dare you presume to suggest I am not a free agent, Mr Crier? I investigated Alex's death as a favour. I signed no contract with your government."

Her irritation was matched by the anger in Forsyth's face. "Now look here, Crier. You've already taken one case away from me. I'm not about to let you take another."

Valentine raised his hands in defence. "I'm sorry. No, you are quite right, both of you. My department was concerned that Alex's death was part of a foreign plot to gain control of British industrial secrets by a foreign power. We do not, as yet, have any evidence of that. We don't know if this murder is connected."

"Of course, it's damn well connected," said Forsyth. "If you'll pardon my language, Miss Anderson."

"I quite agree with you, Inspector."

Valentine sighed. "Look, if it's been planned by a foreign government then it is my business and not yours—" he rushed on as Forsyth prepared to explode again "—but until we know one way or the other, it's all yours."

"All right, Crier. I'll accept that for now," he replied. "But until such time as it becomes your case, I expect to be informed as to what you find."

Valentine looked at Maliha, she nodded.

* * *

The three of them left the comforting lightness of the lift and went out into the foyer. Maliha stopped abruptly. Through the glass of the entrance doors she could see photographers and men with notepads. She hesitated and turned to the concierge behind his desk.

"Is there a back way out?" she asked.

"Yes, miss. But it's been locked."

Valentine came up next to her and leaned against the desk. "Is there any way out that bypasses the gentlemen of the press outside?" Maliha noticed a couple of half-crowns in his fingers. He slid them along the desk.

The concierge reached out and the coins disappeared smoothly.

"A short trip underground, it's a little grubby but not too bad. If that's all right?"

He led the way back past the lifts to the stairwell and down three levels into the shadowy cellars. Maliha noted with some satisfaction that her assessment of the equipment required to power the ventilation system was correct. The heat increased to an almost intolerable level as they passed a cavernous room that would have passed for the pit of hell.

The electric lights dangling from the ceiling did little except illuminate the shadows thrown by the white light from the open furnace door. The silhouettes of three stokers took turns feeding its incandescent maw while shadowy boys kept them supplied, transporting wheelbarrows of coal from a mountainous pile on one side above which she could make out a trapdoor.

The next room was almost as hot but lit only by the electric lights. It was occupied by a mass of interwoven pipework that ran in and out of the ceiling and walls. The final room, with a couple of engineers in attendance, was much cooler and contained the turbines that drove air around the building.

She had fallen behind Valentine and the concierge, though Amita had not left her side. She hurried to catch up. The comment by the Inspector about being a woman of substance came to mind. Amita was the reason for the change in attitudes. Now that she had a lady's maid in attendance she automatically commanded more respect. A woman of substance. She found the thought quite pleasing.

Having mounted another three flights of steps they came out into a similar building across the road from the first. They thanked the concierge, who returned the way they had come.

"Have you lunched?" asked Valentine as they stepped from the refreshing cool interior into the sweltering heat and damp.

"I believe it is a little early for lunch."

"Morning coffee?"

She arched a brow at him. He knew perfectly well she did not drink coffee.

"Or tea?"

"Very well. I believe there is a tea house a short distance from here."

They took a table on the first floor and ordered tea, coffee and biscuits. Amita sat a short distance away and took out a book of poems by Gabriella Rosetti she had borrowed from Barbara's library. Maliha approved of her desire to improve herself.

While they waited, Maliha described the victim and circumstances of the death such as they were known.

"Poison is a woman's weapon," said Valentine.

"Both intention and appearance can be disguised, Mr Crier."

"You think it wasn't a woman?"

"I do not think anything. We do not have enough information," she said. "We know that the person got past the night porter and Forsyth says he assumed it was a woman. Apparently it is not unusual for a woman to visit Mawdsley's rooms. Questions are not asked, of course."

"But you say he was alone in his bed."

"Quite so. The murderer must have forced him into his bed and then made him drink the poison. And attempted to make it appear they had been in bed together."

"To cast the guilt on the mistress."

"The mistress is irrelevant. She did not murder him."

"Unless it's a double bluff."

That comment also deserved a raised eyebrow.

He smiled. "But she may have a clue to the actual murderer."

Maliha shrugged. "Perhaps."

They were interrupted by the waitress bringing the tea and cakes. Maliha selected a slice of Battenberg and bit into it. She adored the taste of marzipan.

"But that means we have no leads."

She finished her cake. "Then, Valentine, we shall find some."

v

The Sinhalese offices of the City & Cornwall Mining Company, a business that undertook mining operations from South America to Alaska, were quite modest. They occupied three floors of a modern building in the business district, which was only a short walk from the apartments.

The rains had begun again and were now supplemented by a brisk wind, making the use of the umbrella impractical. The three of them were wet through by the time they pushed open the heavy wooden doors and entered. The circular foyer was large enough for a small Zeppelin and had a chequerboard floor of orange and black marble. The space was ringed with Roman pillars rising through to the next level. A balcony with a polished brass railing ran all the way round, with passages leading off into the offices proper. Above the entrance stretched a row of windows that, on a bright day, would bring natural right into this cathedral of business.

In the centre of the foyer sat a circular desk, manned by two staff in military-style uniforms. Maliha took advantage of her new realisation and allowed Valentine to go ahead of her. She walked across the floor at her own pace with Amita behind her.

The receptionist addressed Valentine as she approached. "Can I assist you, sir, madam?"

She wondered for a moment what Valentine's superiors must think of him gadding about the town in the company of a half-breed.

Perhaps they were pragmatic; she solved their problems and they ignored the issue.

Valentine showed his credentials and a boy was sent upstairs. Maliha would have preferred there to be no warning of their arrival. However, they were forced to wait. After a short delay a young man crossed the room and greeted them, his eyes lingering on Amita for a moment.

He introduced himself as Randolf Mawdsley's private secretary, John Linton. They took the lift, not assisted by a Faraday device in this instance, to the fifth floor and followed the secretary along thickly carpeted passageways until they reached a suite of rooms.

"What would you like to see, sir?"

"I think that would be up to Miss Anderson, John."

The man's eyes flicked in her direction. "Of course, sir. Miss?"

She looked around the secretary's office: bookshelves with a similar selection of books to those in Mawdsley's rooms, just more of them with the addition of several shelves of tax regulations.

"Can you show me his office?"

The secretary went to his desk and removed a set of keys, he selected one and unlocked the door through to Mawdsley's office. He stood back to allow Maliha and Valentine to enter. The room was large enough to have five wide windows along its back wall giving on to a view across the inside of the compound and the industrial beauty of *Sigiriya* itself. Its lights shone under the dark of the clouds, while the rain and mist gave each one a halo.

The room itself had a spartan luxury, the desk was simple but clearly of the highest quality; over the large fireplace was a painting of a rocky storm-swept coast by one of the Scottish impressionists. A sideboard, matching the desk, stood opposite with an ornate set of crystal bottles and glasses.

Maliha allowed Valentine to exercise an interest in the desk. She went to the painting and read the signature in the corner: *William McIntyre*. "Who chose the painting, Mr Linton?"

She heard his footsteps approach as she examined the powerful brush strokes.

"Mr Mawdsley always approved of my choices."

"You have excellent taste," she said. "How long have you been Mr Mawdsley's secretary?"

"Nearly ten years, ever since he moved out here permanently."

"That's a long time."

"He was a good employer," he said, she could hear his voice almost breaking with the emotion of his loss.

"And you must be a good secretary." She turned to face him. He opened his mouth to reply but shut it again and nodded.

"You were aware Mr Mawdsley kept a mistress." She stated it as a fact.

He paused but nodded again.

"And you know who it is."

He did not deny it.

"How many years has he being seeing her?"

"Four."

Once they had finished examining the otherwise unrevealing office, they returned to the outer office and Linton wrote down the name and address they needed.

"You shouldn't feel you are betraying him," said Valentine as he took the slip of paper from the secretary. He looked at the name and was unable to hide the surprise of her identity from his face. He passed the paper to Maliha. "We are not the police. If she has nothing to do with the crime there is no reason for us to reveal her identity. Whether you choose to inform the police is entirely up to you."

Maliha looked at the name.

"One more thing, if you don't mind," said Maliha. "Can we see Mr Mawdsley's appointments?"

He pulled out the diary from his desk. Maliha flicked through it, absorbing the information on each page at a glance, almost as if she were not reading it at all. She passed it to Valentine to pore over the pages.

"He had an appointment with his solicitor today, do you know what that was about?"

"It was a personal matter, he didn't tell me."

* * *

They stood on the steps of the office building, still sheltered from the rain, as people rushed back and forth in the rain, some fighting with their wind-blown umbrellas.

"Why don't you go and see the solicitor, Valentine? I'll interview the woman."

"Take care, Maliha, she may be dangerous."

"She won't be. I have Amita with me."

She stayed where she was and watched Valentine heading off. She turned to Amita.

"Do you know John Linton?"

The maid hesitated before answering in Hindi. "*I think I know his face from … before.*"

Maliha nodded. "Very well. Let us be off."

vi

Maliha located Old Vidu with their carriage and instructed him to take them to the address. It was not far from Barbara's bungalow so she sent him back to the house after dropping them off.

Arriving uninvited and unexpected before lunch was not good manners at all but the police would not respect custom if the secretary were to tell them.

She walked up to the house. It was much larger than Barbara's and newer. It was clearly designed for a hot climate with a raised floor level, verandah, and wide windows. What was unusual was the addition of a balcony over the verandah to the same depth and height, topped with curious curved gables to the sides.

They mounted the steps to the front door, and rang the bell.

To her shame Maliha stared at the parlour-maid who opened the door. She could rationalise her behaviour by claiming she had never seen a negro woman before, but the thought that she might be prejudiced because of someone's race horrified her. It made her no different from the girls at her school who had made her life hell, and justified every person since then that had abused her or insulted her father or mother for their marriage.

She recovered her composure as best she could. "Miss Anderson to see Mrs Mayberry."

"Mrs Mayberry ain't taking visitors, ma'am. She's indisposed."

So she had heard about Mawdsley's death. "Yes, I understand." Maliha pulled a card from her reticule and found a pencil. She scribbled a note on the back and presented it to the girl. "I believe she will want to see me. If you would give her my card."

The girl admitted them and went upstairs while Maliha and Amita dripped slowly on the painted wooden floor. The open and airy hallway was hung with paintings of battle scenes and military heroism.

Maliha turned to Amita. "You stay here when I go up. See if you can persuade the staff to tell you where Mrs Mayberry was last night. I don't think she'll lie to me but it would be good to have independent corroboration."

"Of course, *sahiba*." Amita responded without hesitation but looked slightly concerned. Maliha had no time to give her further instruction as the maid started down the wooden stairs.

"If you'd like to come up, ma'am."

The staircase had a higher rise than she could easily manage and she was forced to take them like someone of advanced years, both feet on each step before going to the next. They passed down a corridor, still with the military imagery, to a door at the far end that opened into a ladies' salon with stylish sofas and low tables. A copy of *The Times of India* had been thrown on to the table, its pages torn and scattered.

Constance Mayberry stood near the window. She was clutching a handkerchief and was making no effort to hide the fact she had been crying. She was not dressed for visitors. The door closed behind Maliha.

"How did he die, Miss Anderson? Did he suffer?"

The tortured image of the stiff body and the blood splattered bed came to her mind. The woman was either a consummate actor or she had had nothing to do with his death. "I do not think death is ever a pleasant thing when one is not expecting it."

Maliha's leg was beginning to ache more. She took a seat in a chair facing towards the window. "How did you meet?"

"Leonard was entertaining business associates and potential partners. Randolf was there with his wife."

Maliha shifted her weight. "I know this is difficult but I have to pry."

"It's your job."

My job? Maliha thought. A professional detective? Like those Pinkertons they have? What a ridiculous idea.

"But you didn't just…"

Constance looked as if she was going to cry. "No, Miss Anderson, we did not simply leap into bed together. Randolf

Mawdsley is fond of opera." She saw Maliha's surprise. "You find that hard to believe? You did not know him. He could be a passionate man. His wife detested the theatre in any form, but I am of the same mind as he." She looked out of the window. "Are you familiar with Tosca?"

"The heroine commits suicide at the end."

"Yes." Constance lapsed into silence contemplating the window and the deluge beyond. "It's like the world is crying."

"Where were you last evening?"

Constance dragged her attention back into the room. "I was here. My husband had guests."

Maliha found herself thinking about Valentine. How would she feel if he were killed? In his job it was not improbable. The thought of it filled her with emptiness. She needed to focus. "Why would you cuckold your husband?"

Constance pulled herself away from the window and sat down opposite Maliha across the ripped newspaper. "You like Bill."

"I call him Valentine."

"He hates that name," she said, and then sighed. "But that was before he met you. Have you kissed him?"

"Of course not."

"Why not?"

Maliha had no answer. The conversation had galloped from her control.

"Have you touched his skin?"

Maliha nodded, she was unsure what words she would say if she dared speak.

"Like electricity."

She nodded again. The world seemed to have shrunk until all it encompassed were the next words from Constance.

"That's why."

Maliha frowned. "I don't understand."

"Because if we don't experience the electricity we end up like poor Margaret Henley. Hysteria takes us and we suffer, one way or another."

"Is it love?"

Constance barked a painful laugh. "I don't know what that is. I needed the touch, the electricity—I needed a man, Miss Anderson."

The vehemence and candour of her words shocked Maliha out of the spell Constance had cast over her. She returned to herself and she had a question.

"You suffered from hysteria before you met Randolf Mawdsley?"

"Of course."

"What treatment did you receive?"

"I was also … a student of Guru Nadesh."

CHAPTER 4

They walked back to Barbara's house through the late afternoon rain, Amita held the umbrella above her head but random blasts of wind blew it this way and that. It was almost useless.

Amita told her the servants had confirmed Constance had been hosting her husband's party the previous evening along with a dozen guests. It would have been impractical for her to have killed Randolf personally. There was always the chance that she had employed someone else to do it but her reactions seemed quite genuine.

The things Constance had said put Maliha's mind in a turmoil. Even if she had been inclined to discuss the matter with Amita it was nothing the maid would understand. And that left her with only one person.

She studied Barbara as they ate dinner. She was in her late sixties, old enough to be Maliha's grandmother at least. Maliha's Scottish grandparents were dead, while the Indian ones had effectively disowned her mother. Prejudice and bigotry were not traits limited to the British. But Barbara had survived a marriage without any attention from her husband, as Barbara had once told her that the only time the General had touched her was to put the wedding band on her finger. The General had different preferences and had died because of them.

Barbara most certainly did not suffer from hysteria the way Margaret Henley did, nor did Maliha herself—as far as she could tell, though at the back of her mind she remembered how she had touched the cold bare skin of Valentine's shoulder, and how the sensation of his skin against hers had given her some pleasure, despite the circumstances. Perhaps it was a sign she was succumbing to this malady.

Once dinner was finished they moved to the library, to read as was their usual habit, with some tea for Barbara and water for Maliha. For ten minutes Maliha stared at the same page of her book wondering how she should broach this difficult subject.

"You seem distracted, dear," said Barbara without looking up from her book. "Something on your mind?"

"Am I that transparent?"

Barbara looked up and smiled. "What is it?"

"I'm afraid I need to discuss a personal matter," she said. "I need some guidance."

The older woman closed her book and laid it down beside her. She raised her head and looked Maliha in the eye "Well, I can try, my dear. To tell the truth I did not ever expect to hear you say you need my advice. So I imagine it must be serious—" she opened her mouth to say something more, hesitated as if uncertain whether to say what was in her mind, then ploughed on "—you know you are the nearest thing to a daughter I have ever had."

Her words caused the breath to catch in Maliha's chest and she felt the sting of tears in her eyes. She tried to speak but the words were stuck.

The smile on Barbara's face softened with kindness. "And if you were my daughter, I could not be more proud. Ask whatever you must."

Maliha fought to keep the tears from her face. She retrieved her kerchief and dabbed at her eyes. "I don't know what to say."

"I did not mean to upset you, I wanted to reassure you that you can ask me anything. Take a sip from your glass and pretend I had not spoken."

Maliha took the time for several sips and settled herself. She had to clear her throat before she could get the words out. "This is a difficult subject, Barbara."

"You know more of my personal life than any person living, Maliha. Ask your question I promise I shall not be offended."

Maliha took another few moments to gather her thoughts and phrase the question in her mind. "Have you ever suffered from hysteria?"

"That *is* a remarkably personal question."

"I'm sorry."

Barbara raised her hand to stop her. "No. I did not mean I would not answer, just that it was unexpected." She took a deep breath. "I do not believe I have. It is difficult to say for certain—could you truly explain a toothache to someone who has never had one?"

"But you've known women who have?"

"Yes, one or two. I do not believe I experienced what they appeared to suffer from," Barbara said. "Do you think you are suffering from it?"

"No—though I do think of Valentine a good deal."

Barbara smiled at that. "Well, I would suspect that's entirely normal. He is a generous man and a gentleman." She frowned. "But this is not about you, is it?"

"These are not matters I would normally think about, Barbara. It is embarrassing and the sort of thing one was punished for—back in school, I mean. Do you understand?"

It was Barbara's turn to look embarrassed but she nodded. "Yes, dear. I know what you are referring to. I went to boarding school."

Maliha reached the heart of her question. The things that she had read in learned books, and how the things she had observed in relationships, in women, in herself, disagreed. But it was hard because she had had it drummed into her that these were not subjects to be discussed.

"The things that are written down, the things we are told, say that—" she cast around for the right words "—that a wife's duty is not something that she can enjoy. That a woman is incapable of the pleasure a man enjoys. But—it's not true, is it?" It all came out in a rush. She knew the answer, she wanted to be right and yet she needed the agreement of another woman otherwise she would not know if she was wrong.

Barbara sighed. "You are asking if a woman can enjoy the touch of a man?"

Maliha nodded and Barbara looked away. Maliha realised just what she had just asked of the woman who had never felt the touch of her husband and yet remained faithful to her marriage vows for the greater part of her life.

Finally Barbara looked back at her, met her eye. "My husband and I may not have shared the marriage bed, Maliha, but there was someone before him. We were," she hesitated, "intimate. So, yes, we can take pleasure in it."

ii

Valentine received a letter from Maliha the following morning. His man placed it on the table next to his breakfast. Under normal circumstances Valentine dealt with his post after breakfast but Jameson had taken to bringing messages from Maliha directly to him regardless.

It was difficult to find good staff, and Jameson had never given any reason for complaint.

Valentine sliced the envelope open with the butter knife and slipped out the letter. It was no more than a summons but he read it over twice just to be sure. It wouldn't do to miss any instruction.

He fetched the atmospheric timetables from the desk and consulted them, estimating travel times. He glanced out of the window where ragged clumps of dark clouds scudded across the otherwise blue sky.

"Jameson?"

The man appeared from the kitchen area. "Sir?"

"Trip to Madurai by atmospheric. Book a return on the eleven-thirty for two. Private compartment. Would you?"

"Of course, sir. How long will you be staying?"

"Overnight at most, probably back this evening."

"Do you require me to accompany you?"

"No, that's fine."

"Is it Miss Anderson that's accompanying you, sir?"

"Yes."

"Perhaps an ordinary compartment would be more appropriate."

Valentine considered, some time alone with her would be pleasant, but he could not be selfish at the risk of her reputation. "Yes, you're right."

It was not quite eight according to the clock on the sideboard. Couple of hours. She said to collect her after ten.

* * *

Valentine strode along the street towards Barbara's house. He had taken the time to complete his correspondence and then boarded an omnibus to fill in time. He was still early. Well, he was not going to wait outside like a fool. One of those treacherous clouds could unload itself on him at any moment. He knocked on the door.

Sathi opened it and stood back to admit him. He was there so often now they did not bother with the formalities. He handed her his hat and umbrella, and walked through into the library.

"Oh, I'm so sorry, Mrs Makepeace-Flynn."

He had not expected her to be there, since she had never been before when he came visiting. What was more she was sitting facing him as he entered and, in all his experience, she had always sat with her back to the door.

"Please sit, Mr Crier," she said with great formality. He felt the kind of fear that was normally engendered by a confrontation with a maiden aunt of advanced years. An event to strike terror into the heart of any unmarried and dissolute gentleman. Not that he was dissolute in general, only on special occasions.

He perched on the edge of the sofa opposite her.

"I will be frank, Mr Crier."

His heart sank. Frankness was frequently accompanied by misery, or so it had been during his lifetime. His unserious attitude had frequently ended him in trouble with authority. And Mrs Makepeace-Flynn, a woman he knew to be comfortable with a shotgun, epitomised authority.

"What are your intentions towards Miss Anderson."

"My—" this was not quite what he had been expecting "— intentions?"

"Intentions. Yes."

"I'm not entirely sure I understand."

The glowering look of displeasure that overtook her face told him he had said precisely the wrong thing.

"You are frequently out with her unaccompanied. I realise that times change and that this is not so unusual or reprehensible in this day and age. But have you considered her reputation?"

Of course he had. He always considered her reputation. It was she that seemed to disregard it. She seemed more concerned with his reputation. But all he said was "I think I do."

"I have come to care for Miss Anderson a great deal. And I would be most displeased if she were hurt."

"It is not my intention to harm her in any way, Mrs Makepeace-Flynn." He got that far and there were more words that needed to be said. "I also care for her a great deal."

Her expression lightened, and he ceased to feel he was in front of a firing squad. "Very well then, Mr Crier. In that case I believe you should consider your future actions in regard to her quite carefully."

The clock struck ten and there were footsteps on the stairs. Valentine stood and turned towards the door. Maliha stepped down the final step—her stick in her hand—she was dressed for travel.

"You have booked the atmospheric?"

"Eleven thirty."

"Why don't you have some tea before you go?" said Barbara. Amita came down behind Maliha. Valentine, seeing the maid so close and in line with her mistress, realised how tall she was, and apparently with the strength of a horse since she carried Maliha's baggage with little difficulty.

Sathi brought them tea while they sat in the library and Valentine related his dealings with the solicitor. It had taken the full force of His Majesty's Government, as represented by Valentine's warrant card, to persuade him to divulge the reason for the meeting with his now deceased client.

"He was changing his will," said Maliha, ripping the wind from his sails.

"Yes, he was changing his will," Valentine repeated without enthusiasm.

Mrs Makepeace-Flynn smiled. "Don't be put out, Mr Crier. Miss Anderson was merely guessing."

It was Maliha's turn to frown. "I do not guess. It was simple and obvious. Naturally Mawdsley would not want his daughter to inherit the business. It was an oversight which he intended to remedy. That's not the important question." He could have sworn she was pausing for dramatic effect, so chose this moment to exact his revenge.

"The question is who knew of his intention," he said, pre-empting her.

Maliha smiled at him. "Quite."

iii

The train clattered through the tube as it crossed the landscape. The day was not as rainy as on her previous trip and she could see to the horizon as they traversed fields, forests and expanses of water.

Valentine had chosen a public carriage in first class, which suited her. The fact that no stranger had joined them suited her purposes even more. They sat opposite one another by the window. A steward had come and gone with tea and a lunch of light sandwiches.

"Why are we going to Madurai?"

She had thought he would never ask. She pulled a note from her reticule and handed it to him. "This arrived yesterday afternoon."

He read through the short note. "Sounds like the Inspector put a firework under the Kochi police."

"Guru Nadesh has an estate just outside the city."

"What would Catherine want with this spiritual … chap?" asked Valentine.

A wave of heat ran through Maliha. She had not been looking forward to this conversation. She had toyed with the idea of not explaining, but that would not work. She suspected it would embarrass him rather more than her.

"Valentine—" she started, then stopped.

"What?"

She pursed her lips and looked down at her hands. "You know Margaret Henley."

"What about her?"

Maliha steadied herself, this was about murder not personal feelings. Two innocent men were dead. "You know how she chases you?"

"I understand she chases almost any man," he said. "You do know that I don't reciprocate in any fashion."

Maliha nodded. "But do you know why she does it?"

Not a question he expected, he sat back trying to divine some special meaning. She allowed him the time. He finally shook his head. "I assume it is not because I am particularly handsome."

Maliha smiled. "That may have something to do with it." She stopped again. "There is a condition some women suffer from ... they become unwell when they lack for ... gentleman's company."

A red flush blossomed on his face. She had not expected him to be an innocent.

"And Margaret suffers from this ... condition."

"She does."

She could see his mind working. He took the thoughts to their conclusion and made the necessary connections.

"And this Guru Nadesh provides ... treatment."

"This is what I have been told."

"But they don't..."

"I do not believe so."

He turned away from her and looked out of the window as the sun broke through and reflected off a river they were passing. The compartment lit up and then went dark again as they moved on.

"Do you want me to accompany you to see him?" His voice was strained. "I am not sure I would be of any help."

Maliha had considered asking him to go with her.

"I do not think that will be the best course of action. I will go in with Amita," she said. "He will think me another possible disciple."

He turned his head away again, this time turning his whole body to face the window. She wanted to reach out and touch him, but someone might see. Instead she said, "Ask me."

He was silent.

"Valentine, ask me."

He pulled himself back to face her with visible effort. He looked her in the eye. "And are you a possible disciple, Maliha?"

"I am not."

"Why did you ask me to come?"

It was a fair question. Why indeed? She could say it was because two people had been murdered and whoever had done it would not hesitate to kill again. Or because, in this investigation, he was effectively her employer. Or because Alex had been his friend and he deserved to be close when truth was discovered.

They were all valid reasons. The truth was more personal.

A shadow caught her eye and there was a knock on the compartment door. The conductor put in his head. "Pardon me, madam, sir, we are approaching Madurai."

* * *

They left the station and crossed the road to the Midland Hotel. The red temple towered behind it. Apparently Valentine's man had decided that staying over was the better option. They registered at the desk and were escorted to their separate rooms.

Maliha changed into something more suitable for road travel and descended to the hotel lobby where Valentine waited. She emerged from the lift and crossed the floor, leaning heavily on her stick, Amita following behind armed with an umbrella. He seemed to have recovered from his discomfiture on the train.

"I have hired a carriage," he said with a grin. "I think you'll like it."

When they emerged into the open she saw a modern German vehicle sitting in the street, four wheels, diesel engine, and the uniformed driver stood by the open back door. The whole vehicle had a covered passenger area sufficient for eight.

"Amita can ride up front with the driver," he said.

"You never cease to find ways to get me alone, do you?"

She realised from the shocked look on his face that perhaps she had been premature in thinking he had fully recovered from their previous conversation on the atmospheric. She put her hand on his arm to reassure him and smiled. "I think that is an excellent plan. Does the driver know where to go?"

He nodded. "He knows the place."

* * *

The carriage was remarkably quiet as it ran along the Madurai streets. The interior was decorated in walnut and upholstered in leather with velvet window curtains. The suspension was of excellent quality and compensated effectively for the poor quality of the roads.

Soon they were out in the country travelling through fields interspersed with collections of shacks—what passed for villages here. The carriage turned off the main route and up a well-tended gravel avenue. The house they approached was typical early colonial but in good repair. There were gardeners at work.

"The guru does well for himself," said Valentine with a caustic tone.

"Grateful disciples perhaps," Maliha said. "Let's pull the curtains and you can just stay in here."

"If you're not back in an hour I'll come in."

"All right," she said. "But there won't be a problem. I'm just going to talk to him."

The door to the mansion was opened by an Indian maid in western clothing. Maliha introduced herself and was admitted.

The place was clean but lacked for furniture and decoration. The bare floor of the hall echoed to her boots and stick. The walls were devoid of pictures and there was no statuary in the alcoves designed for them. There were two possibilities: either the guru had an ascetic taste, or he simply couldn't afford it. Or perhaps it was an attempt at the former in order to deceive.

The maid escorted her to a large reception room, where a clump of sofas and chairs sat in the middle of the room like an island in a sea of emptiness.

She heard the slap of a sandal on the floor and turned to the main door as a man entered. He effected the appearance of a traditional guru with his *dhoti* and *sattai*—both spotless and smooth. But it was not the clothes that made him stand apart. It was not that he was a short man in his fifties with a small moustache and a long nose. It was that he was not Indian at all, he was as British as Inspector Forsyth.

He stopped just inside the door and pressed his hands together at waist height and barely dipped his head, the minimum of respectful manners. "*Namaste*, Maliha Anderson."

"You are Guru Nadesh?"

"I am he."

He moved forward across the room.

"Please sit, Miss Anderson." He spread one arm expansively towards the settees. "I would offer you a tour of the grounds but for the weather." His voice was calm and relaxed.

Maliha glanced out through the windows at the garden, and a sky filled with clouds, before sitting on the settee that faced him, she positioned her stick in front of her and placed both hands on it. With the ease of long practice, the man sat crosslegged on the floor in one smooth motion, with his back to the fireplace.

He beamed a beatific smile in her direction.

"What can I do for you, Miss Anderson?"

He had no regional accent, there was no hint of crystal-cut upper class, nor any roughness of the lower classes. Each word was distinct but without pretension or falseness.

"I am investigating the deaths of Randolf and Alexander Mawdsley."

"How on earth did a young lady like you come to be involved with such things?"

"I was the schoolgirl who solved the Taliesin Affair."

"You must forgive me, Miss Anderson, I take no interest in the mundanities of life. I do not know of this Taliesin Affair. I follow a more spiritual path." He smiled in apology. "I am more curious to know what drives an attractive young woman into such sordid matters."

"It is a question I have asked myself," she said, almost to herself.

"And what answer did you find?"

"I cannot tolerate untruth."

"Truth is not an absolute, Miss Anderson, it is relative."

They lapsed into silence. Yet she did not feel awkward, she leaned back and rested. She realised she had been sidetracked. She knew why: she did not want to discuss the things that happened in this house with a man she had only just met.

And yet even that was not entirely true. If he had been Indian, if he had been old, she would have not had this reluctance. Was this another example of her own bigotry? She was prejudiced because he was white?

No.

Almost as if he had seen a change in her mind he stood. "Come with me, Miss Anderson."

She stood at his command, pushing heavily on her stick. She heard Amita step up behind her, ready to assist if she needed it.

"Does your maid speak English?" he asked.

"She does."

"Then perhaps she should remain here. We may have things to say that should be kept private."

Maliha turned and nodded at Amita, then set off across the floor.

"Take my arm," he said offering his pale bare arm. "You'll find it easier."

She did so and he led her from the room.

v

He guided her across the hall to the stairs, intending to go up them. He must have felt her tense because he stopped.

"There's no need to be concerned, Miss Anderson. You have an enquiring mind, but there are gaps in your knowledge."

"And you will fill those gaps?"

"I will provide you with the opportunity," he said. "But what I offer is not for everyone."

She moved forwards again and they mounted the stairs. At the first turn, she looked out of the window on to well-tended gardens. "You take a great deal of care over the gardens."

"When it is fine my students like to meditate outside."

They reached the top of the flight into a circular space with a dome of glass above. The change between the floors was dramatic. This one was carpeted in a thick pile the colour of dark wine. The wallpaper had an intricate pattern in red on white but it was the statue in the middle that had Maliha blushing: A naked man and woman entwined in a sexual act. She looked away.

"I know, it's quite shocking, isn't it?" he said with a hint of humour. "But it's a statue created by your culture, Miss Anderson. Hundreds of years old. You should not be embarrassed."

He led her along a corridor to the left. There were closed doors at regular intervals along it.

"You want to instruct me?"

"Only if you wish it. I would never force my teachings onto anyone who did not want them."

"I want to know," she said.

"Very well, but I'll speak plainly. Are you ready for that?"

"I'll manage."

"Hysteria isn't a normal condition," he said in the portentous tone of an authoritative lecturer. "It should not exist at all. I have studied its history. It was unknown before the reign of Victoria. Someone decided it was improper for women to enjoy themselves during the sexual act, and this insidious concept infected the culture. It condemned four generations of women to a form of hell, denying their God-given nature, rewriting history and destroying art in the name of this torture."

Maliha listened with half an ear. She was distracted by the paintings on the walls. Each one depicted a sexual act in one form or another. There was no attempt to disguise it with a classical setting. It was simple lewdness.

"In England tens of thousands of middle and upper class women visit their doctors to have their paroxysm induced. I have often wondered whether it was a doctor who created the lie in the first place to make money for him and his cohorts."

The pictures on the walls changed. They were no longer paintings, now they were photographs. Actual men and women. Maliha realised her skin was burning. She could not stop herself from looking at the pictures as they walked past.

"They even developed machines to induce paroxysm, because the doctors suffered from muscular strains from having to perform so many treatments," he laughed. "Only lucky women discover the truth for themselves and have husbands who understand."

"I don't understand what you do here." Maliha tried to keep her voice neutral. "Do you see yourself as some sort of saviour?"

The guru said nothing. They approached the end of the corridor, a wide door before them. She held her breath as he turned the handle and pushed it open. The momentary fear that this would lead into a bedroom dissipated. The room contained no bed, it was a lounge of some sort with comfortable chairs, sofas and low tables. By the window there was an oak reading stand on which sat a large book.

"There are vulgar words that would be applied to my institute by the ignorant, Miss Anderson. But what I do here is teach."

He guided her past the furniture to the window. He let her arm drop and rested his hand on the closed book. Both the front and the spine were free of any writing.

"Are you familiar with the work of the sage *Vatsyayana*?"

Maliha shook her head but he wasn't looking at her. "No." Her mother had mentioned the name when in discussion with her friends but Maliha was not *familiar* with the author.

"He wrote a treatise on love over fifteen hundred years ago, when the Roman Empire was dying."

He opened the book. The title page contained the words *Kama Sutra* and the names of the translators and publisher. This title she knew. It had cropped up once or twice in her extensive reading, always with the hint of scandal. A salacious work for men to read. She felt herself stabilising as if she were a boat that had finally made it to harbour.

"Your students study this?"

He turned to face her. "The physical act of love is no crime, Miss Anderson. It is a route to spirituality. This is the manual of love."

She glanced back at the open book. "Caroline Mawdsley is a student."

"Has she told you she is?"

"She says she was here the evening her husband was murdered."

Guru Nadesh closed the book but continued to rest his hand lightly on the cover. "That is correct. She was here."

"Studying?"

"Yes."

"And do you induce paroxysm for the relief of hysteria, Guru Nadesh?"

There was the tiniest hesitation, a moment when he was not sure of his answer. "Yes, Miss Anderson. For extreme cases, it is the only decent thing one can do."

"What about Selina?"

His composure splintered. "Selina is not a student," he growled, with a tone that verged on disgust.

* * *

Valentine stayed back in the seat as Maliha clambered awkwardly back into the carriage with Amita's assistance. He suppressed the instinct to assist her just in case someone was watching.

She moved across in front of him to the far side of the compartment and sat heavily. Amita shut the door and climbed into the front. Maliha did not turn to look at him but kept her eyes fixed out the front. The engine growled into life and the gravel crunched as the vehicle drew away from the house. A sigh escaped her lips. As the vehicle, turned more light filled the carriage and he noticed a redness in her cheeks. Her hands still clung to her stick.

Valentine slid closer. "Are you all right?" He stopped when she raised her hand.

"Stay back there, on that side."

"What's wrong?" A dozen thoughts crowded through his mind, none of them good. "What did he do?"

"Nothing. He did nothing." She still did not look at him. "We talked."

"I should have come in with you."

"That—" she seemed to be searching for the words "—would not have accomplished our aims."

He felt uncomfortable and silence stretched between them. The carriage drove out of the gate and took the road back to Madurai.

"At least you had Amita with you."

"Yes."

There was more silence. Her behaviour demonstrated something had happened but the knowledge of what the guru was involved with meant he could not ask.

"Did he corroborate Catherine's alibi?"

"Yes."

"Back to the Fortress in the morning?"

"Yes."

They said nothing more until the carriage rolled up in front of the hotel. He stood back from the door and let Amita help her out. He had received the firm impression that she did not want to be close to him. She stood straight and stretched her back a little, pushing on her stick.

"Send a message to Forsyth. We need to get access to Mawdsley's apartment again."

CHAPTER 5

i

At nine a.m., after a modest and quick breakfast, Maliha had Old Vidu drive her to Randolf Mawdsley's residence with Amita in attendance. There were no longer any members of the press besieging the building and they mounted the steps to the entrance unmolested.

The door was locked but a quick rap on it brought a figure striding towards them through the gloom. As the light hit him it resolved into the concierge. He peered through and seemed to recognise her. He turned a key and let them in.

"Morning, Miss." He rummaged in a pocket and handed her a key. "If you could drop it back when you're done."

"It's a terrible thing to have happen in these apartments."

"Mortifying, Miss. Mortifying. Never had nothing like it before."

She went to walk away then stopped.

"What's your name?"

"Baines, Miss."

She came back to him, putting a smile on her face. "I'm sure you know everything that happens in your apartments."

"I don't pry, Miss," he said too quickly. "My gentlemen have their privacy."

"Of course not. But Mr Mawdsley's lady caller."

"I never saw her face, not before and not that night."

She smiled. "I understand that, but she smelled of roses, didn't she?"

The reminder of Constance's scent had an effect. "She did, Miss. Always roses made me think of spring back home. I used to look forward to seeing her."

"But not that last night."

His face became a caricature of someone making an effort to remember. "She smelled like fruit, I swear."

"Oranges."

He looked amazed. "Yes, oranges, that's what it was.

Maliha smiled. "Yes, I imagine she did."

They called the lift and were treated to the short period of reduced gravity as it rose to the seventh floor.

On the way to Mawdsley's room they passed another resident, a man in his thirties overdressed for the temperature, which suggested he was a recent arrival. His eyes followed her, and as they passed he reached out and touched her wrist.

His hand was ripped away and there was a dull thud as his head hit the wall. Amita's right forearm pressed against his neck and her other hand was located below his waistband. Maliha took in the situation with an embarrassed glance and continued down the corridor. There was a muffled cry of pain behind her.

Amita caught up with her as she was turning the key in the door. With the door closed behind them, Maliha turned to her maid.

"We don't want any trouble."

"No, *sahiba*. I did not hurt him—" she hesitated "—too much."

"I'm glad to hear it."

"And now he will be unsure when a girl is a girl."

Maliha chose not to enquire further, and went to the book shelves. She ran her finger along the journals, checking each date in turn. "Ah yes, I thought there was one missing. December 1883 to March 1884."

They went back to the foyer in silence and the concierge let her out of the door with a polite good-bye.

The humidity was high and the sky was covered in thick cloud, but there was no rain. Where was Valentine?

"Amita, I'm going to Mawdsley's office. Get Old Vidu to drive there and catch me up if you would."

She took the umbrella and set off along the road. She preferred being out of doors. For the first half of her life she had had the freedom of the gardens of her parents' home and, on occasion, had even escaped that. She had had her own friends. Then she had been sent to the confinement of boarding school and British weather, even if the south coast had slightly better climate than the rest.

Now she was her own woman, even if she did not have command of all her income, but she could never return to the freedom of her childhood days.

Where was Valentine? Why hadn't he come? As the question formed in her mind she knew the answer. She had treated him abominably and not specifically requested his presence. And why? Because if she had not pushed him away she would have done quite the opposite.

It was hysteria. The guru did more than just treat it, he caused it. And there was no doubt in her mind that he was perfectly aware of what he was doing. She would have been happy to continue her life without experiencing the desperate craving that had possessed her body at the mansion, and which, in the back of her mind, she knew still lurked. It had been awakened now and might never be returned to its box.

Just thinking about it made it stir within her. And yet how could she not? Somehow it was part-and-parcel with the murders—and it had nothing to do with the Stines.

She arrived at the office, Amita was waiting for her. They went in and were greeted by the reception staff. A few minutes later John Linton arrived. Once more his gaze lingered on Amita slightly too long before giving his attention to Maliha.

He escorted them to the lift but before he had a chance to press the button for the top floor Maliha stopped him.

"Mr Linton, I need to see the company records for 1883. You have those here?"

"Yes, Miss Anderson. Can I ask why?"

"I am afraid that is a police matter and potentially one of national importance."

"I do not wish to be awkward, Miss Anderson, but neither the Inspector or Mr Crier are with you. I do not think I can allow that without someone in authority."

It had crossed Maliha's mind that he might be awkward, and she knew the innocent but seductive woman ploy would be unlikely to work in this instance. Unfortunately there was only one thing she could use as leverage and it was not something she was comfortable with. But there were two deaths to be resolved, and a devious monster to be dealt with.

"Mr Linton, if you do not let me see those records I will be forced to make public your history with my maid."

His already pale face turned ashen. He clasped his hands together but they did not stop shaking. He stared at Amita, who remained impassive.

"What could you know?"

"Let us just leave it with the fact that I do. Amita has not told me any details, I'm not sure I wish to know them, but she will if I ask."

"But you keep her on as your *maid* despite that." He was now confused as well as fearful.

"That is my business," she said. "Let us look at this from another viewpoint, I am attempting to discover the murderer of your employer. If you show me those records I will be able to do that."

"You won't tell anyone?"

"I will reveal neither the fact you let me see the records, nor your other activities. All I am looking for is corroboration of something I already know."

The colour did not return to his cheeks but his hands had stopped shaking when he pressed the floor button.

ii

They exited the office building into another bout of rain. Amita raised the umbrella and guided Maliha round a corner to the vehicle. Parked a short distance behind it, puffing quietly, was a steam carriage from which two men were approaching: Inspector Forsyth and Detective Constable Devilal Choudhary.

Both raised their hats as drew closer. "Glad I caught you, Miss Anderson."

"Inspector. Constable."

Forsyth grinned. "Detective *Sergeant* Choudhary has some information."

"Sergeant?" said Maliha turning to him. "Congratulations. I take it you resolved your ... questions?"

"Thank you, Miss Anderson. For the moment at least, I think."

Forsyth's grin turned to a frown but he did not enquire what they were discussing. "Let's get out of this confounded rain. It may not be as bad as Bombay but I can do without it."

"There are tea rooms around the corner," said Maliha.

Forsyth hesitated as if he were going to make another suggestion. It was getting on towards lunch and she imagined he would probably prefer something stronger than tea.

* * *

They sat and ordered. Maliha had chosen the same table where she had spoken to Valentine. She felt a vague annoyance when she thought of him, she had not received any communication from him since Madurai. It might have been only yesterday evening, but it seemed much longer.

"What did you find in Madurai?" Forsyth asked without preamble.

"Guru Nadesh is a white man gone native, Inspector."

Forsyth studied her face absorbing the information. "Is he, indeed?"

"British. London and the Home Counties I think. No distinct accent anyway," she said carefully.

"And what does this guru do?"

"Teaches Hindu scripture." She certainly did not want Forsyth to make any further enquiries on that subject, so she forestalled him. "I think he and Caroline Mawdsley have some sort of history."

"So he could be providing her with an alibi," said Forsyth. "Better see if we can trace him back to England."

"She might be giving *him* an alibi."

"Any hanky-panky between them?"

"Was that entirely necessary, Inspector?"

"I'm not going to beat about the bush, Miss Anderson. We both know the sort of cases you've been mixed up in. You're no delicate flower."

Perhaps not, she thought, but it would be nice to be treated that way. Instead she said, "I couldn't say. He's not short of a penny or two. I don't think even grateful students would be enough to support the estate he's using."

Forsyth sat back in a very self-satisfied way and looked at Choudhary.

"Terence Timmons," said the Sergeant.

"Who is Terence Timmons?"

"We looked up the Land Registry. He owns the estate this Guru Nadesh occupies."

"I was not aware Land Registry operated in India," she said.

"Only for larger estates and new properties being built in the cities," replied Choudhary. "They only keep track of the monied classes."

Maliha could have sworn he said that with some satisfaction. His previous, personal, difficulties had been the disparity between working for the British Empire while wanting to see them ejected from his home.

"Have you interviewed him?"

"Difficult man to pin down is Mr Timmons," said Forsyth. "According to his staff he's not currently in the country."

"When will he return?"

"They don't know. Comes and goes as he pleases, has a private flyer."

"And what does this Mr Timmons do?"

"Nothing specific, but apparently he plays the London stock market quite successfully."

Maliha examined the last piece of her cake idly. The case lacked focus. The jigsaw pieces they had so far didn't even seem to belong to the same puzzle. She speared the last piece of cake with her fork and ate it, then pulled on her gloves.

"I have to think," she said as she stood. The men climbed to their feet with her. "Thank you for sharing your information, Sergeant Choudhary. It seems we have yet another random fact with no bearing on the murders." She looked at Forsyth's wry smile. "Do you have any other leads? The mistress?"

"Dead end on that."

"Yes, I imagine it would be," she said, thinking of how distraught Constance had been. Maliha wondered if she would be heading back to study with the Guru in the near future now that her opera partner was gone.

Forsyth's gaze suggested he guessed he knew the identity of the mistress. She hoped he trusted her enough to leave Constance be. If the case did not resolve soon, Forsyth would be forced to follow up and would break poor John Linton easily, and then destroy Constance's marriage and hurt even more people.

She came out of her reverie, took her leave and headed back to the carriage.

As Old Vidu drove the carriage back at an easy walking pace Maliha wanted to see Valentine. Needed to see him.

She pushed the feeling away but directed Old Vidu to stop the carriage at the park. Amita handed her out and followed at an appropriate distance as she strode along the gravel paths into the green lawns, trees and flower beds of Albert Park, where a few months ago she had watched the slums beyond the Compound wall burn. She could have stopped it but had not because to do so would have tipped the hand of the murderer. People had died though she had been able to mitigate it using the *hijra*, Amita's people.

The rain had stopped again but there were no other promenaders. No one to watch her as she stood at the top of the hill, staring out across the buildings of the Compound. To her right, the steel and glass of *Sigiriya* created a glowing halo in the misty atmosphere.

An atmospheric traversed the tube at the bottom of the hill some half a mile away, its carriage lights flickering through the windows.

A zeppelin was moored in the commercial air-dock alongside a smaller British passenger flyer and, further off, a dozen smaller cargo ships of a dozen different designs.

Spots of rain hit her hands and face. Amita raised the umbrella again within moments. Maliha could feel her closeness as she tried to take advantage of the umbrella's protection without touching her mistress.

There was one fact she had not revealed to the Inspector. A fact that gave her some leverage, and could be used to wheedle out further information which might lead them somewhere towards the truth.

She needed to get back to Kochi to talk to Catherine Mawdsley; if it were to be done then best if it were done quickly. And for that she required Valentine. She could travel by atmospheric but that would take longer, and it would be helpful to have a family friend with her.

She satisfied herself she needed him for practical reasons, and not because she was desperate for his company.

iii

She sent Amita home to pack an overnight bag for her and directed Old Vidu to drive to the only address she knew for him, his apartment. It was most improper, of course, but there was little option. He was unlikely to be there because he worked in *Sigiriya* itself, and that was a place she had no authority to enter.

Even Old Vidu looked disapproving as he helped her down from the carriage. The idea of a young unmarried woman visiting a man. It was quite unacceptable. She did not care. She needed to get to Kochi.

She mounted the steps, ignoring the rain that was now teeming down and soaking her dress and hat. She pushed through the rotating door and was presented with a small foyer, and a man of at least sixty sitting at reception. The look of his face was a combination of uncertainty and nascent aggression—all he would be seeing was a native girl and that would never bode well. She took a deep breath and summoned the spirit of Barbara Makepeace-Flynn.

"It is imperative I speak with Mr Crier. If you would be so good as to send to his rooms. I will wait." She thrust out one of her cards, and he reached for it instinctively.

"Miss … Anderson?" The discrepancy between her colour and name revealed itself as a frown on his face. Maliha was about to deliver a scathing blast in order to get him moving when she noticed his badge—the Amalgamated Union of Pipe-Fitters, Steam Engineers and Boiler Makers.

"Quite so. I am Alice Anderson. Are you familiar with the Anderson valve?"

He was taken aback at the change of tack but nodded.

"My father," she said.

"I knew Mr Anderson," he said almost in awe. "I mean, I met him once or twice. I was an engineer. How is he?"

"He died. Earlier in the year."

There was an awkward moment. He looked down at her card again. "Mr Crier left this morning, he's not come back."

"Perhaps his man will know where he is or how to contact him?"

"Why don't you go up?"

She muttered surprised thanks, took the lift to the third floor, and found apartment twelve. There was a slight smell of boiled cabbages in the hallways and the decoration was of a lesser quality than other places she had visited. But still for single gentlemen of the middle classes.

The door was opened and the clean-shaven face of Valentine's man looked out and down. "Miss Anderson, I presume. I'm afraid Mr Crier is not here."

"You're Jameson?"

"Yes, Miss." He stepped back from the door to allow her entry. She made her way through the small hallway into the sitting dining room. "May I assume the matter is urgent?"

"Yes, it is imperative I go to Kochi this afternoon."

"Very good, I shall pack a bag for Mr Crier and take it to the air-dock."

"But Mr Crier himself?"

"I will be able to telegraph a message to his office when I reach the dock. He will arrive forthwith."

Maliha was astonished and pleased at the efficiency of the man. "I shall return home then proceed to the air-dock myself."

"Very good, Miss. Only—" he stopped for a moment, a behaviour she thought was quite uncharacteristic even though she had never met him before "—if I may make so bold, if you have something appropriate for the air-plane you might consider wearing it for the journey?"

Her face warmed. He was suggesting she wore men's trousers. "I will certainly consider it, Jameson. Thank you for the consideration."

iv

"Bill, could you come into my office for a minute?"

Valentine looked up from his work, laboriously transcribing his notes on his surveillance of Chinese trade delegation. There was some dispute over the ownership of an ice bucket—one of the specialised cargo vessels that cut ice from the Himalayas and transported it to population centres.

As far as he could tell it was really nothing to do with the British, and as long as they kept their dealings to simple negotiation there would be no reason for the His Majesty's Government to become involved. Thankfully that was the conclusion of most of his enquiries. He laid down his pen and pushed back his chair. Perhaps one day he would rate a secretary of his own.

He glanced out of the window. His office was located in one of the towers that rose from the top of *Sigiriya*. It gave him a view to the south across the Naval Yards and Army barracks. There were always infantrymen marching to and fro in their precise lines. From this distance they were less individuals and more a single creature moving with organisation under one directing intelligence. He fancied he could tell how experienced they were by their precision.

He laughed at his own foolishness. Who was he trying to convince? What chance was there that he would get a secretary? War was coming, perhaps not soon, but it would not be long and it would be a war that had only been hinted at in the last Boer conflict. That war had pitted trained and mechanised soldiers against farmers. Even the Chinese had not fully developed their machines when the British put them down. And that had been a bloody war.

War would come and he would have to fight. It was not that he was afraid of fighting, and he loved his country and his King. But Maliha had opened his eyes to so many things.

"Bill?" The voice was faint having travelled through two sets of doors and a carpeted corridor.

"Sorry, sir, just coming."

He hurried out, two doors down and into the larger, more attractively furnished office of his direct senior, Sir Bertram Kingsley. He looked old-school with his immaculate suit with perfect tailoring and impressive moustache, but he was as up-to-date in his understanding of international diplomacy as any man Valentine had met.

"Sit down, Bill."

That was code for a private chat. Valentine closed the door and came to sit in the leather-upholstered chair facing the desk.

"Your American holiday?"

"Yes, sir."

Sir Bertram consulted the papers on his desk, even upside down Valentine could see it was his report. In his position even holidays needed to be accounted for. Treachery was a very real threat. There was a long silence.

"Is there a problem, sir?"

"Look, Bill, I have been a great supporter of your work. Very fine work it has been too."

Valentine could sense the "but" hanging in the air.

"You are aware that Balinese girl could have been quite useful to us."

"Yes, sir." He must know that he took her to the USA. It would not take a great intelligence to join the dots and he had made a point of not putting any falsehoods in either the report on the Balinese incident, nor the one about the holiday. He had merely omitted to mention everything. There was a time when he would not even have considered doing such a thing but times had changed.

"And this Maliha Anderson."

"Yes, sir."

"Is there anything personal between you?"

Typical of the man to be so forthright, threw one off one's guard. She used that trick too.

"I admire her a great deal, sir," Valentine said. "She has an astonishing intellect."

"Make a good spy, would she?"

"Are you thinking of recruiting her, sir?"

"Let me explain my problem, Bill." He paused as if to gather his thoughts and arrange them in the most effective manner. "Since your first encounter with this young lady—and she is a *very* young lady, let us not forget—your behaviour has become somewhat erratic." He held up his hand to ward off any interruption. "She is clearly, as you say, very bright for a girl and as such might be considered an asset.

However, her involvement in the Balinese case resulted, as far as I can see, in the death of the perpetrator."

"She also ensured we did not lose any secrets."

Sir Bertram frowned. "Indeed, and that is the only reason I am talking to you now. I will not order you to discontinue your relationship in the middle of an investigation but if this does not have a satisfactory conclusion—and I mean satisfactory for *this office* and not satisfactory in the sense of some misguided sense of justice—if it does not, we will have a similar conversation to this one. One in which I will be less reasonable."

* * *

The interview with his senior left Valentine in a concerned state. He understood why he had been given a dressing down, gentle though it may have been—but he was not foolish enough to think it any less than a shot across the bows. If he gave Sir Bertram any further displeasure he could expect a full broadside.

Yet when the messenger brought the telegram from Jameson informing him that Maliha needed him to fly her to Kochi immediately, he was happy to throw his pen down and change into his flying things.

He paused at the door of his office and turned back. He did not believe in premonitions, yet when he looked into the room he could not escape the feeling it belonged to some other world. A world of which he was no longer a part.

He shrugged it off.

The lift carried him to the bottom of the building and he stepped out into the bustling walkways of the top of *Sigiriya*. Although the British had built across every square yard of it, they had kept some of the broken walls and gardens of the original buildings. It made him sad to see such destruction in the name of progress.

Directly above them, seven thousand miles up, hanging in the same position, in defiance of gravity, was the Queen Victoria Void-station: the glittering jewel in the crown of Empire.

He set off between the buildings and took the almost vertical funicular railway that ran down the stone outcrop ferrying the workers down to the Compound.

He stared across the air-docks. He could see that the *Alice* had been wheeled out in preparation and was being refuelled. Jameson was there, and he thought he could make out Maliha and Amita crossing the tarmacadam surface.

The sight of her recalled the events of the previous day. He was still unsure how he should feel. She had pushed him away despite his desire to comfort her. This was a difficult case for her but he knew she would not give it up regardless of the embarrassment it might cause.

His view of the dock was interrupted by buildings as they approached the ground.

He resolved to be himself. He would pretend that nothing had happened between them and that she was not out of sorts. He understood she was not upset with him personally, just discomfited by the whole adventure.

No doubt they would wrap it up in no time at all, and everything could get back to normal.

v

Maliha was pleased that Valentine did not question her before they took off. He did not ask why, only where and how fast. Jameson informed them that he had booked tickets on the atmospheric for himself and Amita, and they would rendezvous with their employers either in Kochi or at the Mawdsley residence. Despite the audience, she had allowed him to lift her into the plane. There came a time when practicality must be more important than dignity. But she resolved to set Amita to providing some appropriate clothing for future trips in the *Alice*.

The take-off on tarmacadam was smoother than over grass and the *Alice* shot into the sky. Maliha was grateful when they had breasted the clouds and levelled off so that he could reduce the engine speed and the noise. The cloud cover was more broken and she watched the terrain below slipping away. They passed the monstrous body of a Zeppelin only a few hundred feet below them. The sun reflected off its rippling balloon envelope.

She settled back into the seat and closed her eyes. They could not converse, so why not rest.

She came awake as if rising to the surface of the sea from a great depth. Valentine was shaking her arm gently. She did not pull away, and turned her head towards him to show him she was awake, but his eyes were focused ahead. She lay her other hand on top of his, just as she had before. She saw him glance at her hand on his and then he turned his face full to hers and grinned.

He extracted his hand gently and placed it back on the steering column.

She looked out and saw they were over the Indian mainland with the mountains of Kerala to the right and the sea to the left. Though the sky was clear around them, ahead she could see a solid bank of cloud.

Valentine put the air-plane into a steep descent that left her stomach behind. She laughed out loud. She found everything about the air-plane to be a delight. She had never been inebriated but thought this must be what it felt like, to be loose and free without a care in the world.

Below the cloud the rain was like a wall ahead of them. Maliha flinched as they hit it. The sound of the rain beating against the metal skin of the air-plane increased the noise level. The wind must have been unpredictable as the *Alice* bucked like a horse and tossed from side to side.

Maliha watched Valentine, his hands glued to the column, moving it back and forth compensating for the gusts, his eyes fixed rigidly ahead, flicking occasionally at the height and velocity gauges. Lightning flashed around them. She gripped the restraining straps. She could not think whether they were more or less likely to get hit if they were flying, but one thing she was certain of, the Faraday device—a metal grid that spanned the entire lower part of the ship from stem to stern and wingtip to wingtip—would not take kindly to such a vicious burst of electricity.

Valentine clearly felt the same. He reduced speed, which seemed to alleviate the effects of the wind, and brought the ship to a lower altitude so they seemed to be skimming across the tree tops.

* * *

Even though it was only mid-afternoon when they finally flew over the Mawdsley residence, the heavy cloud made it feel almost like night. It was difficult to make out the house, let alone the landing field. It took two passes to alert the ground staff to prepare the landing field, but presently the lights were lit and Valentine brought the *Alice* down for a very bumpy and abrupt landing.

With the canopy open they were both drenched within moments. The gardeners-cum-ground crew unloaded their baggage as Valentine lifted Maliha from the plane and did not put her down until he had squelched across the grass to the gravel path. She did not complain. One of the men had found an umbrella and with it Maliha and Valentine made their way to the house.

After the activity of the previous week with the visitors, the Mawdsley house was very quiet, filled with a deathlike silence. The house lights were off and they were greeted by a butler Maliha did not recognise. A young chambermaid was provided for Maliha, and one of the footmen assigned to Valentine.

Maliha's baggage had managed to resist the rain and both dresses were wearable. She chose the one with the severest cut. The girl dressed her wet hair as best she could after they had tried to towel it dry.

She went down and was directed to a room at the back of the house. She stepped from the main building into the hothouse filled with plants in pots and wide beds. She wondered at the point of having such a room when one only had to step outside. The temperature was almost intolerable.

She saw Valentine ahead of her. He had changed into a casual suit but the limpness showed it was already ruined by the intense heat and humidity. As she approached him, she could see it was stained with his perspiration. His hair was matted against his scalp and dripped with sweat.

He was studying the interior of a large glass dome. The reason for the hothouse was revealed as she came up close. Inside the dome—from which radiated an even fiercer heat—was a terrain of wet rocks and, between them, spilling over them were tendrils from a mottled purple and blue plant, with thin spine-like needles poking up from its centre. It might possibly have passed for Earth-born fauna had not those tendrils twitched and twisted, like worms torn from the ground.

"A Venusian Spiny," said Maliha.

"And alive."

"It's disgusting," said Catherine Mawdsley from behind them. "Unnatural."

"The plants of Venus are not like ours," said Maliha turning to their hostess. "It's a difficult place to survive."

Catherine Mawdsley was dressed in mourning black but she did not appear to be perspiring. Her cheeks were bright pink.

"My husband acquired it because he could. He did not appreciate it beyond its monetary value and the fact he owned something that no one else did." Contempt dripped from every word. "He had no love in his heart. He cared for nothing except the material. He lacked any sense of the spiritual."

"Is that why you killed him?" said Maliha. "To move him onto the next cycle."

"I did not kill him," she said without any inflection. "I was with the Guru."

"So he says," she replied. "But then he would, since he is Selina's father."

Catherine Mawdsley staggered as if she had been struck and reached out for the wall, her hand slipped on the slick surface. Valentine moved forward swiftly and caught her before she fell.

Maliha eyed her without sympathy. "She is suffering from the heat."

vi

The mistress of the household did not protest at them taking her out of the hothouse, much to Valentine's relief as he supported her out of the intense heat and into a small sitting room. He called for the staff to bring ice from where they had stored Alex's body, and someone to operate the *punkha* in the ceiling.

Catherine was drifting in and out of consciousness. How long had she been in the hothouse? Was she trying to kill herself? Had she realised why he and Maliha had returned to the house?

If Maliha was right—*Of course I'm right, Valentine*—then perhaps Catherine was trying to end her life.

One of the maids persuaded her mistress to drink some boiled water flavoured with lime and, as the minutes went by, Catherine seemed to come back to herself. Maliha stood by the window, staring out into the cloudy evening. Rain beat against the window.

The blocks of ice and the circulating air had reduced the temperature in the small room to the point where he was almost tempted to think he was cold. Catherine sat up straighter in her chair.

Maliha looked round at her movement and turned. She looked hard at him then flicked her eyes towards the door. He went over and shut it, then stood with his back to it, out of Catherine's view.

* * *

Maliha crossed the room without any hurry. They would not be interrupted. She settled herself across from Catherine.

"Why did you come back?" Catherine said. "I did not invite you."

"What is Guru Nadesh's real name?"

"George Kennington."

"Selina knows he's her father, doesn't she?"

Catherine twisted in her seat. "Bill, take this girl away. I did not invite her. You're always welcome, of course, for Alex's sake, but I must ask you to be more careful in your choice of companion."

"No, Catherine. Miss Anderson is here at the behest of His Majesty's Government. You will answer her questions."

"Don't be ridiculous, how could His Majesty want *this*—" her voice was filled with scorn "—to represent him?"

"Do you need to see my warrant, Catherine?"

Maliha let the discussion play out. She smiled inwardly. She was almost absurdly pleased at the support Valentine was providing. It meant he trusted her, and that was something to cherish.

Catherine turned back in her chair and faced Maliha once more. Her face was set, not with hate, but with defiance.

"Selina knows he's her father," Maliha said.

"My daughter is a goddess. The man who sired her physical body is irrelevant."

"She knows he's her father."

"Why do *you* think she is?"

"Both she and Mr Kennington have the same nose. It's quite distinctive and bears no resemblance to either yours or your late husband's."

"That's no proof."

"On the contrary, the new science of Genetics says it is proof. And I would not be surprised if Mr Kennington's natural hair colour is red." Maliha was satisfied with the shocked look on Catherine's face that confirmed it. She continued gently. "Let us say at this point that both I and Mr Crier know what it is he does, what he teaches and his other activities with hysterical women. However, when I asked him whether Selina was one of his students, he had the decency to be disgusted at the idea."

She proceeded quietly but insistently. "Why would he be disgusted when he plies his trade with who knows how many women? Because she is his daughter and, even in the depths of his depravity, *that* would be a step too far." Maliha noted that Valentine was looking pale at that thought. "But there was one other factor."

Catherine hesitated. "What?"

"Even though you removed the relevant journal from your husband's shelves, company records show he was not in England when Selina must have been conceived."

The older woman wilted and Maliha returned to her original question. "Selina knows he is her father, doesn't she?"

Catherine nodded.

"And Selina killed Alex."

Maliha was surprised when Catherine not only did not respond immediately, but looked up with what could only be described as a sly expression on her face.

"No."

"Yes, she did. She had her horse crush his skull with its hoof."

"No," said Catherine. "I killed Alex, and I killed my husband to stop him changing his will."

"Yes, I know you killed your husband, but Selina killed—"

"No. I did it. I killed my son. I will write whatever the police need. A statement, isn't that it?"

Maliha could think of nothing to say.

*　*　*

Maliha was still on the chair in the small sitting room when Valentine returned. As far as he could see she hadn't moved since he'd taken Catherine to her bedroom and locked her in with her maid. He had charged one of the men to stand guard outside, making it quite clear that if Catherine were to escape the man would be charged. Another was sent into Kochi for the police, and to send a message to Inspector Forsyth.

"You did it again," he said in a quiet voice that he hoped contained some encouragement. She did not look happy.

"Are you a complete idiot?" she snapped.

He contemplated a facetious line to the effect that he was not a complete idiot, merely a half-wit. However, the murderous expression on her face suggested that might not be the best choice.

"She's confessed."

"To protect her daughter from the gallows," she said. "I thought you wanted to find Alex's murderer."

"But Selina?"

"The damage to Alex's shoulder showed he was still holding the reins, and *facing* the horse. But the hoof mark was the wrong way round for a horse in front of him. It was a different horse. Selina can make a horse count with its hoof, what's to say she can't train one to stamp? I took measurements. We can match the size of the hoof mark to a specific horse—and it will be the one Selina was riding."

"But if Catherine confesses to the crime, there won't be a trial, and if there's no trial any other evidence will be ignored."

"This is wrong," Maliha said.

"And when she's dead, Selina inherits," he continued. "Which remains a potential problem."

"You and your precious government. Don't you see, Valentine? This still makes no sense. Why did she kill him at all?"

CHAPTER 6

i

Barbara passed *The Times of India* to Maliha across the breakfast table. She took it with a sullen expression, glanced at the headline and dropped it in disgust.

The newspaper was filled with the news of the apprehension of the murderer of both Alex and Randolf Mawdsley, with lurid inventions about Catherine's evil and warped mind. They skirted round any attempt to explain why she should do such a thing. The court date had been set for the following week, and the journalists were doing the best they could to make the most of that, since there would be no courtroom drama they could string out for weeks.

"Read it already?" Barbara asked. Maliha was like a delicate flower, she wilted when life did not suit her.

"It's indigestible."

The addition of Amita to the staff had improved Maliha's appearance and style, Barbara thought. Maliha and the strange world she brought with her resembled a visit to the fair that went on day after day.

Barbara took the newspaper and opened it at the crossword. She picked up her pencil and examined the clues. They always had an easy one to get started. She scratched a word. She could feel Maliha's discomfort and annoyance like a cold light playing across the breakfast table.

"You're scowling," she said without looking up.

"I don't know what to do." And she sounded like a child who had had her favourite toy put into the cupboard as a punishment. It was easy to forget she was only nineteen. Still a child really.

Maliha pushed back her chair and went to stand at the window looking out. After a dry spell that had lasted three days since she'd got back from Kochi it was raining again. Barbara had lived through so many monsoons—more than Maliha—they no longer meant anything.

"Why is she lying, Barbara?"

Barbara put down her pencil, the crossword would have to wait. "You think she's doing it just to spite you?"

"Yes!"

"Is that likely?"

"If it had not been for me, she and her daughter would have got away with murder. The only way she can thwart me now is by claiming to have killed her son as well."

"You don't think she's doing it to protect her daughter?"

Maliha was silent.

"You think she wouldn't have done the same if the police had been the ones to find her out?"

Maliha whirled round in anger and frustration. "They should have realised Alex's death was murder in the first place. It was obvious."

Barbara smiled to herself. "I told you you were like a daughter to me."

Her words stilled the passion in Maliha. "I … don't—" she stopped as if the sentence could not be finished, and restarted "—thank you is not sufficient to express my feelings, Barbara."

"I know I cannot replace your mother. Nor would I want to," she said. "But that is not why I mention it again. Come, sit."

Maliha returned to the chair she used for breakfast, opposite Barbara. "No, Maliha, here, beside me."

Maliha perched on the edge of the chair facing her. Barbara took her hand. Her small and delicate fingers were cold. "I do not say you are like a daughter to me lightly." Maliha opened her mouth to speak but Barbara shushed her with a raised finger. "Though we've known each other for only a few months, I have come to love you as a daughter. This, in its turn, means I would lay down my life for you."

Whatever words Maliha had planned were lost.

Barbara remembered Lucknow. She had been young—as young as Maliha was now—she and her mother had sought safety there when the rebels attacked. She had treated the wounded and held the hands of the dying. She had been willing to give her life to protect people she did not know, she had loved a Captain.

"You mean regardless of how bad Catherine might be she will still give her life for her daughter."

Barbara nodded. The memories she had unearthed made her voice untrustworthy.

Maliha's hand tightened on hers. "Or for the man she loves."

"She killed her husband."

Maliha smiled. "Yes. She did."

* * *

Maliha climbed the stairs at a slower pace than she normally would. Her realisation about Catherine Mawdsley dictated a certain course of action, something that if she revealed her intent to anyone, they would prevent her, and by main force if necessary.

Amita was reading by the window. She had moved on to *Romeo and Juliet*. It was not one of Maliha's favourites. Amita stood immediately and put down the book, ready to receive instruction.

"Sit down, Amita, I need to talk to you." She corrected herself. "I need to ask you some things."

Amita sat obediently. Maliha went to the window, she did not want to look at Amita's face.

"I want to ask you about … before."

"Before, *sahiba*?"

"The men."

"I do not think that would be good for you to hear."

Maliha closed her eyes. "I know enough about the details."

"You helped Lochana Modi. We all know that story."

The woman who was not a woman but loved like one. Maliha hardly knew her but had helped to bring her justice, at least. But what Maliha needed to know had nothing to do with love.

"Before, Amita, when you were paid—what did you feel?"

"Feel?"

"I mean, emotion, feelings, what did you think of them?"

"*Sahiba*, mistress. Do you truly want to know?"

"I need to know."

"I felt nothing."

"Didn't you hate them? Or despise them?"

"Why would I hate them, *sahiba*? They gave me money and I could eat. Why would I despise them? They are like me."

"But didn't you despise yourself?"

"I did what I had to do, *sahiba*."

* * *

Maliha had Amita pack her a case while she wrote three letters and, after lunch, when Barbara had gone out to see the girls, she arranged for a carriage to take her to the station.

She bought a second-class ticket and boarded the atmospheric to Madurai. The carriage was crowded, with passengers split evenly between white and brown. There was a family with children. The wife wanted to talk and Maliha learned they were heading all the way to Bombay by atmospheric as far as Nagpur, where the atmospheric line ended, and then by cargo flyer the rest of the way. It was the cheapest route. Her husband had obtained a job providing tuition to the children of the gentry.

Ordinary people. Maliha realised she was never around ordinary people.

At Madurai she hired a horse-drawn cab and gave the driver his instructions. He glared at her. A woman alone, going to *that place*. But he did not refuse the fare.

And, by late afternoon, she was hopping awkwardly down from the cab.

The sun was out but the humidity seemed to make the air steam.

The cab crunched away up the drive, leaving her standing alone with her case.

ii

Barbara was tired. It had been a long day and she had arrived back to find Maliha gone with no hint as to where. Barbara always put on a brave face but she knew her age was catching up with her.

She sat in the dark in the drawing room. Before the electric, Sathi would have come to light the gas or the candles. Now it was so easy to do oneself the servants no longer had to, and it was no longer part of their chores. So she sat in the dark because it was easier than aggravating the aches that came with the rain.

When the General had been alive she had had little to look forward to. Their marriage had been a sham but she had made the best of it. Muddled through, because that was what one did. Played the hand you were given.

Then Maliha had taken the cards from her hand and re-dealt them. She was just a girl but had taken the truths Barbara had held dear, and the lies that she used as her defense, and turned them upside-down. Barbara knew she was regarded as an old battle-axe. It was an image she cultivated to keep people at arm's length.

She had told Maliha she was like a daughter to her. The truth was simpler. Barbara considered that she *was* her daughter. She was not yet of age, she needed a guiding hand, someone she could confide in. She needed a mother. Barbara smiled at her own arrogance, to think that she had any right.

They had met in difficult circumstances but the girl had faced her, and the bastions of lies had shredded. Barbara had told her everything. It was an effect Maliha seemed to have on people: when she spoke, you could not lie to her. Except Catherine Mawdsley had.

A violent banging on the door snapped her from her reverie. It paused, as if waiting for a response but when it did not come soon enough, the banging resumed.

Barbara pushed herself to her feet. Her muscles, set so long in one position, protested and ached. Perhaps she should get a stick, like Maliha's. She saw Sathi cross the hall to the door.

"Where is Mrs Makepeace-Flynn?" Mr Crier's voice was strained and urgent, filled with desperation.

Where was Maliha? She wondered. She had thought perhaps she had gone out with Mr Crier on some adventure—there was little chance it would be on some social jaunt. But if she was not with him...

As she walked, her joints stretched and relaxed. By the time she reached the door she was moving as well as she ever did nowadays. The sight of Mr Crier was not something she had seen before. He was red and out of breath, he had neither jacket nor hat, and he was soaked to the skin. He clutched an envelope and letter, both as wet as he was himself.

"What is the meaning of this commotion, Mr Crier?"

"Please tell me she is here," he panted. Had he run all the way? Sathi stood back, she looked as if she was hoping to relieve him of his outdoor things but he had thoroughly confused matters by not having any.

"I cannot do that. She is gone. I thought she was with you."

"Oh dear Lord," he cried. "She has gone to *him*."

A cold hand clutched Barbara's heart. "The Guru?"

He nodded once. Barbara clutched the door frame. "Why would she do that?"

Electric vehicle lights swept the windows and the panting of a powerful steam engine filled the room. Sathi went to the door and opened it as Inspector Forsyth flung himself through it. He was dressed for the weather and touched his hand to his bowler when he saw Barbara.

"Is Miss Anderson about, Mrs Makepeace-Flynn?" he said. "I need to discuss this letter with her."

"She's gone." Mr Crier's voice was almost a wail. She knew his imagination was delivering painful images, because hers was doing the same. But now was not the time to succumb to panic. "Sathi, make tea, and have Old Vidu bring some towels for Mr Crier. Gentlemen, please come in, but if you would forbear from standing on the rugs or sitting, I would appreciate it."

No one sat.

"Give me your letter, Mr Crier," she said and took it from him. The ink had run in the rain and her letter to him was illegible. "Perhaps you can remember what she said?"

"She had something she had to do, and not to follow her."

"And your letter, Inspector?"

"She asked me to come to the house at this time," he replied and flipped open his pocket watch. "I'm a little early. Is she all right?" The gruffness of his voice betrayed his concern.

"She's gone to *that man*." Mr Crier's voice was almost hoarse, she wouldn't be surprised if he hadn't given himself a chill. Young love could be so foolish.

"Guru Nadesh, so called," Forsyth growled. "Lawrence Edward Renfrew is his real name, at least the last name he was known by. He wears names as it suits him."

Barbara felt a coolness fill her, a calmness of repressed anger. "He is known to the police?"

"If it is the same man, and I believe it is. He has several warrants for arrest back in England on a variety of charges including theft by deception, fraud, assault, posing as a doctor and inappropriate conversation."

"Assault? He's violent?"

"The assault charges were brought by husbands in regard to their wives. Likewise the *conversation*."

"We catch your drift, Inspector, I don't think we require any more of that sort of detail." Barbara hoped to spare Mr Crier some pain, but it did not seem to be working. Sathi arrived with the tea. Mr Crier refused it.

"Drink the tea, Mr Crier."

He did as he was told. Barbara glanced up and saw a shadow lurking outside the door. "Come in, Amita."

The girl edged into the room, as if ready to bolt at any moment.

"You knew where she was going?"

Amita nodded. "She tell me I must not say anything. She gave me a place to be."

"I am not angry with you. None of us are."

Mr Crier looked like he might blame her. Barbara glared at him and he said nothing.

"We must go after her, of course," said Barbara.

"She will already be there, she will already..." he broke off.

"Mr Crier, you are not helping her with such outbursts, and you are missing the obvious," she said and realised she sounded like Maliha. "It's not that I don't understand but you really must pull yourself together. Inspector?"

"Aye, Missus. She told me to come here."

"She wants us to go after her."

"Why the deception?" Mr Crier asked, his voice was superficially calmer but still contained desperation.

"You would have let her go into that man's clutches?"

He shook his head.

"Quite so. She believes she needs to do this, but she expects the cavalry to arrive."

The Inspector frowned. "That's easy to say, but the last train to Madurai's gone and I don't think Mr Crier's flying contraption is much good in the dark."

There was a short period of despondency until Mr Crier raised his head. "I can get a train—at least His Majesty's servants can get one running."

"Very good," said Barbara. "I will have to change."

"You're not expecting to come?" said the Inspector.

"Most certainly I am. If she is doing what we all believe she is, she will need me."

They did not offer any further argument.

iii

The room was lit with electric, but the illumination was deliberately muted. There was a small brighter lamp at the dressing table. She had spent nearly an hour staring into the mirror, studying every contour of her face. Her hair hung loose almost to her waist, and without conscious thought she ran the brush through it again and again.

The dinner she had been served was of good quality, enough to appease any hunger but not enough to weigh too heavily. The Guru had not greeted her on her arrival, nor he had been there for the meal.

She had been shown to her room. It was decorated predominantly in red, including the curtains and bedspread. The sheets of the wide bed were cream satin. On the bed was a blue silk shift that would reach her ankles, a thin dressing gown of a lighter shade of blue, and white sandals.

None of the staff had spoken a word to her. No one had asked why she was there. It was taken for granted. There was only one reason why an unaccompanied woman would appear on the doorstep. Was she really here because Catherine Mawdsley had lied? Or for something else?

There was a book on the bedside table. It contained erotic images; once again they were not illustrations, but photographs. She had turned the pages and looked at every picture. It was like a compulsion. The feeling of being out of control filled her and it disturbed her.

She knew what was expected of her. The clues were all there. He would not come to her, she must go to him: she must offer herself. It was always about control.

So she had removed her clothes, one item at a time, carefully folding or hanging each one. When the last item was removed she glanced up at the mirror, as if to catch herself without her mirror-self realising she was looking. All she saw was the white scar that ran down her thigh.

She lifted the shift over her head and allowed it to slip down her body, the material scraping gently across her skin. It fitted perfectly. She put on the dressing gown and tied the sash in a one-loop bow. And finally pushed her feet into the sandals. She looked at her reflection again. The quality and material of her clothing revealed her natural shape.

She sat at the dresser again and tied her hair back, holding it in place with an ivory comb that had been a gift from her mother when she left for boarding school.

She looked at her watch on the dresser. It was nearly ten o'clock, the time she usually went to bed. The wry thought did not raise a smile. She looked once more at her reflection and wondered what Valentine could possibly see in her. Well, after tonight, that would no longer be a concern. Probably for the best. His pash for her needed to be wiped out, otherwise it would ruin his career.

This was a sure way to deal with that problem. Two birds with one stone.

She stood up and looked down at her walking stick leaning against the dressing table. She wouldn't need it tonight. She limped towards the door.

iv

She barely recalled the walk along the length of that dark passage. Even the ache in her thigh seemed to recede. She did not look at the images on the walls, but focused her attention on the door at the end. The journey took an eternity that was over in the blink of an eye.

The door swung away from her soundlessly when she pushed it without knocking. Warmth poured from the room along with the scent of citrus and jasmine. Candles threw light and shadows across the walls.

She did not see him at first. He was standing stock-still by the fireplace. A fire had been lit, but was now just low red embers, enough to drive the damp from the air.

"You can enter if you want to."

Her feet seemed rooted to the floor, as if her whole body was rebelling against her intent. Strange, she thought, shouldn't it want its natural release? She stepped into the room and closed the door behind her. One of the windows was open and the sound of rain beating down outside filtered into the room.

"You can sit down anywhere you wish."

He was looking at her, every part of her. Embarrassment swept over her. Only through sheer will did she prevent her arms from trying to hide her body. She was not naked. She desperately wanted to flee but she looked at him, now dressed only in his *dhoti*, his upper torso bare, and took a step forward, then another. Finally she stood just the other side of the fireplace. She noted the ginger tinge of his body hair with satisfaction.

"Fear of the unknown is natural," he said. "But you must free yourself of it."

"Do you teach Hinduism or Buddhism?"

"The one does not deny the other."

She stared into the embers of the fire, feeling the warmth on her cheeks and through the thin material that hung about her. She had been standing so long without support that the pain in her thigh began to nag.

"Why are you here, Maliha?" The question was not aggressive, it did not threaten, it merely echoed the thought that still echoed in her mind.

"I need answers, Guru Nadesh," she said without looking at him, she could see his bare feet lit by ember light.

"What do you need to know?"

She wanted to turn away but was aware that any movement would reveal the shape of her body with even more clarity.

He answered her silence. "You seek balance between the four goals. Western society is devoted to wealth and prosperity with no respect for the other three—and it engages in the active suppression of Kama," he paused perhaps hoping for some sort of confirmation. She did not speak, but held herself still. "You know about harmony and the cycle of life, but I can teach you Kama."

"Kama is not only about the physical expression of love."

"The Sutra teaches all the aspects of family and devotion, but it all begins with the conjoining of man and woman."

Her heart jumped. There it was.

She closed her eyes, she could still see the ember glow transformed in colour behind her eyelids. She reached to the sash at her waist.

"Wait," he said. His hand, strangely cool to the touch, gripped her wrist. She did not flinch. "This is not some sordid bordello, Maliha. It is a place of learning."

"Then teach me." The words came out like some half-strangled cry.

"Sit."

He guided her to a soft and yielding sofa that faced the fire. She sighed as the pain in her leg faded to a distant ache. She still had her eyes closed.

"Here," he said and pressed a glass tumbler into her fingers. She grasped it with hands and brought it to her mouth. It was deeply scented with flowers, she sipped it and felt a thick sweet sensation spread out across her tongue, leaving a tingling and burning. She swallowed. She opened her eyes and looked at the dark golden liquid.

"What is it?"

"A million blooms."

"Mead," she said. "I do not drink alcohol."

"You are overwrought. You can learn nothing unless you are relaxed. It is distilled poetry." He loomed over her still. "Sit back, let your muscles become loosened."

She pushed herself back until her spine rested against the leather back, and her feet were in the air. The seat was too big for her. She took a sip of the intensely sweet liquid. It slid across her tongue and burned her throat.

"Breathe in deep … very good … and let it out. In again … hold it for a moment .. And let it out."

She felt the tension dissolve, whether it was the alcohol or the breathing. She realised that her body was weary, she drove it so hard every day, she never listened to it—because she hated it so much for betraying her. And now it was betraying her again, or perhaps not, she was not sure any more.

"That's good. You see? You feel better already."

Maliha felt the tears dripping from her eyes. Betrayed again.

"Do you know why you're crying?" Again it was not asked with amusement or accusation, just a question. *Do I know?*

She shook her head. "It doesn't matter."

He took the glass from her hand and placed it on a table. He crouched by her bare feet and placed his hand under her left ankle. He lifted her foot and removed the sandal. He placed his hands on either side and pressed the sole with his thumbs. A shiver ran through her. She raised her hand as if to stop him as a strange tingle ran through her from her foot up, along her leg, through her body and out through the top of her head.

He smiled, and she was shocked as she recognised it was genuine. "We are taught we must not touch each other's bodies. And yet it can be a most potent activity. This I learned from the Chinese."

She leaned her head back as his thumbs dug first into one foot and then the other and the electrical energies continued to shoot through her.

"It must be difficult for you," she said in a voice so quiet it barely traversed the distance between them. His hands paused. "Please don't stop, please." He continued to manipulate her feet. She brushed her hand along her thigh and felt the ridges of her injury red hot and inflamed.

"What must be difficult for me?" he said finally. His fingers kneaded the muscles and she shivered from the bursts of tension that exploded in her thigh.

She managed to recall what she had asked him. "Having to wheedle out the information from your students and pass it on to your benefactor. Never receiving benefit for the information."

His hands slowed but did not stop. "On the contrary, I have everything I need."

Every woman you want, she corrected.

He sat next to her, took her hand and proceeded to press it as he had her foot. She sighed, opened her eyes and stared into his. She was more languid than she had been in her entire life. She was momentarily distracted by a light flashing across the window.

She gently pulled her fingers from his grasp and took his hand in hers. She pulled it towards her and pressed it against her breast. She closed her eyes.

"Teach me," she said.

v

She thought of Valentine as the Guru's arm went under her legs and lifted them onto the sofa. She lay supine, defenceless, as his hands stroked her. They massaged her neck, moved across her stomach with gently scraping nails, stroked her breasts, moved down her legs. She was breathless.

"But—" she was almost panting "—you wanted Catherine."

His hands tensed on her body. "Don't stop, please don't stop." His hands continued to move, more roughly now. "But you must tell me, you must."

She was broken in two. Her body responded like an animal, desperate for his touch. Her mind clinging to reason on the edge of the precipice of lust.

"Yes, I wanted her. I want her. But you found her out."

"I—" she started to speak but reached out instead, grabbing him by the shoulders and pulling him close. She could feel the heat of his skin against hers. "I want you."

His hand clutched her shift, and ripped it from her, exposing her body.

Breathless. "And she wanted you."

His mouth came down on her, biting with exquisite pain.

"She killed for you."

He stopped. She looked down across the landscape of her naked body at his grinning face. "Catherine never had an original thought in her head, but she loved to play. Yes, she did as she was told. So did Selina. And so will you. Look at you, Miss Anderson, a wanton like all of you. Just waiting for me to set you aflame."

His hand did something delicious. She groaned, her body arched of its own volition. She stretched back her arm. Her hair was a tangled mess. Her hand came to rest on the comb. She looked him in the eye, pulled it from her hair and slashed it across his face.

He jerked back, staggered to his feet, hand to his face as blood oozed from a dozen parallel lines. He stared at his bloody fingers. Then he looked up, away from her, towards the door.

"Lawrence Edward Renfrew. You are under arrest for conspiring to murder Randolf Mawdsley and Alexander Mawdsley—what—"

A dark figure from nowhere slammed the Guru against the wall next to the fireplace. The figure grabbed the Guru by the throat and smashed his head against the mantel. Again. And again. And again.

Two more figures rushed past the sofa and tore the first away from the limp figure of the Guru. Now without support he slumped into the bright embers. There was an excruciating wail as his skin burned. The struggling first figure slammed his foot down on the Guru's stomach.

"Oh Christ. Choudhary, keep him off." The Inspector pulled at the Guru's twitching body as Choudhary wrestled Valentine to the floor.

Maliha watched the events as if they were moving pictures on a screen, as if they had nothing to do with her. Forsyth yanked at the body but somehow it was caught on the upward points of the grate. He was making no sound and his eyes stared at her in accusation.

Then Barbara was there. She covered Maliha's nakedness, and drew her to her feet. She was joined by Amita's strong arms and together they supported her as they led her from the room.

vi

Barbara opened the post. Nothing of interest except a letter from her solicitor confirming that her instructions had been carried out. She sighed and glanced at the newspaper. Catherine Mawdsley had not been hanged for the murders, but instead she had been incarcerated in a mental institution.

The death of Renfrew/Kennington himself had not made the papers at all. Inspector Forsyth and Mr Crier had ensured that no news of it leaked out. According to Forsyth, Selina had become even more introverted and equine-obsessed after the death of her real father. She would not speak to anyone except about horses. The evidence of the hoof size was declared to be inconclusive.

The doorbell jangled in the distance. She glanced at the long case clock in the corner, ten o'clock. That would be Mr Crier. He had written to say he would call. Every day. She had put him off for ten days, Maliha had refused to see him until today.

He was not the man she had known, and if she had not known who he was she might not have recognised him when he stepped through the door. He appeared to have aged a dozen years or more. There were dark circles around his eyes though his man continued to dress him impeccably, and ensured he was clean shaven, but where before he had been full of life now he was like a somnambulist.

She did not greet him, not because he was out of favour but simply because, since the events of that night, such social pleasantries lacked any real substance. He went to the window and stood silhouetted against the light, as featureless as a spectre.

Maliha stepped through the door. She had abandoned the loose French fashions she had favoured and returned to the constricting British fashions, and that was not the only change. Barbara was still unaccustomed to the lack of her walking stick. Whatever else had happened that night, Maliha had got up on the third day and discarded her stick. She still limped but it was nowhere near as pronounced as it had been. Maliha stopped in the centre of the room looking at Mr Crier.

Barbara gathered up her letters, placed them in the bureau and left them alone together.

* * *

The anger in him still burned. It was like a volcano threatening to explode at any time. It had been unchanged since the moment he threw himself at Renfrew and dashed his brains against the wall, and watched the monster burning in the grate.

In those moments when the volcano was quietest he recognised that it was the satisfaction he had experienced as he watched that man die by his own hand that was the most disturbing. He had revelled in the horror. But the rest of the time the volcano bubbled and he did not care. He delighted in his anger.

She had refused to see him. He had saved her, he had killed the devil who had abused her. And she spurned him.

"Maliha—"

"I see you found your solution."

"What?"

"You petty bureaucrats, you found your way around the problem of Selina."

He realised what she was talking about. His mind was hot with anger but he controlled his words. "With Catherine alive, Selina does not inherit."

"You pervert the courts for your own ends."

"I have resigned," he said.

She shifted slightly, favouring one leg. She was not carrying her stick. "And this is why you wanted to see me?"

"I thought you'd be pleased."

"I cannot think of anything that is less relevant to me."

"I did it because of you."

"*Because of me?* What does that mean? Everyone makes their own decisions, Mr Crier. You cannot blame someone else for them."

"What have I done to be so abused by you? I thought we had reached an understanding."

"Clearly you failed to comprehend me at all."

He strode across the room and grabbed her by the arms. She did not pull away but the expression on her face was defiant.

"Feel free to touch my body, Mr Crier. With or without my permission. Clearly you see it as your right."

"What have I done to warrant this, Maliha?"

"You will refer to me as Miss Anderson."

"What have I done to offend you so? I killed the monster that defiled you, what more could you want of me?"

"I do not want anything of you, Mr Crier." Close to, her eyes were red, as if from crying, yet they were completely dry. "I did not ask you to kill him. I did not go there for you to kill him. If I had wanted him dead I could have stabbed him, or shot him, or poisoned him. Where was the justice in his *death*? When Selina Mawdsley walks free?"

He stared into her deep brown eyes, almost black. His mind was numb.

"Don't you see?" she said, her voice breaking as if she were crying, yet still there were no tears. "Can you not see what you did? You made my actions, my sacrifice, my humiliation—you made *me*—into nothing. Anyone could have *killed* him, only I could make him confess. And you took that away."

Glacial understanding spread through him, chilling him to the marrow, quenching the volcano that burned in his heart and turning it to ice.

He knew there were words he ought to say, but he did not know what they were.

* * *

His hands dropped from her. He turned and left. She heard the front door slam and the house was left in silence.

She could still feel where his arms had pressed against her. Part of her ached to call him back but she could never do that. She would not bring any more destruction into his life.

What had she said to Choudhary when he asked her how she reconciled the two worlds she lived in, the Indian and the Empire? She had said there was no distinction, that she took each aspect just as it was, because every person whichever side of the line they were on, was simply a person.

She had been wrong. You could not ignore the differences. She was not part of the Empire, she was Indian. And that meant one thing with complete certainty: She could not remain here.

It was a pretty low dive for someone like Crier, thought Forsyth. He pushed open the door into a pub close to the Navy barracks, dimly lit, filled with the smoke of cheap cigarettes and thrumming with voices. Sailors sat in the snugs and at tables, talking, playing cards or cribbage. A few whores flirted, looking for trade. They'd be Madam Chan's girls.

It was stifling hot.

Forsyth wove his way between the tables peering at the faces until he spotted Crier leaning up against the bar nursing a pint. He had fresh bruises on his face and people seemed to be avoiding the space around him. Forsyth could almost feel the anger emanating him.

He took off his bowler and dropped it onto the counter beside Crier, who didn't look up.

"You did it again, didn't you, Crier?"

"Go to hell, Forsyth."

"There's a fair chance of that, but you'll be there with me."

"What do you want?"

"I'll take a pint of heavy, kind of you to offer."

"Like I said. Go to hell, Forsyth. I don't have to talk to you." Crier downed the last of his beer and made to leave. Forsyth put his hand on his shoulder and forced him back onto the stool. Crier winced in pain.

"You owe me, Crier. You took another case away from me," said the Inspector without much malice. "I'm once again a laughing stock."

"Don't look at me, I'd see her hang. Take it up with my former employer. I'm sure His Majesty would be happy to explain it to you."

"Let me buy you a drink, Crier."

William Albert Valentine Crier looked at the Inspector. "Don't mind if I do."

*   *   *

When she heard Maliha finally descending the stairs Barbara climbed to her feet, ignoring the aches in her joints. Old Vidu and Sathi had got Maliha's remaining bags for the journey stowed on the carriage. Most of her luggage had gone on ahead.

As Maliha came down into the hall, Barbara reached the door. She knew what to expect but it was still a shock. Maliha wore a bright yellow and red *sari* over a blue *choli* and had a *bindi* on her forehead. She looked like a native except for the slight hint of European features in her face, but perhaps they were only there if you knew.

Since the visit from Mr Crier two weeks ago, Maliha had become steadily more withdrawn. She had stopped coming to breakfast and only ate in her room. She did not even request the newspaper.

Then the day arrived when she had come down and announced she was returning home to Pondicherry. Barbara had not tried to dissuade her. She had no authority over Maliha, but her heart was breaking.

And here she was. Barbara desperately wanted to hug her, and stop her from leaving. But that would not be proper, that would not be *British*.

Maliha went to the open door, then turned back to her. With a natural reflex she pulled her silk headscarf forwards over her head. She pressed her palms together and bowed her head deeply.

"*Namaste, mata-ji.*"

~ end ~

Read **WIND IN THE EAST**
The next amazing book in the **Maliha Anderson** series.

ABOUT THE AUTHOR

Steve Turnbull was born in the heart of London to book-loving working-class parents in 1958. He lived with his parents and two older sisters in two rooms with gas lighting and no hot water. In his fifth year, a change in his father's fortunes took them out to a detached house in the suburbs. That was the year *Dr Who* first aired on British TV, and Steve watched it avidly from behind the sofa. It was the beginning of his love of science fiction.

Academically Steve always went for the science side, but he also had his imagination—and that took him everywhere. He read through his local library's entire science fiction and fantasy selection, plus his father's 1950s *Astounding Science Fiction* magazines. As he got older he also ate his way through TV SF like *Star Trek*, *Dr Who* and *Blake's 7*.

However, it was when he was 15 he discovered something new. Bored with a maths lesson, he noticed a book from the school library: *Cider with Rosie* by Laurie Lee. From the first page he was captivated by the beauty of the language. As a result he wrote a story longhand and then spent evenings at home on his father's electric typewriter pounding out a second draft, expanding it. Then he wrote a second book. After that he switched to poetry and turned out dozens, mostly not involving teenage angst.

After receiving excellent science and maths results, he went on to study computer science. There he teamed up with another student and they wrote songs for their band, with Steve writing the lyrics. However, they admit their best song was the other way around, with Steve writing the music.

After graduation Steve moved into contract programming but was snapped up a couple of years later by a computer magazine looking for someone with technical knowledge. It was in the magazine industry that Steve learned how to write to length, to deadline, and to style. Within a couple of years he was editor and stayed there for many years.

During that time he married Pam (who also became a magazine editor), whom he'd met at a student party.

Though he continued to write poetry, all prose work stopped. He created his own magazine publishing company which at one point produced the subscription magazine for the *Robot Wars* TV show. The company evolved into a design agency, but after six years of working very hard and not seeing his family—now including a daughter and son—he gave it all up.

He spent a year working on miscellaneous projects including writing 300 pages for a website until he started back where he had begun, contract programming.

With security and success on the job front, the writing began again. This time it was scriptwriting: features scripts, TV scripts and radio scripts. During this time he met a director, Chris Payne, who wanted to create steampunk stories, and between them they created the Voidships universe, a place very similar to ours but with specific scientific changes.

With a whole universe to play with, Steve wrote a web series, a feature film, and then books all in the same Steampunk world and, behind the scenes, all connected.

Join the mailing list at http://bit.ly/voidships